Hidden Part 2

A Michael Sullivan Mystery

LINDA BERRY

Hidden Part 2

First Edition, October 2017
Second Edition, November 2019

ISBN: 978-0-9998538-7-0

Published in the United States of America

www.lindaberry.net

This is the much-anticipated final chapter to the HIDDEN saga, and it does not disappoint! Author Berry has a knack for bringing her characters to life, and I especially enjoyed Marine veteran Sully. He has grit and a strong sense of right and wrong. As Sully struggles to readjust to civilian life and bring a ring of murdering horse thieves to justice, we are provided a view into a softer side of this hard man, and that is only one of the many delights of this story. Throw in the stunning landscapes of Central and Eastern Oregon, and we have a modern western classic.
—Dave Edlund, *USA Today* bestselling author of the Peter Savage Thrillers

Five Star Reviews from Amazon Readers

—I will read anything by Linda Berry! Having read HIDDEN PART 1 I was on tenterhooks until I could read part two. Beautifully and evocatively written, this story immediately drew me in. Do yourself a favor and read it pronto!

—Grit and then some. HIDDEN PART 2 is the adventurous sequel that masterfully takes you to the satisfying end of the trail with captivating turns along the way. Once I started it, I stampeded to the finish with plot sidetracks that added depth and complexity to the engaging journey.

—Captivating characters, rich plot, plenty of beautiful and poetic descriptions. HIDDEN PART 2 is a multifaceted, captivating book that maintains and improves upon the promises of the first volume. The story, already rich and intense in the first instalment, picks up pace and emotional involvement as it progresses. The narration is filled with beautiful descriptions, often mirroring the characters' feelings. The personality traits of each one of them are, however, more defined, vivid, and intense. Highly recommended.

—Loved this book! Complex characters and a storyline that has two stories combined into one. Sully is working hard to leave the war behind him and to get the family farm going in the right direction. Justin has been given the opportunity to train with a former bull riding champion and finally feels like he has a home. They each decide to track the horses stolen from various ranches in the area. As their search intertwines so do their lives.

To the men and women in uniform
who put themselves in harm's way to preserve
the freedom of our great country,
and to the talented athletes who compete
so fearlessly in rodeo

Books by Linda Berry:

Hidden Part 1

Hidden Part 2

Pretty Corpse

The Killing Woods

The Dead Chill

To learn of new releases and discounts,
add your name to Linda's mailing list:
www.lindaberry.net

ACKNOWLEDGMENTS

I AM DEEPLY GRATEFUL to the many friends who contributed their time and knowledge to the development of Hidden.

A special thanks goes to Joan Steelhammer of Equine Outreach, a horse rescue organization where my volunteer work blossomed into a life-long love of horses. I owe a debt of gratitude to Gracie, my stunning gray-dappled mare, who gave me the joy of unfettered companionship for many years.

For their unwavering friendship, support, and continued belief in my work, I owe a big thank you to JT Gregory, Tim Rubin, LaLoni Kirkland, Sarah Persha, Lindy Jacobs, James Koukis, Mike Lankford, Mark Fasnacht, and Katherine Mattingly

I am deeply grateful for my initial readers, who read my book for pure enjoyment and gave me encouraging feedback: Katherine Mattingly, Bob Kruger, my lovely sister Francine Marsh, and my dearest friend and husband, Mark Fasnacht.

I'm thankful to my toy poodles, Rogie and Jackson, who helped fashion the character of Butch.

CHAPTER ONE

AN HOUR AFTER DAYBREAK, Sully sat at the table with Joe and Travis finishing a breakfast of ham and eggs. The mood in the kitchen was quiet and sullen. Sully's bandaged head throbbed, and the three men had barely spoken. Joe sat hunched over his plate like a beaten dog, wearing a stricken expression. Sully knew his dad blamed himself for Mateo's death, but he felt little sympathy. A good man was dead, his wife widowed, his children fatherless, and murderous thieves were still running around the county with impunity. All because of a careless decision Joe had made.

Sully watched through the window as the sheriff's Yukon pulled to a stop outside the house. Following a light rap at the door, Matterson shuffled into the kitchen. A day's growth of stubble darkened his face, his uniform was rumpled, and his eyes were red-rimmed. Clearly, he'd been up all night.

"Morning Carl," Travis said with a note of sympathy. "Coffee?"

Matterson nodded. "Thanks. I could use a cup."

Travis got up, filled a mug with black coffee, and handed it to him. "Long night?"

"Too long." Matterson removed his hat and joined them at the table with a squeak of leather from his holster. He sipped his coffee with a look of appreciation. "How're you folks holding up?"

Joe shrugged.

"We're okay," Travis said.

"How's the head?" he asked Sully.

"They said I'll live," Sully said dryly. "Bunch of stitches. No concussion." Sully waited expectantly. Matterson never talked shop before getting a feel for the temperature in a room.

"That's fortunate." Matterson ran a large-knuckled hand through his thinning hair and cleared his throat. "I went out to Mateo's place last night. Talked to his widow, Rosa."

Matterson had their full attention.

"Needless to say, she's a wreck. Poor woman. But she didn't seem surprised. She said Mateo hadn't been himself since Monty's murder. Mateo did all of Monty's hoof work, and the two were tight. Mateo knew the horses as well as his own kids." He fell silent and thoughtfully sipped his coffee.

Sully connected the dots. Adrenaline buzzed through his system. "Mateo helped the thieves steal Monty's horses?"

Matterson nodded grimly. "He was there that night."

"The horses trusted Mateo, that's why they followed him out," Travis added.

"Right. He was the lead man. This gang he got hooked up with assured him no one would get hurt. But right away, they killed the dogs. Then they killed Monty while Mateo was leading the horses out through the creek. Rosa said he didn't know about the murder until he read it in the paper the next day. He'd been eaten up with guilt ever since. Couldn't work. Couldn't sleep."

"Why didn't he come forward?" Sully asked with a touch of anger.

"Scared shitless, apparently. Rosa said he didn't want any part of the thefts, but one of the gang members threatened him. Mateo and his wife were undocumented." Matterson paused for effect. "If deported, Mateo would have lost his ranch, and everything else he'd acquired in the last thirty years. After the murder, Mateo was going to confess, regardless, but the gang warned him to keep his mouth shut or they'd kill his family."

The room went silent as everyone absorbed the gravity of the situation.

"I think Mateo knew he was a dead man. A loose string." The lines around Matterson's mouth tightened. "I believe he wanted to come clean before they got him. That's why he called you."

"Who was he working with?" Sully asked.

"That, we don't know."

Sully's disappointment was mirrored on the faces of Travis and Joe.

The sheriff ran a hand over his haggard face, rubbed his eyes with his knuckles.

"How will Rosa and the kids manage without Mateo?" Joe asked.

"Mateo had some life insurance. They'll be okay. Also, her brother lives with them. He's a farrier, too. Learned everything from Mateo. He can take care of his brother's clients. The pastor's going out with a bunch of neighbors to take food and help around their ranch."

Sully saw relief wash over Joe's face.

"What about Gunner?" Travis asked.

"Rosa said Mateo didn't have anything to do with that. He told her one of the thieves had a special interest in Gunner. Had an eye on him for years. Wanted him for himself. When Mateo herded Monty's horses past your ranch, that particular thief made a side trip, alone, and took Gunner."

Anger tightened Sully's chest, but looking at his father's hollow eyes, he kept his mouth shut.

Matterson finished his coffee in a gulp. "That's all the info we could squeeze out of Rosa." He pushed his chair back and stood over them for a moment as if contemplating something more to say … but … he nodded, settled his hat on his head, and walked out the door.

CHAPTER TWO

SULLY STEPPED out of the cool barn into the sunlight as a truck hauling a livestock trailer eased to a stop in front of him, brakes groaning. Several bovine yearlings moaned pitifully from the back, their frightened eyes peering through the slats. No doubt, it was their first time separated from their herd. Sully recognized the driver, Roth Henderson, before he saw the Sterling O emblem on the door. An old friend, Roth was a good horse and cattle man, who had worked on the Sterling spread for nearly a decade. Sully knew him to be a competent, easy-going man, but when the circumstances called for it, he could be tough as nails. Roth climbed down from the cab, his weathered face stretching into a toothy grin. "Hey, Sully. Been a while."

Sully shook Roth's out-stretched hand. "Four years."

"Missed seeing you at rodeos." Roth tipped up his hat and his eyes came out of shadow, revealing deep lines fanning outward from the corners.

"My bronc riding days are over. Military cut my career short. Just happy to be back ranching."

Roth's passenger rounded the cab and stood towering over them. Under the shade of his dark hat, the man had a long, hollow face, dark brooding eyes, a bull neck, and a solidly packed frame. He looked like he could wrestle a bull to the ground with one arm.

"This here's Bear." Roth nodded at his companion. "He's taken over my job as livestock foreman. I don't wanna be on the road so much anymore."

In a display of hubris, the man's hand swallowed Sully's in a grip too tight for comfort.

"Sorry to spring this visit on you," Roth said, hitching his thumbs into the pockets of his jeans. "We were over at Petersons' dropping off yearlings, and he told us you've got a really fine reining horse you're looking at selling."

Sully nodded. "That I do. Chico. Wanna take a look?"

"We'd be obliged."

"Just finished grooming him up." Sully led the two men down the long row of stalls to the back of the barn. Chico jutted his head over the gate, whinnied, and watched them with large, expressive eyes. Sully pulled a treat from his pocket and offered it on the palm of his hand. Chico nimbly accepted.

"What do you say?" Sully asked.

Chico bobbed his head up and down, tossing his dark mane.

The two visitors laughed.

"Sully's a hell of a trainer," Roth said to Bear.

"I see that."

Smiling his appreciation, Sully haltered Chico and led him out of the barn, his metal shoes clattering on the cement floor. Outside, the gelding's sleek muscles rippled in the sunlight.

"He's a beaut," Bear said, gliding a hand over the horse's shoulders. "Looks about seventeen hands. Strong haunches." He pulled his cell phone from his breast pocket and started taking photos of Chico from all sides.

"He's the spitting image of Gunner," Roth said. "Same refined head and straight profile."

Sully's smile faded. He lifted off his hat, replaced it. "You hear about the horse thefts here a month back?"

"Who hasn't?" Roth said, eyes sparking with anger. "Goddamned murdering thieves."

"Killed Monty," Bear added gruffly, stuffing his phone back into his pocket. "Stole his whole herd."

"You knew him?" Sully asked.

"Yeah. Bought a couple horses from him last year for Hank. Handsome animals. Fast."

"He spent his whole life perfecting that lineage," Roth said. "Now poof. Gone."

"Monty was a good friend," Sully said sadly. "Gunner was stolen the same night he was killed."

Both men looked startled.

"Sorry to hear that," Roth said, shaking his head. "Hell of a shame what this county's coming to, when murderers can waltz onto a man's property, kill him, and steal his horses."

"And get away with it," Bear said bluntly.

The foreman's words hit Sully like a punch, and he said with bitterness, "They won't get away with it. Only a matter of time before they're caught."

Bear shrugged, revealing a glint of contempt before a dull blankness fell across his eyes.

Cold bastard.

"Now another murder last week," Roth said heatedly. "Mateo Gonzalez was a good friend. Took care of Hank's horses for years." He scratched the back of his neck. "Why would anyone want Mateo dead? Think his murder's connected to Monty's?"

"Very likely." Though he knew for a fact the two murders were connected, Sully kept his tone noncommittal. The sheriff had advised him to keep details of Mateo's death quiet during the investigation, especially Mateo's connection to the horse thefts. He didn't want rumors and half-truths leaking out to the public, or the killers finding out what the law knew.

"This sudden uptick of horse thefts and murders can't be a coincidence. They gotta be connected." Roth waited, searching Sully's face.

Sully looked away, and the men stood in awkward silence, listening to the wind rustle leaves on the huge cottonwoods next to the barn. "Let's wait and see what the sheriff digs up," Sully finally offered.

Calves bawled from the truck. Roth jingled his keys. "Well, we better hit the road. Get these doggies delivered."

"I'll talk to Hank about Chico," Bear said, pulling his hat low and concealing his eyes in shadow. "I expect he'll be interested."

Sully nodded, stroking Chico's silky neck.

The men climbed into their truck. Roth cranked the engine, and their lumbering load groaned out of the driveway. Sully stood watching, thoughts of murder and horse theft swirling through his mind. He already knew the sheriff's investigation had turned up nothing. Whoever killed

Mateo covered his tracks. Ballistics had no match for the bullets that killed Mateo, and the killer left no other evidence.

The prophetic words of Roth's new foreman echoed in his head, that the thieves would never be caught, leaving Sully with a cold feeling in his gut. The man had the sensitivity of a bulldozer. Sully refused to believe the murders of two good men would not be avenged. Like Matterson said, sooner or later, they'd make a mistake.

Turning his thoughts back to Chico, Sully hoped Bear would prove instrumental in pushing the sale through. Hank's operation was first class, and he wasn't one to dicker on price. If he bought Chico, the gelding would be in good hands, and that would take some of the sting out of losing him.

As he led Chico back to his stall, Sully's thoughts turned to Maggie. It was Sunday, their weekly dinner date. A little fizz of excitement had started strumming in his veins when he woke up that morning and stayed with him all day. He liked Maggie. He liked everything about her. The more time he spent with her, the more his feelings deepened, and the more dangerous it felt. Maggie wasn't an available woman. Never would be. With her position in life, her success and money, she was way out of his league. Still, he often found himself fantasizing about her, imagining what it would be like to kiss her, to hold her in his arms. When they were together, he felt a keen attraction to her, and he often fooled himself into thinking she felt the same way. Then reality would set in with a sharp sting, and he would try to force thoughts of her out of his mind—but that was impossible. The way her body felt when he hugged her goodbye last week breathed just below the surface, never fading.

Sully headed to the house to get cleaned up, trying to neutralize his feelings. Right now, just being in Maggie's company, and getting away from horse theft, murder, and ranch problems filled an unquenchable need.

CHAPTER THREE

AS HE PULLED into her driveway, Sully spotted Maggie. Dressed in shorts and a tank top, she was kneeling in the dark soil of a flower bed in a patchwork of colorful flowers. She put down her pruning shears, lifted a gloved hand to shade her eyes, and walked over to meet him. Admiring her athletic figure, he climbed out of the truck toting a cardboard box.

"Is it seven already? I lost track of time. I'm a mess."

No makeup, hair pulled back in a ponytail, knees caked with soil, she looked beautiful to Sully. "No worries. We're just grilling outside, not attending the governor's ball."

"You're so easy," she grinned, pulling off her gloves. "I'll get cleaned up and meet you out back. There's wine in the fridge."

"Deal." He felt a sense of comfort as he followed her into the house, as though this was his second home. She disappeared down the hallway. He made his way to the kitchen, took out a bottle of Merlot and two glasses, and went outside to crank up the grill. He felt himself starting to unwind from his long work week, which had been both physically and mentally taxing. The day's lingering heat warmed his face, but the sun was not oppressive, and the wind blew a clean scent of juniper across the yard. A few white wisps of clouds stretched across the evening sky just above the tree line.

Maggie joined him shortly, carrying steaks and skewered vegetables on a platter. She had changed into a short, gauzy summer dress, her auburn hair loose around her shoulders. Her blue-green eyes stood out against her tan like pieces of stained glass. He marveled at the feelings she stirred in him, just by walking up to him.

With a look of keen interest, she studied the assortment of herbs he'd dug up from the garden and planted in small clay pots. She took them out one by one and placed them in the center of the table. "These smell heavenly. Let's see. Thyme, rosemary, oregano, and basil." She flashed him a good-natured smile. "I'm not sure I should thank you. This means I have to cook more."

"Or you can just look at them. That's all I do."

Her eyes brightened. "I'll find a use for them."

The steaks hissed as he placed them on the grill.

"What's this?" She picked up a quart-size mason jar from the box.

"The best barbeque sauce you've ever tasted. Compliments of my mom."

She unscrewed the lid, stuck in a finger and put it in her mouth. "Wow. Delicious. How'd she get so many flavors to hit your taste buds all at once?"

"A lifetime of experimenting in the kitchen."

"Lucky you." She turned her attention to the steaks smoking on the grill. "I like medium rare."

"Me, too." With a long-handled fork, he flipped the steaks, then stood soaking in the view of the valley and Maggie's beautiful landscaping. Like his mother, she was a talented gardener. The yard was a riot of color and texture. Flagstone pathways cut around blossoming bushes and ornamental trees, and birdbaths and feeders attracted a flurry of birds.

"I'd like to meet your mom sometime, and your dad. You never talk about them." She poured wine into the glasses, handed him one. "I'm still waiting for you to invite me over."

"Honestly, Maggie, I don't see that happening for a while. Dad and I aren't getting along." He watched as a Downy woodpecker drove finches and swallows from a feeder. His gaze met hers. "Plus, I want to paint the house first."

"Sully, things don't have to be perfect. As far as your dad, I'm a therapist. I can handle him." She took a sip of wine, her eyes gently observing him. "I won't judge, even if your dad's a complete lunatic."

"You're getting close." He flipped the steaks and arranged the vegetable kebobs on the grill.

"They're your family. I already like them, just for raising such a wonderful young man."

"Not that young."

She smiled. "Definitely mature."

At that, he smiled.

Within minutes the steaks and veggies were perfectly singed, and he slipped them onto the plates. They sat in cushioned seats at her patio table, and he realized he was ravenous as he cut into the tender beef. "Good beef," he said out of the side of his mouth.

"Good sauce. Give your mom my thanks."

"Will do." He chewed and swallowed, admiring the graceful line of Maggie's neck and shoulders, her expressive hands and long slender fingers. "My mom wants to move back to the ranch."

She arched her brows. "Your parents are getting back together?"

"No. Not even close. She's moving into a little cottage we have out on the creek, away from the house, and Dad. She'll have her privacy, and will still be able to garden, ride the horses, work with the animals. Things that make her happy."

"She rides?"

"Wonderful rider. She also does most of the veterinary work. Or used to, anyway."

"It must be hard for her to be away from all that."

He felt his throat tighten, thinking about his mother's isolation and loneliness. "Very hard."

A breeze lifted Maggie's hair and her bared shoulders glowed in the dimming light. Her eyes were clear and curious. "Will your parents be able to get along?"

He shrugged and stabbed a piece of steak. "It'll be an experiment. She can't stay where she is. Never leaving the house."

Maggie blinked. "Why doesn't she leave?"

He hesitated, not sure how much to tell her. "Emotional issues."

Maggie chewed for a moment. She sipped her wine, set her glass down. "Do you want me to visit with her? I specialize in treating these kinds of problems."

He mulled it over. "Part of me says yes, part says no."

"I understand." She gazed steadily into his eyes. "You don't want me to insert myself into your messy family affairs."

"Right."

"You believe it will influence my feelings for you."

"Right again."

"Nothing could make me think less of you, Sully." Their eyes met and for a long moment a feeling of tender friendship passed between them. She gave him an easy smile. "Why don't you think it over? Maybe discuss it with your mom." Her voice was light and friendly, no hint of therapeutic prying. "Whatever she and I talk about would be confidential. No ripple effect." She sipped her wine. "And of course, I'd be doing it as a friend. Free of charge."

"Thank you for the offer." He didn't see it happening. His mother was too private. Too stubborn.

It was pleasant eating and drinking with the sweet scent of flowers in the air. Twilight deepened, the sun melted into a red and orange sea across the mountains, and an amber glow colored the valley. Overhead, Venus winked at them.

Sully watched Maggie's skin turn to gold, her eyes to jade. When they finished dinner, she stacked the dishes and took them inside, then returned shortly with another bottle of wine. She lit two votive candles and refilled their glasses. "You know, there's a lot about you I know nothing about. I don't mean to pry, but I care enough to want to share your personal life."

He was feeling relaxed from the wine, the mellowness of the evening, and Maggie's gentle company. "I thought I was an open book."

"You are. With a lot of chapters missing."

He stretched his legs under the table and clasped his hands behind his head. "Ask me anything. You get five free answers without penalty."

"Okay. Why are you at odds with your dad?"

"Ouch. You go straight for the jugular. Couldn't you ease into that one slowly?"

She looked like the Mona Lisa, an inscrutable expression on her face. "Sully, I was serious when I said nothing you tell me will dampen our friendship. If anything, I'll feel more invested."

"Invested how?"

"Stop stalling."

"There's not a lot I can tell you. In my family, we were raised to keep secrets. We're good at it. I have a war chest buried in the basement brimming with classified information. I talk to my horses. Outside the family, only equines know what goes on with the Sullivan family."

She sat silently waiting, eyes boring a hole in his forehead.

"I don't even confide in Travis," he said defensively. "My closest friend."

She crossed her arms and continued giving him the silent treatment.

"Is this a rite of passage?" he asked.

"Yes. For our friendship to advance to the next level."

"What's the next level?"

Her smile was open to interpretation. "Put the key in the lock and find out."

Intrigued, Sully rambled, telling her everything that happened over the last week: his father disappearing from the ranch, how he and Travis tracked him to the gorge, how Sully got attacked and was knocked out, how he discovered a body in the gorge and thought it was his father, and finally, the sheriff showing up, and Joe stumbling out of the Yukon. And last, but not least, it turned out the dead man was an old friend.

Maggie never once interrupted, but when he finished, she looked astonished. "Holy shit, Sully."

"What?" He couldn't remember ever hearing her curse before.

"It's like you live on another planet! I go to the grocery store, to the gym, do laundry. You hunt murderous horse thieves, get assaulted, find dead bodies."

It made his skin prickle to think about it. He scratched his head. "When you put it like that, yeah. It is out of the ordinary."

"You have a gift for understatement."

"I have a gift for burying my feelings. Trust me, it wasn't an easy week." Several moments of silence passed while he struggled to keep his emotions stifled. They pressed hard against the vaulted door of their cell, eager to surface. With a feigned look of complacency, he sipped his wine. "So is that enough secret sharing for one night?"

"You knocked the wind out of me."

"So what's my reward?" he asked with a wicked lilt to his tone.

Silence. She looked at him with a level, steady gaze, and asked softly, "Are you flirting with me?"

"No. Yes. I mean … maybe. What do you want the right answer to be?"

"The wine is making you silly. You're toying with me."

"No, I'm not. I am flirting. Hell, don't friends get to flirt a little?"

"Of course. It's harmless. Just unexpected. I'm old enough to be your mother." Her tone didn't convince him. He heard something in it. Something wistful.

"You're Eric's mother. Not mine. You're not that much older than me. Only fourteen years."

"Women get pregnant at fourteen."

"What I mean is … I don't think of you as an older woman."

"Thank you. I'm flattered, I think."

If she could see his expression, she'd know exactly what he was thinking. He thought she was sexy as hell, and he wanted to go beyond friendship. The candles had burned down low and sputtered, casting flickering shadows across their faces. He longed to see her expression, get a clue how she felt about his lame attempt to gauge her feelings. Rein it in, he told himself sternly.

CHAPTER FOUR

CODY RODE BUSTER to the arena and was told by Nelson that Justin had outmatched all five bulls Hank had put under him that afternoon. A rugged, seasoned cowboy, Nelson didn't impress easily, yet today she felt his excitement stirring the air around him. "Those five bulls aren't even close to the monsters he'll face at top rodeos," she said.

"Still, the kid looked good." Nelson slapped dust from his jeans with his hat and placed it back on his head. "Real good."

"We'll see how well he does on our big boys." She knew Hank had just been warming Justin up these last four weeks on minor league bulls, focusing on technique, and she had assumed it wasn't going well. Justin sometimes came into dinner limping, or nursing an arm or wrist, and from the talk around the table, she knew he was hitting the dirt as much as he was staying on board. Sustaining injuries in bull riding was the norm in this business. Some injuries could put you on the sideline for weeks, and everyone knew it was just a matter of time before the "big one" ended a career. She admired Justin for his courage, for going into the arena day after day and facing life-threatening injuries.

Cody tethered Buster and climbed on the rail above the chute to join her father. Hank barely took notice of her. Bear herded a bull down the narrow passageway leading from the holding pen and slammed the metal grate behind him with a loud clank. Her breath caught. The bull was Crash Course. "What're you up to, Dad? He won't last two seconds on that bull."

"Don't expect him to." Hank pulled his hat down to block the sun. "But it's time he got a taste of the real thing."

A tingle of fear passed through her, which she tried to suppress. This was a dangerous profession, but Justin was an adult. He'd made his own choice to take it on.

Agitated by his captivity, Crash Course snorted and flung his weight against the sides of the chute. The earth seemed to wobble. Roth cautiously adjusted the flank strap while Hank worked the rope around the bull's sizable girth.

Cody sensed a heavy presence and turned as Bear strode up beside her. It unnerved her that such a big man could move so quietly. To make conversation, she asked, "What's your take on Justin?"

"Shovels shit pretty good." Bear shot Justin a sour look and spit on the ground. "You'd think the kid was Lane freaking Frost, the way your dad coddles him."

"Dad knows what he's doing," she said heatedly. "Justin's been working his tail off."

Bear eyed her for a long moment, and she felt chilled by his cold expression.

He put up his hands. "No offense intended." With a sideward glance, he ambled off into the arena to assist the other hands.

Cody always felt uneasy in Bear's presence. He shared some of the more loathsome traits of her ex, Buddy Jack. Like Buddy, Bear was strong and handsome, and he could lay on the charm with silky smoothness, which worked on her sister like a love potion. It had the opposite effect on Cody. Bear's assumption that he was her equal because he was the 'fiancé' stirred her indignation. He was an employee of the Sterling family, and he should show appropriate humility. Sarah hadn't yet set a wedding date, and Cody prayed she never would. Her sister had never sustained a relationship beyond a couple of years, and Cody hoped Bear's expiration date would rear up soon. In unguarded moments after he'd downed a few beers, she'd caught a malevolent glint in his eyes when Sarah talked to other cowboys. That same look in Buddy's eyes had been a prelude to violence. She had learned to back away, fast. And hide.

Forcing barbed memories of Buddy Jack back into some hidden vault, she joined Justin, who was rubbing sticky rosin into the palm of his gloved hand. He had the whole testosterone thing going on—the consummate pro in his protective vest and smooth leather chaps lined with long fringe. It dawned on her with a jolt that he was outfitted in her father's old rodeo duds, inscribed with the brand names from his former sponsors. Hank's total commitment to Justin hit home like a nail under a sledgehammer. With his lean athletic build, she realized Justin could easily pass for Hank at that age, or more profoundly, his son.

Justin glanced over at her and nodded. "Miss Sterling."

"Hey." She studied him for a moment, suppressing her apprehension. "Think you're ready for Crash Course?"

"Hell, yeah."

She shoved her hands into the pockets of her jeans. "Don't underestimate this bull, Justin. He can hurt you, bad."

Strapping on his helmet, he flashed her a confident grin. "Your dad thinks I'm ready. I trust his judgment."

She almost advised him to abort the ride, to keep practicing on minor bulls, but she caught herself before her lips formed the words. That would've shown lack of trust in his ability, not the strong leadership a cowboy needed from management. His good mood was contagious. She found herself smiling back and realized she had to watch herself around him. His quiet, down-to-earth manner could be completely disarming. She'd already been seduced more than once into lowering her guard, even laughing and flirting a bit when they played poker, now almost a nightly routine. "Hang tough," she said in an assertive tone, as much to herself as to Justin.

"Hang tough. Got it." He made a thumb's up gesture, his tone slightly mocking. With no outward sign of fear, he climbed over the railing, descended into the chute, and straddled the back of the massive bull. She glanced around and saw that Bear's gaze had shifted to her sister. Sarah was standing on the sidelines dressed in tight jeans and a low-cut T-shirt, her attention focused intently on Justin. Everyone, Cody realized, had their eyes on Justin. Billy, Roth, and Nelson were mounted on top-notch quarter horses in the ring, looking alert, ready to rush to his aid if necessary. There was a hush in the air. This was the moment of truth.

Cody climbed up on the chute next to her father. Below them, Crash Course was wild-eyed, snorting and butting his head against the gate. Keeping his balance, Justin clenched his gloved hand tighter around the stiff rope handle. He looked up, flashed those neon blues, and nodded. "Let 'er rip!"

Bear swung the gate wide open.

The bull launched himself into the arena as though jet propelled, then turned back toward the chute and did a hair-raising spin. He leapt into the air as though weightless, legs kicking out to one side before coming down and hitting the earth like a tank, lifting a voluminous cloud of dust. A chill of excitement raced along Cody's spine. The bull's unpredictability was the Sterling trademark. Justin, she saw, was holding on with everything he had.

"Hang tough!" Hank shouted.

Crash Course continued his spine-ramming leaps and spins, and to Cody's surprise, Justin didn't fly off his back. His style was rhythmic and instinctual, but mostly he was tenacious as hell. It wasn't possible for him to loosen his grip! The rope would have to snap to get him off the bull's back. Her jaw dropped a little. Justin was as much a natural performer as Crash Course. Champion stock.

The buzzer sounded at eight seconds and Justin dismounted fluidly, avoiding the 2000 pounds of muscled steel that could easily crush his bones. Nelson and Roth shot forward on their horses and herded Crash Course out of the arena, leaving behind a billowing trail of dust.

Excited voices cried out all around. Cody and Hank exchanged a look of astonishment. Justin had exceeded even her dad's expectations. How had a novice rider stayed on a bull that had outmatched dozens of cowboys holding world titles? She and Hank joined Sarah and the cowboys who were high-fiving Justin and whooping it up. Everyone wore a shit-eating grin.

Brimming with elation and pride, Hank slapped Justin soundly on the back. "Hell of a ride! Hell of a ride!"

Justin's tanned face flushed red with pleasure.

Cody sensed the bonds of friendship deepening between Justin, her family, and the hands. She was thrilled to see a vitality restored to her father's spirit that had dimmed after her mother's death. Strange, she thought, Justin had taken full possession of her dad's attention, yet she felt no resentment. Just the opposite, in fact. A release of pressure. Living under the hot glare of her father's demand for perfection shifted to Justin's shoulders, providing Hank with something she and Sarah had never been able to give. Justin flourished under Hank's rigorous supervision. A win-win all around.

Cody's gaze fell upon her sister, and to her dismay, Sarah morphed into a full-blown groupie—eyelashes batting, her body clinging to Justin like a Velcro viper. Cody watched with sympathy as Justin tried to disentangle her arms from his neck. Sarah finally backed off, hands clasped like a disciple in ecstatic prayer, face glowing with adoration.

Bear remained on the sideline, beefy arms crossed, harpooning Justin with little darts of malice. The foreman's glare abruptly shifted to Cody and she felt the heat of his animosity before he shifted his expression into neutral. Bear felt threatened by Justin, with good reason. He'd just become invisible, his status as foreman and boyfriend eclipsed by Justin's phenomenal talent. With a stiff grin fixed on his face, he joined the group and shadow boxed Justin's arm. "Looked good out there, dude."

Despite his achievement, Justin wasn't bouncing his ego around all over the place. His banter with the ranch hands remained modest and polite, but more spirited.

"Let's get these bulls stalled, and then we'll all meet up at the house," Hank said with exuberance. "It's barbeque time." He and the hands gathered up the horses and headed for the holding pens where the bulls had been temporarily housed.

As Cody watched, Sarah bypassed Bear, locked arms with Justin, and tried to steer him toward the house. Cody recalled what a rabble-rouser Sarah had been in high school. She made it a habit to date several guys at once, swearing loyalty to each while trying to conceal one from the other. Secrets don't stay hidden in a small town. A continuous soap opera played out, season after season. Memorizing her favorite lines and shenanigans, Sarah emulated the actors on the shows she watched every afternoon. Fistfights, drunken brawls, and jealous rages were commonplace. Hank and Olivia tried to calm the waters, soothe the ruptured nerves of other parents, and even bailed their sons out of jail.

The family thought Sarah finally settled down when she married Chase Hillman and moved to his small spread in Tumalo. Their relief was short-lived. Sarah cheated with Chase's best friend, Neil. A year later, jilted by Neil and going through a divorce, she was back at the family ranch. Not to be deterred, Sarah hit on both Roth and Nelson in her time, but the two were smart enough to choose their jobs over a few lusty romps in the hay. Bear had not shown the same restraint. Employed for two years, he seemed to think being foreman and cavorting with

Sarah came as a package deal, and insured him a cut of the family business when they married. Sarah had been wearing his ring for a year, but she squirmed like a jellyfish when Bear tried to pin down the wedding date.

At twenty-seven, she showed no sign of maturing, and seemed oblivious to the hornet's nest she had just swatted.

"Go on ahead, Sarah," Justin said, pulling his arm away from hers while shooting a sideward glance at Bear. "I gotta get my gear packed."

"Okay. I'll save you a seat." Sarah caught up with Bear and they left together, though not wrapped in each other's arms as usual.

Cody untied Buster and led him to the railing where Justin was unfastening his chaps. "What was it like riding Crash?"

He glanced up and flashed a high voltage smile. "Most insane eight seconds this side of an electric chair."

"You looked good out there. You've got a solid future as a pro."

"Thanks. All the credit goes to your dad. I couldn't have ridden that bull a week ago." He slapped dust from his chaps and folded them over the railing. "Every time I got tossed in the dirt, Hank helped me see where I was going wrong. He inspired me to pick myself up and try again."

"Dad's big on practice and discipline."

"That's why you ride as well as you do. You were lucky to grow up with him." He settled his brown Stetson over his sandy hair, shading his eyes, and nodded at Buster. "By the time you get that horse groomed, you'll be late for the barbeque."

"No worries," she said.

"I'd be happy to help." He added playfully, "Maybe you'd like to interrogate me some more."

"As long as you don't use a fake name again, that bridge doesn't need re-crossing."

"Won't make that mistake. Though I thought Alex Hamilton had a nice ring to it."

"Leave it to the historians."

Justin fondly stroked Buster's neck. The gelding lowered his head, relaxing. "Hey, buddy." He glanced at Cody. "He likes me."

Justin's arm was brushing hers, his hand nuzzling Buster's velvety mouth. He had stepped into her hemisphere, disrupting her protective field. Cody felt the heat from his body and picked up his scent; leather and a faint sweetness, like grass hay. His blue eyes held hers in a mesmerizing gaze. Her mind emptied of thought. She stood motionless, as though in a trance. She couldn't move the tiniest muscle in her tongue to speak.

"You should trust your horse," he said quietly. "He knows a good guy when he sees one."

Justin's closeness stirred a sweet, piercing ache. A longing to be kissed. It scared the hell out of her.

"You okay?" he asked, brow creasing.

Cody realized her face had hardened into her usual stone mask. She stepped away from him and rounded Buster, stumbling a little. Feeling a little detached from her body, she placed her boot in the stirrup and mounted, then exhaled sharply as though getting rid of a nasty odor. Justin was dangerous. Like Buddy, he could rob her of reason. Looking down her nose at him, she said curtly, "Buster liked my ex, too. And he was a psycho."

Justin squinted up at her with a bewildered expression.

She pressed her heels into Buster's sides and the gelding took off at a trot, quickly putting a safe distance between her and Justin. No doubt, he thought she was a nut job, and he'd be right. Cody understood she was emotionally damaged. Splintered. Broken. She was doing her best to fit the pieces of her life back together, but the edges didn't quite match up, and probably never would. Her reality always felt a little askew. She shuddered, sensing the ominous presence of her ex-husband loom up behind her, though she knew the feeling was irrational. Buddy was barricaded behind thick stone walls and steel bars. Too late in the marriage game, Cody came face to face with the monster who hid behind his handsome guise. By then he had become her jailer, controlling her every move with the very real threat of violence.

She felt a sudden rush of shame and was catapulted back through time. A memory ignited in her mind of Buddy's fist slamming into her face, crushing bone and cartilage, and she experienced a metal taste in her mouth, a byproduct of fear. Cody cursed Buddy under her breath. In the future, she would kill in a heartbeat, with whatever she could get her hands on, before allowing a man to violate her body and soul.

CHAPTER FIVE

AS CODY FINISHED brushing Buster, she heard shrill voices echo across the stalls. Peering over the gelding's withers, she saw Sarah and Bear enter the barn, their bodies backlit by the late afternoon sun. Bear spit out Justin's name in a fierce rumbling of anger. Sarah prowled in front of him like a cat, agile and restless, driven by something unquenchable, her red hair tumbling around her shoulders.

Bear's arms suddenly snaked out, grasped her waist, and jerked her around to face him.

"Let go!" Sarah struggled, her palms pushing against his chest.

He pulled her tighter.

"Damn you! Let go!" Sarah wrenched herself free, struck Bear violently across the face, and bolted from the barn. "Stay away from me. We're done!" Her words reverberated through the barn like gunshots.

Wow. Dramatic. As good a scene as any Sarah had ever performed. Better than Scarlett O'Hara striking Rhett in "Gone with the Wind."

Sarah's rebelliousness thrilled Cody. Bear showed all the telltale signs of a batterer. Controlling, arrogant, jealous. In a moment of rage, he could snap Sarah's neck like a chicken bone. Cody wished she'd had the courage to leave Buddy while they were still dating. Instead she married the bastard and dive-bombed into hell.

She stood motionless in Buster's stall, watching Bear. He pulled a flask from his hip pocket and tipped it skyward, his pronounced Adam's apple rolling as he drained it. Wiping his mouth with the back of his hand, his eyes did a sweep of the barn. Cody withdrew, but not before making fleeting contact with his malignant stare. The barn was quiet except for the muffled sounds of horse hooves. A full minute passed before she peered out again. Bear was gone.

Despite the warmth of the barn, Cody was trembling. The episode between Bear and Sarah hit home, unearthing memories of Buddy's last drunken rampage. Her mind traveled to a place where her deepest fears resided, and she felt a watery feeling in her stomach. Her hands rose to protect her breasts as horrific memories flickered through her mind like an old movie reel.

Impatient to get to his hay, Buster prodded her from behind, startling her out of her grisly travelogue. She wiped her sweating hands on her jeans, took a few deep breaths to compose herself, and left the barn. By the time she reached the house, Carlos and Maresol were slapping steaks and ribs on the huge outdoor grill. Under the canopy of giant fir trees, Hank and the ranch hands were popping open beer bottles and wolfing down appetizers. The dogs, parked at the grill at full attention, whined for scraps. Outside the huddle of men, Bear stood leaning against the massive red trunk of a ponderosa, pulling on his beer with a grim expression, his right cheek still colored from Sarah's slap. He caught her stare and held it defiantly until she glanced away.

Cody felt detached, as though watching the world from behind a veil. Wanting to stay in her safety zone, she entered the house through the side entrance, dashed up to her room and locked the door behind her. The decor hadn't changed since high school. She felt a complete disconnect from the teenager who picked out the velvet curtains, floral bed linens, and Impressionist paintings of horses and ballerinas. When she got engaged to Buddy three years earlier, she had a built-in expectation of happiness, as though a sprinkle of fairy dust came with the wedding vows, ensuring happiness ever after. Men were the weaker sex, she firmly believed, and could be controlled as easily as a horse. She married Buddy thinking she had the upper hand. To this day, the extent of her naïveté still shocked her.

The coin always flipped to the other side. Good times take a turn for the worse. Even her parents weren't bulletproof. She and Sarah were left dazed with grief after the speedy decline of their mother's health. Following two weeks of blinding headaches, Olivia was diagnosed with a brain tumor, and she died soon after, following a courageous battle with cancer. Vanished. Stripped from their lives. Her father turned into a ghost, teetering on autopilot, numb to the outer world, focused inward, living on memories. The passion fueling his life had been sucked out of him and buried with Olivia. Cody was useless to her father. Battered and emotionally paralyzed, she was unable to even help herself.

Five months after her mother's death, Cody landed in the ICU hanging on to life by the thinnest of filaments. Covered in Cody's blood, Buddy was thrown into jail in a drunken, drug-induced haze, charged with first-degree attempted murder. When the facts of the case emerged, and X-rays revealed the injuries Cody had sustained over the course of her three-year marriage, Hank was stunned. He never had a clue. No one did. Cody kept the abuse masterfully hidden.

She returned home from the hospital humiliated, unwilling to be branded a victim, and ignoring everyone's advice to get counseling. She spoke to no one about her abuse, never left the ranch, and strived to become invisible to men. As camouflage, she wore over-sized men's clothing. This provided an illusion of substance, filling the space around her with layers of protection.

So much for happy endings. Frozen in graceful poses, the ballerinas staring at her from the paintings on the wall seemed to leer at her.

Cody showered, wiped the steam from the mirror, and took a cold, hard look at the damage. Six red scars carved into pale skin. The one on her neck was small, just missing the carotid artery. Even in his deranged state, Buddy knew not to execute a killing blow. He had another plan in mind. The two scars on her abdomen were almost perpendicular, the exact size of the blade of his hunting knife. Thrust in and out. The other three were jagged and horizontal where the blade sliced through her breasts from left to right, the middle one dissecting her nipples.

After Buddy completed his butchery, he stumbled out of the bedroom and passed out in his vomit in the hallway. Cody dialed 911, almost bleeding to death before the sheriff arrived. Buddy's intent was mutilation, he told the sheriff later, so no other man would want her. He succeeded. Once round and smooth and soft, her breasts had been a point of feminine pride, an alluring offering to the opposite sex. Now, like her soul, they were disfigured. The doctors told her reconstruction could make her breasts pretty again, but Cody wasn't ready. She couldn't bear the thought of anything cutting through her flesh. Not now. Not for a very long time.

She opened the drawer of her nightstand and pulled out her Colt .45. The cold steel felt good in her hands. Raised with firearms, she handled guns well and was an excellent shot. She'd bought the Colt as soon as she was released from the hospital. The pistol was small and lightweight, with great accuracy and stopping power. If she'd had it the night Buddy attacked her, he'd be rotting in his grave right now instead of a prison cell.

Cody laid the Colt on the marble counter and turned her attention to her immediate needs; combing her wet hair, applying moisturizer, brushing her teeth. As she camouflaged the scar on her neck with makeup, thoughts of Justin filled her mind. She pictured his blue eyes squinting at her in the sun, his unflinching composure when he straddled a bull that could easily kill him. He stirred in her a desire to be feminine again; to flirt, to laugh, to feel empowered by the power she held over a man. Fear soiled those vibrant emotions. Her yearning to come out of hiding felt both irrepressible and life threatening.

She studied the offerings of her closet. Clothing from her former life hung to one side; clingy dresses that accentuated the swell of her breasts, her tiny waist. Up front hung her new wardrobe: half a dozen men's shirts, extra-large, and as many pairs of jeans. She pulled out a plaid flannel shirt that was so big she could pull it over her head without unfastening the buttons. After wiggling into a pair of baggy Wranglers, she ran a belt through the loops and cinched it tight to keep it from falling off her hips. I'm the abominable snowman, she thought as she looked at her reflection in the mirror, envisioning herself through Justin's eyes. She knew it was irrational, but she tucked the Colt .45 into the waistband at the small of her back and covered it with the baggy shirt.

The smell of grilled meat drifted through the open window along with the sound of muffled voices and laughter. Feeling substantially bulked up and as upholstered as an easy chair, she summoned her composure and left the safety of her room.

CHAPTER SIX

WHEN CODY stepped out on the back porch, the melting sun had drenched the yard in a golden glow, deepening the tanned complexions of men who worked outdoors all year. Laughing, looking relaxed, and nursing bottles of beer, the ranch hands huddled under the fragrant canopy of fir trees. Bear smoked, still rooted to the ponderosa, watching the festivity with dark, brooding eyes. Strings of tiny white lights twinkled in the branches, sweet-smelling smoke sifted up through the boughs from the grill, and the background music added a festive mood to the evening.

Cody joined her father at the grill as Carlos laid ribs slathered in sauce across his plate. Cody chose a thick, juicy steak, and followed Hank across the grass to the long outdoor table under the trees. Ignoring his ribs, he sat hunched over his phone, thumbs busy, the dusty brim of his hat hiding everything but his mouth, which slowly curled into a smile.

"Asian markets just open?" she asked.

"Yep. Stocks are up."

"Always good news." She busied herself scooping potato salad and baked beans onto their plates. "Dad, eat."

"Yes, ma'am." He slipped the phone into his pocket, shot her a smile, and bit into a rib.

The screen door shut with a loud clatter and all heads turned to the porch. Cody could practically hear a collective intake of breath as her sister descended the stairs with the poise of a supermodel. Sarah worked out like a fiend, and tonight her sculpted arms and legs were on full display in a short summer dress and western boots studded with rhinestones. She wore her hair in a loose bun, with a few tendrils loose around her long, slender neck.

Cody felt a jolt of envy as she watched her sister's ease around the men. She remembered when she took pleasure in dressing seductively, but now if she bared that much skin she'd feel turned inside out.

Loosened up by alcohol, the ranch hands took special notice of the pretty lady in their midst. Roth took Sarah by the hand and spun her around in sync to the music, then ushered her to the front of the line ahead of Justin, who flashed her a dazzling smile. Sarah shot back a grin as bright as high beams on a moonless night. Cody could almost see the sparks fly. At the end of the line, Bear's posture stiffened, and his face darkened a shade.

Justin leaned in close to Sarah and made some remark that must've been sidesplitting, judging from her high-pitched laughter. Even the dogs looked up from their scraps. Cody felt a tightening in her chest as she watched them. Sitting in her shapeless, over-sized clothes, she felt about as attractive as Quasimodo.

Hank wiped barbeque sauce off his mouth with a napkin and shot Cody a quizzical look. "What's up with Sarah and Bear? She's been giving him the cold shoulder all day."

"She broke up with him. Now she seems to have Justin in her sights."

Surprisingly, her father smiled.

"You approve?" she asked.

"Well, hell yeah. You know how I feel about Bear. Good man on the job. As a family member, not so much."

"You think she's a good match for Justin?"

"Couldn't find a better man," he said, eyes sparkling. He turned back to his ribs, gnawing hungrily.

Cody sat dumbfounded. After just a few weeks, Hank was ready to usher Justin into the family circle. Apparently, Justin was here to stay, yet the thought of him transplanted into the family as Sarah's boyfriend made her stomach knot. Fighting his maddening attractiveness, while watching her sister fearlessly embrace it, seemed like an endless form of torture. A shadow fell across her plate and she looked up to see Justin holding two frosted bottles of Corona in one hand, his plate of food in the other.

"You look a million miles away," he said. "Thirsty?"

"Thanks." She took one of the beers and ignored him, leaving him standing awkwardly over her chair.

"Join us," Hank said enthusiastically, motioning with a rib bone to the seat next to his, normally occupied by Bear.

Justin settled across from Cody, and immediately got to work on his steak with his knife and fork. Like the other hands, he wasn't bashful about eating with speedy efficiency. Between bites, he and Hank talked shop, evaluating the smallest details of Justin's performance that afternoon.

"You were swinging your free arm a little too much," Hank said. "That made your hips twist a bit. A little more so, and you would've hit the dirt."

"Yeah, I felt I was off balance at times," Justin said, cheeks packed with food.

"Ease up to where you're nearly sitting on your hand," Hank said. "Stay that way the entire ride, and sit up off your butt. That'll put all of your weight on the inside of your thighs."

Cody couldn't help adding. "Then you're holding on to the bull with your thighs and feet. You ride the buck, not the bull."

"Yes ma'am. I'll remember that," Justin said with a touch of humor, his gaze locking onto hers. "Ride the buck, not the bull."

Feeling her face heat up, she turned her attention to her steak, appreciating beef so tender it practically melted in her mouth. Though she avoided looking at him directly, she was keenly aware of the warm energy emanating from his body.

With a jingle of bracelets and a whiff of cinnamon, Sarah lowered herself next to Justin as gracefully as a flower bending in the breeze. They shared a smile.

"Crash came out of that chute today ready to kick some serious ass," Sarah said. "You one-upped him."

"He was hotter than a firecracker," Roth said, joining them with Nelson and Billy in tow. The ranch hands dove into their food as though dinner was an eating contest.

"That was a super clean ride," Billy said. "Crash was really bucking."

"I fought him all the way," Justin said, eyes flashing with excitement. "He made a left, turned back to the right, and started a spin.

Faked me out when he jumped out of that spin."

"Yeah, I thought you was in trouble right there," Nelson said.

Hank removed his hat and ran a sunburned hand through his flattened hair, spiking it up like a punk rocker. "All in all, a damn good afternoon."

"What bull are you gonna surprise me with tomorrow?" Justin asked.

"No work tomorrow," Hank said. "Take the day off. You've earned it. Go into town."

"Can I go?" Sarah piped up. "I need a few things."

"Take both girls," Hank said. "Cody, you need to get off the ranch, too."

"She doesn't wanna go," Sarah said, giving Cody a warning glance.

Cody frowned. Would her sister ever learn the art of subtlety?

Justin's gaze landed on Cody. "Sure she does. Wanna come, Cody?"

She shrugged. "I'll think about it."

Bear sank heavily into the chair next to Sarah, the last to arrive at the table, with no food and a fresh bottle of Pale Ale. He laced an arm across her shoulder. She flinched. He withdrew it, shooting an angry look at Justin.

Cody saw that Bear wasn't going to give Sarah up easily. She worried what a scorned lover might take into his mind to do. Jealousy was a powerful force.

Maresol lit the lanterns on the table. The flames shot up and flickered softly over the table. A couple of moths flew in to dance outside the glass. Forks and knives clicked on plates.

"Sarah, did you get Justin registered for the summer rodeos?" Hank asked.

"Yep. The first is in June, in Sisters," she said. "Coming up in three weeks."

"That rodeo pulls in good bulls, good riders," Roth said.

"Sisters has the highest purse in the nation," Sarah said.

"I've dreamt about doing that rodeo," Justin said. "I've gone as a spectator every year. Can't believe I'm gonna be on the other side of the chute."

"Next you'll be headed to Idaho, then Nevada," Sarah said. "I emailed you the calendar dates, Dad."

"Did you contact local airports?" Hank said. "Justin and I need landing permission."

"Done," Sarah said.

"Good girl."

A silent question hung in the air. Justin was flying? Bear always traveled with Hank by air, while the other hands drove the RV and cattle truck.

"I want Justin's travel time to be short and easy," Hank said. "Since he's competing, he needs to be rested mentally and physically. Bear, you can help Roth with the driving."

"No problem," Bear said, expressionless, but Cody saw a vein pulse on his temple.

"Cody, you'll be flying with us, too," Hank said.

"Me?" She was unable to hide the stark surprise in her voice. She hadn't been to a rodeo with Hank since high school.

"You ready to get involved in the rodeo side of the business?" he asked with a direct stare.

She hesitated. It would mean leaving the safety of the ranch and putting herself out into the world again. She met Hank's gaze head on. "Yeah, I'm ready."

Hank's smile was subtle, but the corners of his eyes crinkled with pleasure. Her father wanted her to play a bigger role in the family business, despite the fact that she'd walked away from the ranch without a second thought when she married Buddy. Seemed all was well and forgiven between them.

"What about me, Dad?" Sarah asked, her red fingernails tapping the table.

Hank's eyebrows arched in surprise. "When have you ever wanted to go to a rodeo, Sarah? You don't like bulls or horses."

"Maybe I'm changing," she said, shooting a smile at Justin.

"Sarah, as long as you keep up your office work, you're welcome to come. You can ride in the motor home with Bear and Roth."

Caught in the lantern light, sparks of defiance flashed in her eyes. "Why can't I fly, too?"

Hank looked flustered. "We'll see, Sarah."

The men never stopped chewing, their eyes darting from Hank to Bear to Sarah, then back to Bear. The muscles in Bear's face tightened, his eyes glassy and bloodshot. In the sudden strained silence, everyone listened to the music coming through the sound system. "You Save Me" was playing by Kenny Chesney. Slow, sensual, romantic. Cody watched her sister do exactly the wrong thing.

"I love this song, Justin," Sarah said. "Dance with me. Pleeeease?"

All eyes turned to Justin, whose fork was suspended halfway to his mouth. His face and neck flushed red. He lowered his fork and wiped his mouth with his napkin, he but didn't rise. "I'm not much of a dancer."

"Oh come on. This is easy. Nice 'n slow." Sarah stood over him, grabbed his hand, and pulled.

"Okay, sure." He got slowly to his feet, took Sarah in his arms and made it quickly apparent that he was a good dancer after all, leading her in a smooth two-step on the grass.   Cody couldn't help but think how good they looked together, athletic and graceful, even though Sarah stood four inches taller in her boot heels. Never taking her eyes off his, Sarah sang along with the lyrics. Cody felt uncomfortable watching, but she was transfixed by the queer expression on her sister's face—a mix of excitement and determination. Cody pulled her gaze away and glanced at Bear.

Scowling deeply, the foreman crossed his massive arms and leaned heavily back in his chair. Before his face moved out of the lamplight, Cody saw the glint of pure hatred in his eyes. It made her flesh crawl. She could feel his wrath rolling across the table.

When the song ended, Justin walked Sarah back to her chair, but he remained standing. "It's been a long day," he said lazily. "Guess I'll call it a night."

Cody noticed his plate was half full.

"Not staying for dessert?" Hank asked, a shadow falling across his face.

"We got chocolate cake," Nelson said. "Maresol made it special for the party."

"Save me a piece," Justin said. "I'm beat."

"What about going to town tomorrow?" Sarah asked eagerly.

Justin glanced at Bear and said in an apologetic tone, "Let's talk at breakfast."

Smart man, Cody thought. Separating himself from a bad situation. Still, Cody felt disappointment as she watched him fade away from the lantern light, draining his bright energy from the table.

"I'll dance with you," Bear said, fingers tightening around Sarah's arm.

She yanked her arm away. "Don't touch me!"

Strained silence.

"I don't know what's going on between you two," Hank said sternly. "But don't bring it to the table. Work it out in private."

The good mood at the table fizzled. Everyone sat quietly eating.

"My apologies, Hank," Bear said, slurring his words. He stood unsteadily, his hand holding onto the edge of the table, and then he staggered away into the darkness.

CHAPTER SEVEN

MAGGIE RELIT the candles, and in the flickering light, she and Sully finished the second bottle of wine. The moon hung in the sky like a bright medallion, casting the yard in silvery light. Sully found it peaceful on the hillside, with the twinkling lights of town spread across the valley below. A small herd of white-tailed deer drifted through the yard, watching them with curiosity, showing no fear. Sully stretched his legs under the table, crossing one boot over the other, and rubbed the tightness in his neck, feeling the fatigue of his unceasing work schedule.

"You look tired," Maggie said, her cheeks flushed from wine.

"Long week."

"Do you ever take a day off?"

"I will this fall. I figure I'll be mostly caught up by then."

She looked at him critically for a moment, and he thought she was about to give him a lecture. Instead, her face softened. "I thought you might want to take some time off next Sunday. It's Eric's birthday. I want to visit his grave."

"Sure," he said without hesitation. "That would mean a lot to me."

She looked relieved. "I thought you might feel that way. I don't want to go alone."

"I'll drive," he said.

"I'd appreciate that." A long pause. "He'll be twenty-three."

Maggie still talked about Eric in the present tense, as though he were just on vacation, and would one day waltz back into her life.

Tears welled into her eyes. She scrubbed away a tear with a knuckle. "I've been kind of a wreck all week. His first birthday ...."

He reached for her hand and they sat together in silence, her eyes as sad as he had ever seen them. With a wan smile, she withdrew her hand

and visibly shivered. "It's getting cold. Let's go in and watch a movie. I'm gonna change into sweats."

They blew out the candles, collected the empty bottles and dishes, and carried them into the kitchen. As was their habit, they stood side by side at the sink, Maggie rinsing off the dinner dishes and Sully placing them in the dishwasher.

"Have you seen *Sideways*?" she asked when the counters were clean and the dishwasher was humming. "It got a bunch of nominations last year."

"No. I've been wanting to, though. Go put on your sweats. I'll make popcorn."

She motioned to him with her finger and leaned forward, thinking she was going to whisper something in his ear. Instead, she kissed him gently on the cheek. A simple kiss, but it sent a cipher of pleasure shimmying through him. They shared a smile and she slipped away.

He stood staring after her, analyzing what just happened. Did that little kiss go beyond friendship? Was she picking up on his feelings, and responding? Get a grip, he told himself. Maggie had never shown any obvious sign that they were more than friends. Sully considered himself a practical guy. He understood the obstacles standing between himself and Maggie. The biggest problem was economics. He was a struggling horse trainer with two years of college. She was a successful career woman with a good salary and a big house. And no doubt, her husband had left her a ton of money. He figured, in her eyes, he wasn't a very attractive prospect. Then there was the age difference, which made no difference to him, but after the comment she made about being old enough to be his mother, he figured it mattered to her. After losing Lilah, Sully didn't want any more heartache, and he certainly didn't want to risk losing Maggie's friendship by acting on feelings she didn't share.

For the remainder of the evening they followed their routine faithfully. He plopped in the recliner. She stretched out on the couch. They ate popcorn, laughed out loud, commented on the movie. Did he imagine it, or had something changed in the way she looked at him, the way she smiled? When she caught his eyes, she seemed to hold his gaze longer than usual. Her smile seemed more vulnerable.

After the movie, Maggie walked him out into the crisp night air, and they stood talking next to his truck. The sky was studded with stars and the fragrance of juniper seasoned the air. As always, he pulled her into a hug as he said goodnight, only this time, he didn't let go, and she didn't pull away. They fit well together, the softness of her body filling in the hard grooves of his. He ran his hands down her back until they came to rest on the curve of her hips. *Contours made for a man's hands.* She smelled like her garden, green leaves and lavender. "I'll pick you up Sunday," he murmured, not wanting to let go.

"What time?" Her voice was barely a whisper.

"Around three. Is that too late?"

"No." She raised her face to his, her skin as pale and smooth as soap in the moonlight.

He put his hand under her chin and rubbed his thumb across her lower lip and almost kissed her, but at the last second, he got hold of himself. He released her, said good night, and climbed into his truck. He drove away slowly, watching her in the rearview mirror, not putting on the radio for once, not wanting anything, sound or movement, to disturb the fragile feeling that still lingered from holding her.

CHAPTER EIGHT

CODY BOTH resented and empathized with her sister. She sat with Sarah for a long while after everyone else left the table. The lanterns had sputtered out and velvety darkness enfolded them like a cloak. As far back as Cody could remember, Sarah had a history of ruining family celebrations with her fabricated dramas, yet their parents had always been lenient and forgiving.

"Your sister's different," her mother had confided years ago, on a day that lived vividly in Cody's memory; her first week in high school. Shy and studious, Cody had inhabited a narrow, boy-like figure all through middle school. The summer before her freshman year, she sprouted hips and breasts, and was thrust into an alien world populated by kids who seemed more mature, more confident, and more at home in their bodies. Boys were taller, more muscular, some even shaved, and she knew from the grapevine that they were having sex with any girl who was willing. As a newly minted freshman, Cody tried hard to navigate the foreign terrain and distinguish flirtation from friendliness.

Complicating the situation was her older sister, whose reputation stemmed from her favorite extra-curricular activity—dating. With her shapely figure and beautiful face, Sarah had her pick of boys. Her weakness was jocks, and she was often seen in the company of one or more over-sized, and overly attentive athletes. Boys flirted freely with Cody, too, assuming Sarah's "hobby" ran in the family. But Cody was cautious by nature, and barely placed a toe across "the good girl line" before shrinking back into her protective shell.

The day that stood in infamy came during her second week of high school. Sarah and a bulky football player, Carson, were laughing it up in the cafeteria, and Sarah playfully plopped into his lap. Carson encircled her in his massive arms and buried his face in the cove of her neck. When he finally pulled away, Sarah wore his brand on her neck—a hickey the size of quarter.

Sitting right next to them, burning with embarrassment, Cody tried to ignore the dozens of students who sat gawking and whispering. The squeak of athletic shoes on polished linoleum sounded an alarm as Carson's girlfriend swooped in like a bird of prey, followed by a trio of tight-faced cheerleaders. Fenced in by their bodies, Cody couldn't see beyond the blazing school logos plastered on their green and yellow sweaters. Insults volleyed back and forth at high velocity, accompanied by some vicious shoving and hair pulling. A really great show. The whole cafeteria was riveted.

Faces flaming, Carson and Sarah bolted from the table with the cheerleaders squawking at their heels. Sitting alone, Cody caught lewd glimpses from boys and smirks from girls. She wished she could shrink into a particle of dust and disappear. Instead, she walked calmly out of the hall with her chin held high, and her posture straight. Once safely barricaded in a restroom stall, she collapsed into tears and relayed her social disaster to her mother by phone.

Olivia rushed to her rescue.

A thunderstorm had rumbled through the valley and warm, moist air circulated through the open windows of the Land Cruiser as they drove back to the ranch. Her mother's trademark silk scarf, wrapped around her head Grace Kelly style, fluttered in the wind. Cody kept her eyes pinned to the steaming asphalt as the desert landscape flew by. "I can't go back there, Mom. I need to transfer to another school."

Her mother tossed her a sympathetic look. "I understand your feelings, honey. I really do. But running away from a problem is never the right answer. I'm proud of you for walking out of the cafeteria with your dignity intact. Self-respect comes from facing a challenge head on, even when you're afraid. Sailing into the storm with grace and courage."

"Why do I have to face *every* challenge? People take breaks from challenges all the time."

"You're not other people." Her mother glanced at her, green eyes leveling a direct stare. "You're a Sterling."

"What about Sarah? She gets away with everything."

"Your sister's different," Olivia said coolly as they passed through the immense stone pillars of Sterling O.

"She sure is." *She's a slut.* "And she's giving me a bad reputation."

Her mother's face tensed, and she silently chewed on her lower lip.

Cody studied her mom's beautiful profile, wishing she were more like her. Olivia had the sleek, glossy style of a thoroughbred, and she always seemed to be in command of her emotions. After college, she did postgraduate work in Paris, and traveled the world before settling down and marrying Hank. A gifted horsewoman, she rode English, wearing tailored riding outfits and polished boots. Cody lived her entire life on the ranch, in the dusty sphere of cattle and cowboys. She could be spit and polished on the outside, but her cowgirl sensibility was ingrained.

"Sarah's brain is wired differently than yours and mine," her mother finally said. "You've always known that. When you were both little, you acted like the big sister. Always taking care of her."

"That was okay when we were little. Not anymore. She's not normal!"

"Don't speak that way about your sister," her mother's voice warned. Olivia pulled into the driveway, circled around back, and parked the Land Cruiser in the garage. Sitting in the dim light after the door groaned shut, her mother met her gaze. "Who's to say what's normal, and what isn't?"

Cody fidgeted with the flap on her book bag. She didn't have an answer.

"We need to accept differences between people, not judge them harshly."

"What's different about Sarah?"

Her mother reflected before speaking. "Your sister is scary smart. She's a whiz at computer science and math, but socially, she doesn't have maturity. Probably, she never will."

"Is that why she says stupid stuff all the time?"

"Think of her as innocent, not stupid. Do you think you can do that?"

Cody shrugged. "I'd rather just pretend I don't know her."

"I'm sorry your sister embarrassed you today. I'll talk to her." Her mother's graceful hand reached over and squeezed hers. "Try to have patience with her. You have the advantage. Little things you take for granted are a huge struggle for her. Most of us come equipped with social antennae. We pick up cues by reading a person's expression, body language, and the nuances in their voice. Sarah isn't good at that."

"She doesn't have an antennae?"

"No, she doesn't. That's why she acts inappropriately sometimes."

"She imitates actors she sees on soaps. She's so dramatic."

"She's doing the best she can, Katie, trying to figure out what response goes with each interaction. She doesn't always get it right, and she doesn't understand why things blow up around her. That's a sad and lonely way to live." Olivia's eyes were soft and pleading, touching chords deeply rooted in family loyalty. "Try to have more patience. Try to understand her."

Cody shrugged, not feeling generous, and mumbled. "I'll try."

"You're the strong one, Katie. Remember that. Promise me you'll always look out for your sister."

"I promise."

"Good girl. Please think about going back to school tomorrow. You have your own friends. You don't have to be part of Sarah's circle."

"I'll think about it." *Avoid Sarah entirely.*

"Don't say anything about Sarah's shenanigans to your father. He worries about her, and he has enough on his mind." Olivia smiled her beautiful smile, her face brightening as quickly as it darkened. Keeping secrets from Hank had been a long-standing tradition between them. Probably the number one reason Cody never revealed the abuse in her marriage. She was the designated daughter. The strong one. The one who didn't upset the order of things.

Cody never honored the pledge she made to her mother that day. Her total and complete avoidance of Sarah became her coping mechanism. It was easier to ignore Sarah than to try to help her. A swollen vein of guilt ruptured on occasion but was stymied beneath the weight of her own crushing problems.

Sarah's voice cut into Cody's rambling thoughts, jerking her attention back to the present.

"Man, the party sure flat-lined after Justin left." Sarah tilted a bottle of Bud to her lips.

"Yeah, it did."

Moonlight filtered through the trees, and shadows swayed over the ground as branches moved with the wind. Roth draped his jacket around

Sarah's shoulders before heading out, but the temperature steadily dropped, and she sat shivering. "What a party pooper." She shook a cigarette from her pack, tucked it between her lips, clicked on her lighter, inhaled deeply, and blew out a stream of smoke. "Did I do something to make him leave?"

Cody waved the smoke away from her face. "Considering you just broke up with Bear, you might have let the dust settle before hitting on Justin."

"I was letting him know I like him. What's wrong with that?"

"Slow down a little, Sarah. Rome wasn't built in a day." Cody swigged her beer. "Why'd you break up with Bear?"

"He's been rubbing me the wrong way. Possessive. Jealous." Sarah wrinkled her nose, extending her arm and flicking her ash. "He's mean when he drinks, and he's been drinking a lot lately." She hiked her dress above her thigh, exposing a bruise the size of a baseball.

Cody gasped.

"He likes rough sex."

"Jesus, Sarah!"

"It's not that bad. I fell out of bed. He didn't hit me."

Recalling Buddy's sadism in the bedroom, Cody's hands got clammy.

"He likes to hold me down, pretend he's raping me."

Cody kept the revulsion out of her voice. "How does that make you feel?"

"Depends on how much I drink." Sarah's lips twisted with distaste. "If I'm drunk enough, I don't care. But when I don't drink, I don't like it. He hurts me."

"Sarah, don't let him hurt you. That's not how you keep a man."

Sarah locked eyes with Cody for so long it made her uncomfortable. "You let Buddy hurt you."

Cody sucked in a deep breath. "That was a mistake. Look where it got me. Nearly dead."

"Why'd you let him do it?" Sarah's expression was as guileless as a child's.

Cody thought for a long moment, choosing the right words. "Buddy was sick. I got sick, too. I let him have power over me. I was afraid of him."

"Why didn't you come home? Tell Dad?"

"He threatened to kill me if I left him." Cody wet her lips. "I believed him. He was crazy when he drank. He would've hunted me down."

Sarah's face softened. "I'm sorry he hurt you."

"Me, too." She tucked a strand of hair behind her ear. "Don't do what I did. Don't let Bear hurt you again."

"He won't. We're done." She swallowed the last of her beer and glanced up at the moon. Her face transformed in the moonlight and her lips widened into a dreamy smile. "I like Justin. He's nice. Shy, and gentle."

"Did Justin say he liked you, too?"

"No. But I can tell he does."

"He thinks you're pretty. That doesn't mean he wants to be your boyfriend."

"He sure didn't seem to like me tonight." Sarah dropped her cigarette into her beer bottle, and it hissed as it went out. "Far from it. He marched away from the table without finishing his dinner." She turned to Cody. "Have any romance advice for me?"

Cody chuckled. "I'm the last person to ask, unless you want to get stabbed a bunch of times." She studied her bottle, realizing she'd never spoken of that night before.

"Why'd Buddy stab you?" Sarah asked.

A grisly kernel of memory darted into her mind.

"Wanna talk about it?"

Cody finished her beer, then found herself reminiscing in a quiet voice. "I was packing my car the night it happened. Fleeing. Terrified. I knew Buddy would eventually kill me, whether I stayed or not. I looked over my shoulder the whole time, at any sliver of shadow that moved. I backed out of the driveway, just seconds from freedom, when Buddy screeched behind me in his fucking Dodge Ram Truck, blocking my car." Cody's fingers clutched the arms of her chair and her words started rushing together. "I backed into the driver's door so hard he couldn't get out right away. It gave me time to run into the house, lock myself in the bedroom, and call nine-one-one. Buddy threw his weight against the door like a wrecking ball. It sounded like the world coming to an end. He burst in and was all over me, reeking of alcohol, his fists slamming into my face. I blacked out. When I came to, he was sitting on top of me, holding me down with his knees, his hunting knife raised in his fist." Cody's hands flew up to her breasts, warding off his knife thrusts as she relived the attack.

"Stop!" Sarah shrieked.

Bolting out of her nightmare, Cody's eyes locked on her sister's stricken face. Sarah's eyes were enormous.

Cody trembled uncontrollably as the violence of old memories pulsed through her body.

"I wish you'd killed him," Sarah hissed through clenched teeth.

It took a long moment to compose herself, to be able to speak. "I thought about killing him lots of times, Sarah. One night I even waited for him with a loaded shotgun in my hands. I pumped it when he came through the door, aimed it at him, watched the fear of Satan pass through him. He pissed his pants. But I couldn't pull the trigger." Cody knuckled away her tears, wiped her nose on her shirt sleeve. "After that, he locked up all the guns. He didn't touch me for weeks. Then it started up again." She shuddered.

Sarah reached over and gently stroked Cody's back, the pain of sympathy in her eyes, not confusion or withdrawal. They sat quietly for a long time, watching a skunk scuttle out of a bush and waddle across the lawn in front of them. There was no sound except the soft rustle of boughs in the wind.

Sarah pulled her jacket tighter at the collar. Her eyes gleamed in the starlight like the eyes of a mountain cat. Her nostrils flared delicately. "My therapist said talking about trauma loosens its power. After listening to you, I'm not so sure."

"You're seeing a shrink?" Cody struggled to pull her attention away from the past.

"A therapist, since mom died. Dad thought it would be a good idea. Dr. Simon put me on anti-anxiety meds. Now I don't feel so keyed-up all the time."

Cody studied her sister's solemn expression. "I could use some myself."

"I'll share mine." They shared a muted smile.

"Is seeing a therapist helping?

"A lot. She's helping me understand why I'm so complicated. Why my thoughts get so jumbled. I do best when I'm alone. Being around people rattles me."

"That's why you stay in the office all day?"

"Yeah." Sarah maintained a rigid silence and looked pale, almost chalk white in the moonlight. "Except when I work out in the gym. It's hard to stop exercising once I start. Dad comes in and makes me quit after an hour."

Cody mulled this over. Sarah and her father shared a pact, an understanding she knew nothing about. Cody shared nothing of her personal life with anyone, especially her father, unless it was to garner his favor. She gave her sister an admiring glance. "You're brave to get help."

Sarah touched her arm. "Come with me sometime. Talk to her."

"Maybe." Cody scowled. *No way.* She didn't want someone dredging up her past, picking at scabs, then trying to comfort her after making it sting.

"We should visit like this more often," Sarah said wistfully.

"Sure. It's been great. Compared to you, I don't feel so fucked up anymore."

They both laughed.

"We're a pair of broken bookends," Sarah said.

"Two squished peas in a pod."

Leaves rustled in the breeze and off in the distance came the neighing of horses. The faint strains of Justin's guitar drifted across the yard from his open window.

"He plays pretty decent," Cody said.

"He's cute, too. Getting back to me and my love-life, what should I do?"

Cody shrugged. "Don't do anything. You don't have to fall into everything that crosses your path. Back off for a while. Let everyone calm the hell down."

"What about going to town tomorrow?" Sarah sighed and her face seemed to crumple a little. "Will you come, too, so I don't make an ass of myself?"

Cody felt her shoulder muscles tense, then slowly relax. Leaving the ranch would be a challenge, but she needed to push herself. "Okay. But don't do your Velcro routine with Justin. I'm not coming as a wrestling referee."

"I'll behave." Sarah pocketed her smokes and linked arms with her sister as they walked back to the house.

Cody felt Sarah shivering through the jacket. Crickets chirped ecstatically in the coolness of the grass. Shadows dipped and bobbed, and somewhere, a calf bawled.

"I've missed you, Katie. You haven't been a good friend since you've been back."

"I'll try harder," Cody said. "For the record, I'm not ready to be called Katie."

CHAPTER NINE

SULLY WOKE from a sleep so deep he felt like he was swimming up from the depth of the ocean. Rain drummed the house and rattled the drainpipe outside his window. As his mind stuttered into consciousness, he remembered today was Eric's birthday, and he and Maggie were going to the cemetery. The weather matched the somber occasion. Tossing the covers aside, he followed the smell of coffee through the living room into the kitchen where he found an older version of himself standing at the counter. Bare-chested, rumpled pajama bottoms, face sprouting gray stubble, hair like dried corn stocks, Joe stood transfixed, watching coffee drip into the pot. Travis, on the other hand, was dressed and shaved, hair neatly braided, dutifully tending to bacon and eggs. Three plates waited on the table with the newspaper.

"Morning," Sully said, scratching his bare chest.

"Morning," the two older men replied in chorus.

Nails clicking on floorboards, Butch trotted up to him, tail spinning like a propeller, mouth curved into a smile, revealing tiny teeth. He did a flawless pirouette on his hind legs. Sully scooped him up and held him against his chest. The rat had really grown on him.

"Make some toast," Joe commanded. "We wanna eat."

Travis shot Sully an amused smile. Both understood that Joe took his singular task seriously, watching coffee drip. Simultaneously making toast didn't fit his job description. Sully placed bread in the toaster, sorted the paper, and leaned against the counter reading the sports section.

Four toasts popped up, Sully buttered them, put four more slices in, and resumed reading. The remaining toast buttered, the food distributed, the men arranged themselves around the table, and occasionally swapped sections of the paper.

"I need help shoeing Whistler today," Joe said to Sully.

"Travis can help you. I'm taking the afternoon off."

"Where ya going?" Joe's eyes were suddenly sharp and alert.

"Out." Sully drained his mug.

"Meeting your lady friend?" Travis asked.

"What lady friend?" Joe asked.

"Where do you think he goes Sunday nights?" Travis asked. "Knitting classes?"

"Maggie's a friend," Sully said.

"Maggie?" Joe's gaze held steady. "How long you been seeing this Maggie?"

"A few weeks." Sully frowned at Travis for bringing up the topic.

"How come you haven't brought her home?"

"What part of 'we're just friends' don't you understand?"

Joe waited for more information. Sully lifted the paper higher, blocking out his intense stare. "Mom's moving back to the ranch," he said, changing the subject.

Joe nearly choked on his eggs.

"Don't get your hopes up. She's moving into the cottage. I'm gonna start painting it this week."

"I'll help you." Joe's voice vibrated with excitement.

"Me, too," Travis said. "We can start taping today."

"Great."

"When's she moving in?" Joe asked.

"Why don't you call her and find out?"

Joe looked down at his plate, said nothing.

What's his problem? Why's it so hard for him to make contact with his wife? Sully folded the paper and placed it next to his plate. "Think you can manage the dishes, Dad? It's your turn."

Joe grunted.

Sully left the table, his mind entangled with thoughts of Maggie.

"Who's this lady friend?" Joe asked Travis.

Sully paused in the living room to listen.

"Mother of one of his Marine buddies."

"How old is she?"

"Dunno."

"Why's he messing 'round with somebody's mother?"

"None of my business. Lay off him, Joe. He's been to hell and back. If this woman makes him happy, let it be."

Long silence.

"You gonna help me shoe Whistler?" Joe asked, voice conciliatory. "I'm itching to do some riding."

Sully showered, dressed, and headed to the barn where he called Maggie, barely making out her words against the ruckus of the storm. Rain pelted the roof and wind thrashed the paddock doors down the length of the barn. The horses stood close to the inside gates of their stalls, ears flicking nervously.

"Yes, I want to go," Maggie said. "We can't disappoint Eric."

"Okay," he yelled into the phone. "I'll be there at three." That was that. Hopefully the storm would ease up. He'd rather stay dry and watch the ballgame on her big screen TV, but he'd do whatever she wanted, just to spend time with her.

***

The wipers worked double-time as Maggie directed Sully down a narrow road that dissected the small military cemetery. Wind wrestled the trees and stretches of uneven ground turned into puddles of boiling water.

"Park here, Sully." Maggie pointed to an alcove on the side of the road.

He parked against the curb so she could easily step over the water surging along the gutter. As he climbed out, he raised his black umbrella and braced stiffly against the wind, then rounded the cab to open her door. Maggie snapped open a red umbrella, the only spot of color in the gray landscape, and clutched a paper-wrapped bouquet against her chest. They kept their umbrellas angled out in front. Water drenched Sully's jeans as he sloshed across the grass holding her elbow, and rivulets of rain streamed down her raincoat and cascaded over her boots. The air smelled of wet earth and freshly cut grass.

Sully's throat tightened with emotion as they approached Eric's grave, marked with a simple white headstone that looked like all the others. Sully hated funerals and memorials. He'd been to too many in Afghanistan. After a Marine's body was shipped home, survivors honored the few possessions left behind—a pair of boots, a rifle, bayonet down, crowned by a helmet—the soldier's cross. A sacred symbol, representing a man's willingness to sacrifice his life for a cause greater than himself. Down on one knee, Sully had said goodbye to his fallen friends, whispering a prayer, touching the toes of empty boots, fingering dog tags dangling from the rifle, conjuring the living spirit of the man, his emotions turned inside out.

Under the protective arms of beautiful old maples, rows of tombstones swept away from them in all directions. He stood next to Maggie on the sodden earth, listening to the percussion of rain on their umbrellas, his eyes tracing a few maple leaves that clung to Eric's headstone, reminding him of the wide-spread handprints of children. Eric's epitaph was modest.

Eric Steeler
May 28, 1983 - March 1, 2006
Beloved Son of David and Maggie Steeler
Eric Gave His Life So We Could Be Free.
His Spirit Lives In Eternity.

Kneeling, Maggie unwrapped her bouquet and gently arranged long-stemmed calla lilies against the stone. Tracing Eric's name with her fingertips, she wished him happy birthday, and then she wept, shoulders shuddering, fingers pressed against her mouth.

Sully's grief came up swift and raw. He closed his eyes against the tears that burned to the surface. He consoled himself with the knowledge that Eric's spirit stood nearby, watching over them, eyes crinkled with laughter. That's how Sully wanted to remember him.

Maggie stood clumsily. He caught her elbow, pressed a firm hand to her back, and steered her toward the truck, their umbrellas colliding. When they were seated in the cab, she smiled sadly, tears or raindrops glistening on her cheeks. "Time heals, but never fast enough."

He nodded, held mute with emotion.

"Let's go get a drink. That's what Eric would do if he were here. He'd be getting bombed. Probably with you."

Absolutely true. Sully started the engine. "Where to?"

"His favorite pub. Beckett's."

Sully got on the parkway and headed south to Bend. After the lumber mills closed in the eighties, Sully watched the former lumber and ranching community transform into a resort town that offered skiing, fishing, golf, and other outdoor activities. The blue-collar atmosphere disappeared, replaced by trendy restaurants, upscale stores, and microbreweries that attracted a thriving tourist trade. The Deschutes River, once clogged with toxic logging material, now ran clean, curling like a cobalt ribbon through the leafy, tree-lined neighborhoods.

It was late afternoon. Sully didn't feel much like drinking, but for Maggie's sake, he'd nurse a designer beer. He pulled into a slot in front of the pub and helped her out of the truck.

As the door of Beckett's closed behind them, they were swallowed into another world. The softly-lit interior smelled like garlic and grilled chicken. The murmur of voices drifted over from the restaurant section. Sully and Maggie occupied two stools at the polished oak bar that faced well-stocked shelves of liquor. The middle-aged bartender, polishing glasses, put down a tumbler and wandered over to them. He reminded Sully of Freud. With his neatly trimmed white beard and observant gaze behind his wire-rimmed glasses, he stood ready to be server or therapist.

Maggie studiously scanned the martini menu before looking up. "A Spaceblaster, please."

Five different liquors, Sully noted. Potent. She wasn't playing around. "You like sushi?"

She nodded.

"Bring her the sushi plate." Sully wasn't about to let her drink a whammer on an empty stomach. "Halibut fish n' chips for me, and a dark ale."

After shaking off their wet jackets, they talked about trivialities until their food and drinks arrived. Then they conjured heartwarming memories of Eric. Alcohol improved their mood. Maggie shared stories of Eric as a precocious toddler. Sully shared pranks Eric pulled on his unsuspecting Marine buddies—one in particular that cost him dearly. "He replaced the whipped cream in a box of doughnuts with shaving cream and left it in the break room for a rival team, a bunch of arrogant assholes. Watching their faces as they chomped into them was funnier than hell, until the NCO waltzed in and grabbed one. Not so funny. Resulted in our whole team getting latrine duty for a week. Ever clean a toilet with a toothbrush?"

Sully and Maggie laughed together, heads bowed close. Eric's presence was palpable, as though he were standing behind them, arms draped across their shoulders.

After eating, they ordered another round of drinks and carried them to one of the pool tables in the back. That's what he and Eric would have done. The two had played pool for hundreds of hours at the base and both became aces, clearing a table of balls in minutes. Now to humor Maggie, Sully played left-handed. One game stretched into another, as did her martinis, and he didn't mind watching her bend over the table to take her shots. In tight jeans, Maggie looked as good as any woman he'd ever seen. In payment for the nice visuals, he let her win three out of five.

Ecstatic, she smiled brilliantly. "I'm seeing double. We better switch to darts."

He laughed. "We better switch to TV. Let me drive you home." While he paid the tab, he watched a handsome middle-aged man approach Maggie where she stood waiting by the door. She smiled in recognition, they spoke briefly, and then she nodded toward Sully. The man caught Sully's gaze, frowned, and said something to Maggie. She stiffened and her smile disappeared. A stab of unease worked its way between Sully's ribs as the man walked back to his table where two women sat waiting.

"Who was that?" Sully asked, joining her.

"Brennen, my colleague at work. We share office space."

"Looks like he upset you."

She shrugged. No smile.

"You okay?"

"He thought we were on a date. He said you were way too young, and you shouldn't have let me drink so much." She hiccoughed.

"What business is it of his?" Sully said, indignant.

"He's just looking out for me."

"By judging you? You're an adult. You can drink as much as you want. You're not falling all over anyone. And I'm driving."

"Obviously, you got me drunk for wicked reasons."

"I'd never take advantage of you." Sully peered above the heads of customers sitting at tables. The man was still watching, glaring. Sully thought about going over and giving him hell.

Maggie put her hand on his arm. "Whatever you're thinking about doing, don't."

"What if we were on a date? What difference does age make?"

She leveled her beautiful eyes on him, and her lips formed a lopsided smile. He knew she was feeling her martini. "That's what you really think? Age doesn't matter?"

"Age isn't a gauge for maturity, or intelligence."

"Or character," she added, with an admiring expression. "Which you have in ample supply."

He felt like kissing her. He always felt like kissing her. Instead, he opened the door and they stepped outside. She put her arm through his and they bent forward in the rain, hurriedly crossing the sidewalk and climbing into his truck. It felt good to have her close, to play the role of her protector. As he drove, they listened to a country station and the muffled rain keeping beat on the roof. He felt a comfortable intimacy and a strong urge to share his feelings, to confess that he wished they *were* on a date, that he wanted many dates, that she surfaced in his thoughts a hundred times a day, that he felt her presence when she wasn't there, that he thought he was in love with her. But now was not the time. Not following the painful afternoon at the cemetery. Not when she was hammered and vulnerable.

CHAPTER TEN

THEY GOT OFF to a late start. It was afternoon by the time Justin finished his chores. He knew he was stalling, worried about the risk of being seen in town. He wasn't thrilled about being trapped in the company of the Sterling sisters, either. Sarah was illogical, moody, and unpredictable, and he didn't appreciate being sexually harassed on the job. Cody, on the other hand, was just plain unreadable, which bothered him even more. He couldn't fathom what thoughts shimmied and swirled beyond her cool gray eyes.

Sarah opted to sit in the back of the Land Cruiser, letting Justin ride shotgun. Out on the highway Cody cut loose, proving to be an aggressive driver, bearing down on slow moving cars like a wolf on a rabbit until they swerved out of her way.

"Back off, Cody," he said at one point, sitting rigid with tension, one hand pressed to the dashboard. "Where'd you learn to drive? Bumper car school?"

"You're kind of a wuss for a bull rider, you know that?" She stepped on the brakes and jolted them before slowing down to the speed limit.

"This wuss would like to live long enough to win the World Title, if you don't mind."

"This car's a tank," Sarah said. "If we crash, we'll more 'n likely survive."

"I feel a whole lot better now." Justin was relieved when they parked downtown on Main Street and Cody separated herself from the driver's seat. Piling out onto the sidewalk, they had a quick pow wow. Sarah was hell bent on shopping, Cody was just along for the ride, and he needed to run an errand. The air held the promise of rain. The clouds looked like clotted milk, while in the far distance above the Cascades, they were forming one huge, roiling gray mass. A hell of a storm heading their way. "Let's make it fast before that storm rolls in."

Sarah hurriedly dragged her sister into a fancy shop called L'Amour Boutique.

Justin hiked three blocks down Main Street to the post office with his hat pulled low on his forehead, his shaded eyes scrutinizing every passing car. He felt a spurt of adrenaline when a blue Ram 500 bore down on him, but he didn't recognize the driver and it barreled past. He exhaled slowly. Inside the small brick building, he bought a book of stamps and picked up mail from his PO Box. Two letters from Avery.

After hustling back to the boutique, he leaned against the stucco wall in the alley and slowly read the letters, rereading the parts where Avery visited their intimate moments. With a stab of guilt, Justin remembered when he kissed her before he left—her look of longing, and frustration, and anger. Avery invited him to visit. He didn't know when he could make that happen, but the prospect filled him with yearning. Justin longed to hold her close, smell her skin, bury his face in the warm cove of her neck, and lay in her arms after lovemaking, talking about nothing in particular. He folded the letters in half, tucked them into his back pocket, and strode into the boutique.

Instantly, his senses were assailed by the sweet scent of candles, new age music, and displays of lacey panties and lingerie. The fixed gaze of a mannequin in a transparent bra and thong panties followed him as he maneuvered down an aisle with his arms pulled into his sides. Feeling as big as an ox and just as clumsy, he reached the back of the store where Cody paced in front of a curtained dressing room. In contrast to the ultra-feminine offerings of the boutique, she looked like a fish out of water, dressed in her usual flannel shirt and Wranglers large enough to fit Chris Farley.

The curtains snapped open and Sarah stepped into the room with the heightened drama of a burlesque queen, wearing an emerald-green dress that fit her curves like skin on a hot dog.

"Wow." He couldn't help staring. "That dress should be against the law."

Beaming, Sarah pressed herself warmly into his arms.

His hands closed around her waist and traced the roundness of her hips. Though fully appreciating the feel of a beautiful woman, he quickly pulled away, not wanting to encourage her.

Sarah grabbed a turquoise dress from the dressing room and held it up to Cody. "This would be killer on you Cody, right Justin?"

He had to admit, the color deepened Cody's gray-blue eyes and added a striking contrast to her pale blonde hair. "Beautiful."

Her face softened and matching spots of color materialized on her cheeks. She met his eyes in a lingering gaze that made his face warm. Justin momentarily found it hard to swallow, and he had a sudden desire to touch her hair, to thread its silky texture through his fingers. He reached out a finger and pushed a loose strand from her eyes.

"Try it on, Cody!" Sarah's excited voice edged in, shattering the tender moment.

Cody blinked, and the spots of color on his cheeks grew darker, angrier. She shoved Sarah's arm away. "No way. I have no use for that ridiculous thing." In a mild fit of temper, she stalked out of the store.

"When's she gonna get over this dressing like a man craze?" Sarah said.

Justin shrugged, still a little mesmerized by Cody's spell. Sarah stepped back into the changing room and snapped the curtain shut.

"I'll wait outside with Cody."

Emerging minutes later with a bag in each hand, Sarah led her two reluctant companions into the high-end shoe store next door where she proceeded to try on seven pairs of western boots.

Cody scowled, hands shoved deep into her pockets. "Sarah, you have enough boots."

"Not chili pepper red with black piping and blue alligator inlays. What do you think, Justin?"

"I think you should donate the money to the humane society."

She gave him a funny look, and bought two pairs of boots.

Mind dulled with boredom, Justin was relieved to escape the boot store, but he shuddered when Sarah suggested browsing through a few antique shops. He and Cody obediently trailed behind her. Justin volunteered to carry Sarah's bulky bags and tried not to collide with china and crystal sitting precariously close to the edges of tables and sideboards. He and Cody watched mindlessly for an interminable period of time while Sarah tried on an endless array of sparkling jewelry.

After the brain-numbing shopping spree, they locked the bags in the Land Cruiser and the girls asked Justin what he wanted to do.

He smiled.

Sarah left to do more shopping while Cody accompanied him to the Beaverhead Historical Museum. Feeling in no need to hurry, Justin took his sweet time inching down every corridor. He read every caption on every panel with great interest and studied closely the photos of native peoples. He admired beautiful handcrafted baskets, beadwork, and headdresses displayed behind glass, and imagined out loud to Cody the joy and hardship of living off the land with no grocery stores, plumbing, or electricity.

Surprisingly, Cody was equally enthused. Her face lost its carefully arranged expression, and her mouth tipped into a genuine smile. "Growing up, we did a lot of horse camping in the back country with Dad. I loved being swallowed up by nature, living off what little we could carry on our backs. Far away from the madding crowd."

"Far from the Madding Crowd. Thomas Hardy. I loved that book."

"Me, too. I've read it three times." They rounded a hallway and stepped into a wide corridor lined with panels of photos. "Here's my favorite part of the museum," she said.

This section of the museum paid tribute to the Sterling family. Dozens of photos chronicled Hank and Olivia's ancestry, their marriage, and the expansion of Sterling property from ten to fifty thousand acres of prime Oregon real estate. Sarah and Cody were now the youngest members of a dynasty spanning four generations. Cody listened attentively as Justin pointed out the highlights of Hank's rise to rodeo fame.

Cody was especially captivated by the pictures of her mother. In the photos, Olivia was elegantly dressed at civic events, or perched on the backs of champion horses like an English aristocrat. The last photo, Justin noted, was taken ten months ago.

"That was right before we found out she had cancer." Cody's eyes suddenly grew soft and misty, and her shoulders slumped with grief.

"I'm sorry about your mom," he said gently.

"Thank you."

She met his gaze and that same paralyzing connection held him mute. Some irresistible force drew them together. "Don't cry," he whispered roughly. Stroking her back, he felt the curve of her spine through the thick flannel shirt.

When she pulled away, he brushed her lips with a kiss as light as a whisper.

"Where are you guys?" Sarah came huffing around the corner, carrying more bags.

Cody stepped away from Justin, cheeks burning with color.

"Enough boredom," Sarah said. "I'm starved. Let's go refuel at Chuck's."

"Let's head back to the ranch," Justin said. Chuck's was a popular hangout. He didn't need to tempt fate any further.

CHAPTER ELEVEN

HOMER MET Sully and Maggie at the door in a frenzy of tail wagging and body wiggling.

"Hi, Homer," she laughed.

"Hey, fella." Sully scratched the fur around his floppy ears.

Once Homer's excitement siphoned off, Sully and Maggie shed their boots and hung their wet coats on a rack in the hallway.

"Let's watch the game," she suggested, unwinding a scarf from her neck.

"Music to my ears." He followed her into the living room and headed for his usual spot on the recliner. With a sleepy smile, Maggie patted the seat beside her on the sofa. "Sit with me."

He made a detour around the coffee table and settled beside her.

Looking a little cross-eyed, she laid her head on the armrest, her legs scrunched up between them. Homer circled the carpet and curled up at their feet. "I want you to come over Friday night," she murmured. "I've decided to have a party."

"What kind of party?"

"A back to the living party. It's time to come out of hibernation. See my friends again. That's what Eric would want. I got that at the cemetery."

"Sure, I'd like to meet your friends." Sully suppressed a smile. Maggie wanted to introduce him to her friends, which signaled a hallmark in their relationship. He placed a pillow on his lap and patted it. "Stretch out your legs."

She complied, and he started massaging one of her feet. He found her stress points and worked at gently kneading out the tension.

"Hmmm. You're good at that."

Sully had a lot of feeling stored up for Maggie and was happy to funnel some of it into his handiwork. She released a series of soft little moans and drifted to sleep before he started on her second foot. After covering her with the quilt she kept folded over the back of the couch, he grabbed the remote and tuned into ESPN, the Red Sox versus Yankees, and gave the game his rapt attention.

During the seventh-inning stretch, he let Homer out to do his business, grabbed a cold Moosehead, and settled back to watch the Red Sox blow the Yankees out of the stadium. The pewter sky spit rain at the windows and the cadence of the storm lulled him into a feeling of well-being. Occasionally he turned to Maggie just to watch her sleep, untroubled, the frown lines smoothed from her forehead.

When she woke and found him sitting beside her, her lips curved into a beautiful smile. "How long was I out?"

"Couple hours." He muted the hockey game he was watching.

"That long?"

"Yes, ma'am. Dead to the world. I tickled your feet and painted hearts on your face, but you didn't respond."

She laughed.

"Coffee?" he asked.

"Absolutely."

"I'll make a pot."

She yawned prettily, stretched with the grace of a cat, and followed him into the kitchen. "Want a sandwich to go with the coffee?"

"I can always eat."

"Let's see what I can throw together." Her eyes flashed with good humor. "Hand me a mixing bowl out of the cabinet." She pulled a few items from the fridge and carried them to the island, got out a cutting board for Sully, and instructed him to chop celery and apples into very small pieces. After mixing together tuna, walnuts, raisins, and mayo with his ingredients, Maggie spread the mixture on crusty sourdough bread, crowned each with tomato slices and pepper-jack cheese, and grilled them to perfection in the toaster oven.

"You make a hell of a sandwich," he said between bites.

"My specialty. How was the game?"

"Depends on whether you're a Yankee or Red Sox fan."

She shrugged.

Sully knew she didn't follow sports, but he shared the highlights of the game anyway, and Maggie listened attentively. While nursing their second mug of coffee, she took out catering menus and asked his help selecting appetizers for her party. They circled a dozen.

They retreated to the living room and watched "Jerry McGuire," their feet propped on the table side by side, eating popcorn from the same bowl. He took pleasure in being near her: feeling her body shudder with laughter, the casual way her hand lighted on his arm or knee. It appeared a comfortable intimacy had evolved between them. When the film ended, he glanced at his watch. Time to go. The day had melted away too fast. He wanted to stay stretched out beside Maggie, enjoying the warmth of her body and this feeling of contentment, but chores waited at the ranch. "I better get going."

"So soon?" She looked genuinely disappointed, which tugged a little at his heart.

"Yep. Duty calls." At the door, he pulled on his jacket and boots and she walked him out to the porch. A quiet rain fell, and the air was perfumed with juniper. It'd been a challenging day, but together, they'd gotten through the gut-wrenching visit to the cemetery.

"Sorry I slept through most of the evening."

"No worries. I liked watching you. You look pretty when you sleep."

"Except for the drool."

"Yeah, that and the snoring. I had to turn up the volume to drown you out."

"Really?"

"No. Come here." He pulled her into his arms. She snuggled closer, tilting her face up to his. With no hesitancy, he kissed her, slowly and deliberately.

"That was nice," she whispered.

He kissed her again. Long, slow, deep.

With a sigh of pleasure, she pulled away, her eyes dreamy in the porch light.

He let his hands slide down her arms and gently squeezed her hands before releasing them. "Goodnight, Maggie."

"Goodnight, Sully."

He strode out into the cool fresh rain, climbed into his truck, and drove mindlessly, intoxicated by her kiss and the startling realization that Maggie shared his feelings. She cared about him, too. More than a friend. Like him, she wanted intimacy. He pulled into the ranch forty-five minutes later, barely remembering the drive home. As he climbed the porch steps, the wood creaked beneath his feet, and Butch's sharp, insistent barks came through the kitchen door, bringing him back to earth. His thoughts turned from Maggie to the list of chores awaiting him.

CHAPTER TWELVE

"ANOTHER MARGARITA with Cuervo Gold, please," Sarah said to the server.

"Another Deschutes Pale Ale," Justin said.

"Nothing for me. I'm driving." Cody was still nursing a virgin Piña Colada.

Tucked into a cozy booth, Justin sat across from the two sisters in the bar at Chuck's, the most popular restaurant in Beaverhead, Sarah's over-size orange handbag taking up half his seat. They worked on a variety of appetizers: fried mozzarella sticks, crab-stuffed mushrooms, a large bowl of steamed clams in garlic broth. Justin pulled a clam away from the shell with a ridiculously tiny fork and popped it into his mouth. The ale took the edge off his anxiety, but his eyes routinely scanned the people milling around the bar. One more drink and they'd be safely on the road. He took a long pull of ale and ate the last of the mushrooms.

"Shopping with us must've felt like hard labor," Cody said, her voice barely decipherable above the bass thrum of hard rock music spewing from the speakers.

Justin gave a little bow, and said with a touch of old-fashioned chivalry, "It was an honor to escort the two beautiful Sterling sisters."

The sisters responded with identical smiles.

Both had been on their best behavior, and he had a great time sharing his passion for history with Cody in the museum. He wondered about the strangely erotic and hypnotic spell she cast over him today. It had to be a response to Avery's sensual letters, which left him feeling aroused and sensitive. He figured the attraction would fade when they got back to the ranch and all its distractions.

Relief washed over him when the waiter plopped down their check tucked into a black plastic jacket. "My treat, ladies," he said, pulling out his wallet, and taking a last sweeping survey of the people in the restaurant. The bartender, a good-looking blonde in tight jeans and low-cut sweater, was chatting up a couple of cowboys who'd just rambled in. Justin's body went cold. The men stood with their bodies angled away from him, but he'd know them anywhere. The younger man had broad-shoulders, a muscular body, dark tousled hair, and chiseled features. The older man was barrel-chested with a weathered face, a hook nose, and gray hair that had thinned noticeably since Justin had seen him last. The old man turned and honed-in on Justin as if by radar. He blinked and widened his eyes in surprise.

Justin felt a white-hot jolt of adrenaline. "Holy shit."

The sisters stopped in mid-sentence and followed his gaze.

The old man nudged the younger one. They dissected Justin with steel-edged stares.

"That's Jabe McKinley and his son, Kenny," Sarah said. "They look like they wanna kill you."

"They do."

As the three watched from the booth, the men spoke quietly, then abruptly left the bar.

"Let's get out of here." Justin's anxious breathing grew more uneven. "Get the car. Pull up in front. I'll pay."

The sisters mirrored a stunned expression.

"Now!" The intensity of his tone triggered movement. They gathered up their belongings and fled the restaurant.

Justin hurriedly pulled bills from his wallet and threw them on the table. He watched from the front door until the Land Cruiser approached, headlights cutting through a good downpour, then dashed from the restaurant. Before he stepped off the porch, a blue Dodge Ram truck screeched to a halt between him and the Land Cruiser. The old man and his three sons poured out, muscles bunched, faces twisted with fury. Kenny, Jim, and Dan had him pinned against their cab in seconds flat.

Justin struggled but he was held tighter than a pig in a truss. Everyone quickly became slick with rain, hair matting foreheads and clothes shrinking against skin.

"Justin Powell," the old man said with primal ferocity. His neck muscles bulged, and a vein throbbed in the center of his forehead. "I knew we'd catch up with you one of these days."

"Let me go, you sonuvabitch," Justin growled.

McKinley encircled Justin's throat with a large gnarled hand and squeezed, his lips pulled back from his teeth. "You think you can mess with me, boy, and get away with it?"

Justin tried to speak but couldn't push words past the vise on his throat.

Two blurry figures moved into his periphery. "What the hell are you doing?" It was Cody, angry as hell.

"Stay back, ladies. This man is dangerous." Glistening in the rain, McKinley swung back his arm and threw a power-packed punch into Justin's gut.

Exploding flashes of pain coursed through Justin's abdomen and radiated outward. He gasped for air. Pinned down good with his head pressed against the truck, he couldn't breathe. Before the fist slammed into him again, he jerked up his right knee and pistoned McKinley in the groin. The old man shrieked and staggered backwards, then sank to his knees, clutching himself and groaning.

Justin kicked and squirmed and pulled. The three brothers tossed expletives around like grenades, trying to hold him down. Avoiding Justin's flailing legs, Kenny lunged at him from the side, one powerful arm pulled back like a sling, ready to launch a blow.

Justin braced himself.

A figure leapt upon Kenny's back, arms and legs tightening around his neck and torso. *Sarah!*

"Get off me, you crazy bitch!" Kenny spun in circles, trying to shake her loose.

Justin struggled and kicked. Dan and Jim held tight.

Old man McKinley got to his feet and staggered over to lend Kenny a hand.

"Back the fuck away, or I'll shoot!" A voice rang out sharply.

All four McKinley men froze.

Blinking against the rain, Cody stood gripping a Colt .45 with both hands, its barrel aimed at the old man's head. Sarah slid off Kenny's back and joined her sister. Cody turned the gun toward the three brothers, her hands as steady as a SWAT cop. "Get the hell away from Justin. Now!"

They stepped away.

Justin bent over and retched his guts out.

"Hands up," Cody barked. "Don't even twitch, or I'll shoot your fucking ears off."

"Her aim's spot on!" Sarah's voice vibrated with excitement.

Arms jutted skyward.

No one moved.

Kenny sneered. "You're making a big mistake, Katie, defending that piece of shit."

"Screw you."

"Put the gun down. Walk away," the old man said coldly.

She ignored him.

"Put the gun down. You understand me, Katie?"

"Maybe if you use smaller words," she said.

"Justin's a criminal," Dan hissed.

"And you're a family of saints," she said. "Four against one. Real heroes."

"He raped my wife," McKinley growled. "Stole my money."

"You got proof, take it up with the sheriff."

"This isn't the wild west," Sarah snorted. "And you ain't Wyatt Earp."

"Sarah, help Justin. Get the car!"

Sarah sprang forward, grabbed Justin's arm.

"I'm okay," he said hoarsely, tasting bile in his mouth. White-hot pain kept him doubled over and he was breathing in shallow gulps. He fell into the back seat. Sarah drove the Cruiser around the Ram to Cody. He spied several diners on the porch who had come out to watch the drama. Someone yelled, "We've called the cops."

"Get in," Sarah called urgently to Cody.

Cody backed up to the Land Cruiser, climbed in, and slammed the door, her gun trained on the McKinleys through the open window. "Go!"

Sarah peeled out of the parking lot spewing a wall of water over the men. As the SUV raced away, Justin peered out the back window, watching for their truck. Screeching around a corner onto a narrow residential street, Sarah dodged parked cars, then she made a sharp left bouncing over the curb, and made another hard right. City blocks hissed under the wet tires, and when she hit the highway she gunned the engine and the SUV roared down the asphalt. After a few miles flashed past the windows, Sarah slowed down to the speed limit and Justin felt the tension in the car slowly diffuse. He stopped holding his breath.

"Whew." Cody exhaled a deep breath. "That was close. They were about to beat the holy crap out of you, Justin. You rocked, Sarah! Jumping on Kenny's back like that. He didn't know what hit him."

Sarah laughed, hands gripping the wheel. "You were awesome, too. I thought they were gonna shit themselves when you pulled out that .45."

Cody laughed too, rich and throaty, like her sister. Justin realized it was the first time he'd ever heard her really cut loose.

"Man, that felt good," Cody said. "Giving some fucked up men a taste of their own medicine."

"I'm glad you kicked the old man in the nuts," Sarah said over her shoulder. "What a creepy old douche."

"We're a good team," Cody said. "The three amigos."

"Three Musketeers," Sarah said.

The girls were elated. Justin wasn't.

"You all right?" Cody looked back at him, her expression quickly sobering.

"I've been better." He sat up straighter. His gut hurt like hell, his throat throbbed from Jabe's chokehold, and his mouth burned with the taste of bile. His ego hurt worse. Having his past catch up with him and play out in high drama in front of the Sterling sisters pummeled his self-respect. "I owe you both. I'd be raw meat if you two hadn't acted."

"What was that showdown all about?" Cody asked.

"A pack of lies. Every bit of it."

"You knew it was coming though, sooner or later," Sarah said. "That's why you used a fake name."

"And wouldn't go into town," Cody said.

"Something like that." There was little traffic out in the desert, and he could track cars speeding up on them.

"You gonna talk about it?" Cody asked.

"I'm getting around to it. Don't have much patience, do you?"

"They didn't teach patience in bumper car school. You a rapist, Justin?"

"Look at him," Sarah snorted. "Does he look like he needs to rape women for sex?"

"Rape isn't about sex." Cody's tone turned deadly serious. "It's about domination and control."

"You sound like the voice of experience," Sarah said.

Cody clenched her jaw.

"Buddy?" Sarah asked.

Cody turned her face to the window. Justin saw the desert landscape race past her hardened reflection in the glass. Sarah reached across the seat and squeezed her sister's hand.

The three lapsed into silence, listening to the steady drum of rain and the swish of wipers. Justin felt the wind pushing against the Land Cruiser. A truck rumbled by in the opposite direction, its headlight gilding their profiles.

"You never answered, Justin," Cody said abruptly. "Did you rape Jabe's wife?"

"Hell no."

"She's old," Sarah said. "If you boinked her, it was mercy sex."

"She's a lot younger than the old man," Cody said.

"Look, I didn't rape Jessica. If anything, she raped me. Foster care placed me at the McKinley ranch. When Jabe left town, Jessica started sneaking into my room at night."

Sarah gasped. "The old pervert!"

"How old were you?" Cody asked.

"Seventeen."

"Why didn't you tell anyone?"

Justin slouched in his seat, wishing he could disappear. This was the last conversation he ever wanted to be having with anyone, especially Cody. "I felt guilty, I guess. Sleeping with a married woman. I blamed myself. I figured I must've been giving her the wrong signal. Jessica told me if Jabe ever found out, he'd kill us both, so I kept quiet."

Silence by intimidation. Cody knew all about that. "There's a name for what she did. Statutory rape."

"I never looked at it that way, since I consented. She was older. I trusted her judgment."

"Rape. Plain and simple. How'd she treat you during the day when her husband was around?"

"Looked right through me like I wasn't there." He glanced out the window at the tufts of sagebrush bending in the wind. They were now on

Hank's property, passing through the big stone gate.

"How'd the boys treat you?"

"Like hired help. Made me do all the shit jobs." In the dark car, not looking at their faces, the alcohol coaxed out of hiding the parts of his life he'd kept secret. "They ate in the dining room as a family, while I ate in the kitchen with the dogs." He brooded for a long moment, remembering how the old man shoved him around when he didn't move fast enough, and then his sons started taking up the practice, mostly for sport. A living hell. The loneliness and confusion he felt living under their roof surfaced as a dull ache in his chest. He studied Cody's profile, trying to gauge her reaction. The sisters probably thought he was lower than pond scum.

"I'm sorry you were placed in that terrible situation," Cody said. "They're the criminals, Justin, not you. You should report Jessica to the sheriff."

"My word against hers. Who's gonna believe me? They're rich. I'm a nobody."

"Don't talk that way about yourself," Sarah said, catching his eyes in the mirror. "You're a good person."

The three were quiet for the rest of the drive. Justin was wet and cold and the air in the car felt poisonous from his memories. He needed to go for a long hard jog to clear his head.

Sarah pulled into the driveway behind the house. The three exited the car and hurried into the house. Justin stood with Cody in the dining room, soaking in heat from the fireplace. He could hardly bear to look at her. When he did, she didn't recoil. She didn't say a word. She put her arm around his waist and pulled him close. He breathed in the scent of her hair and waited to feel different, to feel lighter now that she knew. He felt no relief.

Cody pulled away. "We're gonna go talk to Dad."

"No. I'm not getting your dad involved."

"He's already involved," Cody said. "After the circus act we performed in the parking lot, it'll be all over town tomorrow. It's best if he hears it from us. The McKinleys will pay for what they did to you, Justin. You can count on it." The kindness in her eyes touched him deeply, gently lifting the edges of his battered spirit.

CHAPTER THIRTEEN

WEARING A STERN expression, Hank listened attentively as his daughters related the story of their violent run-in with the McKinley clan. Hank paced in front of the huge fireplace rubbing his chin, a muscle twitching along his jaw. The four dogs were interwoven mounds of fur, soaking up the heat.

"I'm shocked that this happened downtown," he said. "The McKinleys acted like thugs." He turned to his daughters. "You were both completely justified in your actions. I'm proud of you. You showed real courage tonight. No telling what they would've done to Justin if you hadn't acted quickly. We need to report them to the authorities."

"I don't want to file a complaint," Justin said.

"Why not?"

"I've been enough trouble to this town. Don't want to be at the center of a scandal."

Hank studied Justin for a long moment. "Let's backtrack a little. What stirred up this mess to begin with?"

Justin shifted his weight from one foot to the other. Hank's hot glare was like a spotlight illuminating his stupidity.

"He slept with Jessica," Sarah blurted.

"Who's Jessica?" Hank asked.

"Jabe's wife," she said.

Hank looked startled. "You slept with Jabe's wife?"

Justin's face burned hot up to the tips of his ears. "Yes, sir."

"Explain yourself."

In a halting voice, Justin gave Hank the abbreviated version—Jessica's midnight visits, the secrecy, the underlying threat of death.

"You had sex with this woman for six months?"

"Yes, sir." Unable to meet Hank's piercing gaze, Justin pinned his eyes on the crackling fire as he spoke. "Whenever Jabe was out of town."

"What ended it?"

"Jessica woke me in the middle of the night. Told me to pack my things and get out."

The three Sterlings stood riveted, waiting for more.

Justin shoved his hands in his pockets, looked down at his feet, then raised his head. "She said she was pregnant."

Hank and the girls stood motionless. Embers popped in the fireplace. The roar of rain grew louder. Sarah sank onto the couch. Cody sat on the armrest.

Justin's face burned even hotter, but he forced himself to continue. "She said she was going to tell Jabe I raped her, and I better be long gone when he found out, or he'd shoot me dead."

"Those her words?"

"Yeah. Exactly. They stuck in my mind."

Hank rubbed his chin, paced a little more. "Couldn't Jabe be the father?"

"No. She told me he had a vasectomy. After three sons with his first wife, he didn't want more kids."

"Do you believe you're the father?"

Three pairs of eyes zeroed in on him.

He shrugged. "We used protection."

"Condoms aren't fail proof. Did she have the baby?"

"I don't know." Justin remembered his panicked state after Jessica left his room. "I grabbed my stuff and ran."

"Looking over your shoulder ever since?"

"Two and a half years."

Frowning, Hank leaned against his desk. Outside, the force of the wind made the glass shudder. "Hell of a thing to put on a boy."

Justin didn't like being called a boy, but said nothing.

Hank's eyes narrowed. "What's this about you being a thief?"

"No idea. The old man gave me shit for an allowance. I had less than fifty bucks when I left."

"Did Jessica or one of the boys have reason to take Jabe's money?"

Justin scratched the back of his neck, reflecting. "Maybe Kenny. He had a gambling habit. It caused several family fights. He liked cocaine, too. I caught him using a few times."

Hank crossed the room, placed another log on the fire, picked up a poker and forcefully stoked the embers, lost in thought. Justin watched him, feeling tension in his shoulders. If Hank told him to pack up his stuff and leave tonight, he wouldn't be surprised. He always knew his past would catch up to him one day, and he'd pay the price.

Warm light flickered over Hank's profile as he set the poker aside and studied the flames. He expelled a sharp breath and turned back to Justin. "Well, let me look into all this. We'll hold off on filing a complaint. I'll get an investigator on the case. Find out if Jessica had the baby. If so, we need to get a DNA test."

"That sounds expensive, Hank."

"Let me worry about that." Hank's expression hardened. "If I had my way, I'd have the whole pack of them thrown in jail. Family of hoodlums. Let's see where Jabe hit you."

He looked at the bruise marks on Justin's throat, then his abdomen, which was turning crimson and purple. Hank probed the area with his fingers.

Justin gasped.

"Good thing you got muscle as a shock absorber. I don't think any organs are damaged." He turned to Sarah. "Take a few pictures of these bruises."

Sarah pulled her phone from her purse and snapped photos, more than necessary, he thought. "Nice six-pack," she grinned.

Justin lowered his shirt.

"You kids better get out of those wet clothes. Put some warm food in your stomachs. Justin, take some Ibuprofen and ice your gut. Tomorrow, I want all of you to go about your business as usual. Don't talk to reporters if they call. Understood?"

"Yes, sir," Justin said.

The sisters nodded in unison.

"Now I want to talk to Justin alone."

"I'll warm up some soup for you, Justin." Cody tossed him a sweet smile and followed Sarah out of the room.

Hank settled into a sofa chair, his face tense with emotions Justin couldn't read. He gestured to Justin to take the other. Apprehensive, Justin sank wearily, knowing what was coming. This was where Hank would give him a scorching reprimand and tell him how disappointed he was. Justin had heard the spiel from foster parents too many times to count.

"I know this is difficult, Justin. But I need to understand the details clearly to pass on to my investigator. Tell me about your relationship with Jessica. What happened the first night she came into your room?"

Justin squirmed, took a breath, then started reciting details as well as he could remember. "She woke me up by getting into my bed. She said she'd had a nightmare and couldn't sleep. Jabe was out of town, and she was afraid to be alone, and would I mind just holding her. I was half asleep, confused, a little frightened, to be honest. It seemed inappropriate. But not knowing what to say, I said sure. She moved right up against me. Her hands …." He paused, licked his dry lips.

"It's okay, Justin. Go on."

"Well … her hands started touching me and she rubbed herself against me." Justin paused, cleared his throat. How did he explain sex to Hank? "My body responded, one thing led to another, and then she put a condom on me." Justin stared at his hands, feeling ridiculous. "The rest just happened. I'd never had sex before, but it came naturally, I guess. When it was over, she got out of bed, put on a kimono, and left the room without a word. No explanation. I lay there for a long time trying to figure out what just happened. The next morning if seemed so farfetched, I wondered if I'd dreamt the whole thing."

"You were a virgin?"

He nodded. "Yeah. Over time, Jessica taught me the basics. We didn't talk much, just … you know."

Hank nodded.

Old anger stewed in Justin's gut. He bunched a fist into the palm of his hand, nervously working them together like a ball and socket. "I realize now, looking back, that I was just performing a service. She crawled into my bed and got right down to business. Left right after. Never said a word other than giving me instructions. Telling me what she wanted me to do."

"This only happened at night?"

"Yeah. During the day, she never talked to me, or even looked at me. It was really weird."

"She brought the condoms?"

"Yeah."

"Premeditated rape," Hank said with a touch of anger. "Let me be very clear about this, Justin. None of this was your fault. You're not to blame. Jessica's a sick woman. A sex offender. Her job was to foster you, instead she abused you in the worst possible way." Hank spoke firmly, adamantly. "Relationships must be based on mutual respect. From respect comes trust. Without trust, love can't exist."

"Yes, sir."

"I'll report Jessica, to ensure this doesn't happen to another kid. And to make sure no child is placed in the McKinley home again."

Justin felt himself relaxing. Hank was taking *his* side. No scolding. Just fatherly concern. Talking about Jessica made Justin realize the extent of her cruelty, and how he'd absorbed all the blame, the shame and guilt, and carted it around ever since. Hank's interpretation brought the whole sordid experience into a new focus. Maybe over time the humiliation would fade away.

"There will always be people who'll want to take advantage of you, Justin. That's life. Hardship is inescapable. But many things are within your control. You have choices. In the future, trust your instincts. They'll tell you what's right or wrong. Don't let anyone bully you off course."

"Yes, sir. Trust my instincts. Good advice."

"Well, enough with the lecture." Hank slapped him on the knee and got to his feet, gray eyes radiating warmth. "Get yourself something to eat."

Feeling strong affection for the older man, Justin impulsively threw his arms around him.

Hank held him tight. "Hang tough, son. We'll get through this together."

We'll get through this together. Hank's words echoed in Justin's mind and his throat burned with unexpected emotion. He thanked God with every morsel of his being for guiding him to the Sterling ranch. *This must be what having a family feels like. A father. Sisters.* One sister, he corrected. What Cody was, he wasn't sure. But the feelings she stirred inside him felt far from sisterly.

CHAPTER FOURTEEN

USING A PATIENT TONE, Brennen demonstrated to Maggie how to make cappuccino using his fancy Italian java machine, which ground the fresh beans and dripped rich aromatic coffee into their cups. "This is how you get the steamed milk." The machine hissed, milk spewed from a spout and crowned their cups with creamy foam. Brennen sprinkled chocolate powder on top, submerged cinnamon sticks, and handed one to her.

The coffee smelled heavenly. She sipped and smiled. "Delicious."

He sipped and wiped away a thin mustache of foam, his eyes clear and curious behind the lens of his glasses. "Nice to see you smiling again, Maggie, and getting back out into the world."

"Thanks. I'm ready to be social again. No more hiding in the house. Starting with a party this Friday night."

"A party?"

"Food, drink, music, dancing." She stirred her cappuccino with the cinnamon stick. "A lot of our friends will be there. Can you come?"

"Of course I'll come." He pushed his tortoise shell glasses higher on his nose and put on his Father Freud expression. "What brought on this sudden need to be social?"

She shrugged. "It's time."

"Does it have something to do with the man you were with at Beckett's?" He rubbed his chin. "What's his name?"

"Sully." She felt a lecture coming on, and Brennen had her pinned against the counter in the small kitchen. "What's on your mind, Brennen?"

"Let's just say I was surprised to see you bending over a pool table, drunk, flirting with a young cowboy. What if clients saw you?"

Maggie's good mood fizzed away like air from a balloon. "I wasn't drunk. Well, maybe a little. It's no crime to have fun, Brennen. And Sully's not just a cowboy. As you know, he's Eric's best friend. His squad leader in Afghanistan. He went with me to visit Eric's grave."

He blinked. "That couldn't have been easy."

"It wasn't."

A long pause. "I certainly understand your attachment to Sully. He's your strongest link to Eric."

"Yes, he is."

"How old is he?"

"Twenty-eight."

"I see."

"It was a one-time deal, Brennen. I haven't turned into a bar fly." She maneuvered around him, careful not to topple the foam on her coffee, and heard the floorboards squeak behind her as he followed her into her office. She sank into her swivel chair, set her cup down and kicked her heels off under the desk.

Though uninvited, he sat across from her with an ankle crossed over a knee.

She had work to do, but Brennen looked as planted as a potted fern.

He pushed out his lips, his expression reflective. "How often do you see him?"

"Every Sunday night. Dinner and a movie at my place." *Not that it's any of your business.*

They were both silent. Maggie didn't want to continue the conversation. She clicked on her monitor and scanned her calendar, but Brennen didn't take the hint. He remained seated, and waited until she met his eyes again.

"You're missing the obvious, Maggie. Most people would call that dating."

"We're friends, Brennen. Good friends."

"Sully's getting the wrong idea."

"You know this, how?"

"I watched you two for quite a while. I'd go so far as to say he's deeply infatuated."

Maggie felt a warm glow as she recalled Sully's kiss last night. What a kiss it was ... so gentle, yet urgent. She kissed him back, blissfully, and realized she'd been waiting a long time for intimacy with him. Her fondness for Sully reshaped itself over time, deepening into something far stronger than affection. She would never have acted on her feelings if Sully hadn't started showing signs of romantic interest.

Brennen studied her, and she knew her little smile gave her away.

"Let me point out the obvious," Brennen said, leaning forward, a serious expression on his face. "You're fourteen years older than Sully."

"In all seriousness, Brennen, age is irrelevant," she said, echoing Sully's words at Beckett's.

"Is it?" His stare was an accusation. "You and Sully are both recovering from deep emotional trauma. As a professional, you know this is the worst possible time to jump into an affair. Covering up pain with shots of sexual adrenaline is a temporary fix. In the end, the energy sputters out, and one or both people are left hurting."

"Sully and I are not jumping into an affair, Brennen. We've known each other for weeks. We've spent hours and hours together, just talking, sharing feelings."

He sipped his cappuccino, face inscrutable, the light from the window reflecting on his glasses. "Getting involved with him could be considered unethical."

Maggie felt a tinge of anger. "I'm not his therapist."

"But he knows you're a therapist. Have you resisted taking a professional slant in your conversations with him?" He gave her time to reflect on this. "Is he acting like a patient?"

Maggie crossed her arms, suddenly feeling defensive.

"We both know how common erotic transference is. Clients frequently develop sexual feelings for their therapists. They open up and pour out their souls, and we listen without judgment. They mistake gratitude for love, and often want to act on their feelings. Whether those feelings are real or not, it's important to discuss them thoroughly. Not exploit them."

Maggie knew the truth in Brennen's words. She had worked through transference issues with many patients over the years, and gently helped them sort through confusing feelings. Now she critically assessed Brennen's point of view. It was true, she and Sully had never discussed these feelings of attraction. Just acted on them. *Was* she acting unethically? Was she so wrapped up in her own needs that she was overlooking Sully's?

"Has Sully given himself opportunities to meet other women?"

"No," she said candidly. "He works around the clock."

Brennen's silence hung heavy in the air. "If Sully *were* meeting other women," he said carefully, "younger women, would his interest in you be as strong?"

Maggie turned away from his penetrating stare, gazed out the window. The rain was moving in soft veils across the parking lot and trees were waving their branches like seaweed underwater. The mass of gray clouds pressing down on the earth suddenly felt suffocating.

"Maggie?"

"I don't know."

"Maggie, face facts. He's a young man. With needs. It's easy for him to just show up at your house and take advantage of the situation."

"He's a perfect gentleman."

"Waiting to make his move."

It sounded sordid, but no more so than the stories she heard every day in therapy sessions.

"Plus, he's a cowboy." Brennen's voice sounded skeptical. "Do you think he's going to move off the ranch into the suburbs? Or are you thinking of moving in with the pigs and the goats?"

She had never thought that far ahead. "It's horses. Performance horses."

"Do you know anything about horses?"

"No, but ...."

"Riding a pig or a horse is all the same to me. A lot of manure. A lot of hard work. No vacations."

Again, she saw the truth in Brennen's words. "He works seven days a week from morning until night," she thought out loud. "And he cares for his father."

"What's wrong with his father?"

"Stroke."

"How's the ranch faring?"

"Not well. He's trying to turn it around."

A long silence stretched between them. Brennen removed his glasses and polished them with the edge of his cardigan, then replaced them. "Maggie, this man may not be the prize you imagine him to be."

The corners of her mouth pulled steadily downward, and she knew disappointment showed on her face.

Brennen's voice softened. "I'm sorry, Maggie. I'm giving it to you with both barrels." He leaned back in his chair, hands relaxing on the armrests. "I just want to steer you away from more grief."

Maggie forced a smile. "I know, Brennen. I appreciate your frank words."

They were both silent. "Why not invite a couple of younger women to your party?"

"Why? To bait Sully?"

"To test him. See what he does when opportunity falls directly across his path."

She sat quietly, seeing the logic, despising the method, and the possible outcome.

"It's best to find the stress fractures early."

Feeling the sudden need to be alone, she opened the top file on the stack of folders on her desk and stared blankly at her notes. "My patient will be here shortly."

Brennen took his cue and walked to the door, paused to glance back at her. "Give yourself a few months, a year, to get your head on straight. If you and Sully still have strong feelings for one another, at least you'll know you didn't use each other as a Band-aid."

She cleared her throat. "Thanks for the upbeat conversation, Brennen."

He smiled. "Maggie, I'm always here."

"I know, Brennen. Me, too." Maggie sighed as he shut the door. She immediately started running a debate about Sully through her mind. She could argue that Brennen's point of view was critically biased. He was suffering the aftermath of a terrible divorce, and his wife had dragged him the length of a football field through shards of glass. But to his credit, when it came to assessing the human mind and its desire to skirt unpleasant truths, he was generally spot on.

Maggie could not deny that her feelings for Sully had deepened considerably. She had waded beyond the 'friendship' buoy some time ago, but feeling guilty, and afraid to rock the boat, she kept her feelings hidden. If Eric were alive, the kiss between her and his best friend would never have happened, and as Brennen so deftly pointed out, there were the looming age and financial issues. Sully lived with his father on his childhood ranch, and was a struggling horse trainer. Maybe the alcohol, or the profound sense of loss stirred by visiting Eric's grave, made her willpower cave last night. She deliberately pulled up anchor and headed into unknown waters. Now Brennen wanted to throw her a safety line before she lost sight of the shore. Only she wasn't sure she wanted to be reeled back to her former life, which was one of heartache, too much work, and too little play.

A year had passed since she'd been in a romantic relationship. Her thoughts drifted to Ryan Gable, a sexy, intelligent colleague who'd been a close friend for years. The two shared common interests, passionate ideas, and lots of laughter. When Ryan's marriage was on the ropes and he separated from his wife, he and Maggie acted on their feelings and started dating. For six months, the relationship had been charged with excitement and warm companionship. Sex had been thrilling, and the future looked promising. But in the end, Ryan missed his kids to the point of distraction, and for their sake he decided to give his marriage another chance. That was that. A seemingly perfect relationship skidded off the tracks like a train wreck. The period of loss that followed was painful, and then she just felt numb, and unwilling to put herself out there in the dating jungle again. It was a brutal game of chance requiring too large an emotional investment.

Out of the blue, Sully miraculously appeared in her life. A decent, hardworking, honest man, who offered gentle support and a beam of hope in a dim future. She didn't want that light to go dark, but sometimes the morally right decision to make was the one that hurt the most.

CHAPTER FIFTEEN

CODY ARRIVED first for breakfast. The storm had barreled in with unusual force, and had drummed the walls of the house all night. The indoor lamps cast a warm glow against the bleak light filtering through the windows. After crowding her plate with scrambled eggs, two buttermilk pancakes, and a couple of grilled sausages, she sat at the long, scarred table and poured herself a mug of coffee from a carafe. As she stirred in cream and honey, Sarah swept into the room like the forewarning of a tornado, her face screwed tight with anger. She slapped two rumpled envelopes down in front of Cody. The handwriting was smeared as though water had spilled across them.

"What's this?" Cody picked one up. It was addressed to Justin from Avery Steiner in Arizona.

"Love letters! They fell out of Justin's pocket last night. I found them in the back of the Land Cruiser when I got my packages."

"You read his mail?"

"They were already open." Sarah slumped wearily into the chair next to Cody.

"That makes it right?"

"I wanted to see what I was dealing with. Good thing, too. She's his girlfriend." Sarah's eyes welled with tears. "I broke up with Bear for him!"

Cody swallowed. "Bear drinks. And he treats you like shit."

"Like you said, I shouldn't be getting love advice from you! At least Bear doesn't have another woman stashed away." Sarah chewed her bottom lip. "I still have Bear's engagement ring."

"Sarah, don't even think about it!" Her sister's uneasy expression showed how thin her layer of self-confidence was.

Justin entered the room and the sound of the rainstorm amplified until the door shut behind him. He scraped his boots on the mat and hung his wet jacket on a peg.

Sarah jumped up, shot daggers at him, and fled into the hallway.

He stood looking after her, scratching his head. "Morning, Cody."

"Morning."

He walked to the buffet, looking dusty from cleaning stalls, bits of hay clinging to his hair. He filled his plate, eased comfortably into one of the wooden chairs, and poured a mug of coffee. "What's up with Sarah? She looked at me like I was an ax murderer."

Cody pushed his letters over to him. "She found these."

His face showed surprise. "She read them?"

"I'm sorry to say she did. On the plus side, she'll leave you alone now that she knows you have a girlfriend."

He folded the letters into squares and stuffed them into his breast pocket. "Avery and I are friends. She helped me out after I got robbed and beaten. I owe her, big time." He paused, looked away, then turned back to her. "We don't have a commitment."

"Sarah got the impression from those letters that you do."

His face shadowed, then he gave her a direct stare. "I guess I should break it off with Avery completely."

"A swift cut is generally the kindest."

"You're right. I'll do that in my next letter."

Though it was none of Cody's business, she realized that Justin's private life mattered to her, and she was thankful he shared this intimate information. For weeks, his gentle manner had rubbed against her prickly façade like river water on stone, buffing it smooth. As he peered at her over his mug, she felt the warmth of his friendship. In some secret way, Justin seemed to know what she felt inside, and he would understand anything she said. After the showdown in the parking lot last night, and his heartfelt confession to her family, she felt the bond between them strengthen. Like her, Justin was dragging a heavy cart of baggage through life, just trying to cope.

The door opened and Roth, Nelson, and Billy shuffled inside. They hung wet slickers on pegs and crowded the buffet, boot heels scuffing the hardwood floor.

"Man, it's like being under water out there today," Roth said, as the three sat down with their overflowing plates. "A bigger storm's heading in. Winds up to sixty miles per hour."

The men discussed the storm as they passed around coffee, butter, and maple syrup. "We need to batten down the hatches after breakfast. Stash everything that might blow around. Lock the stall doors."

"I'll head down to the bottom pasture," Nelson said. "Herd them cows ready to calve into the birthing shed."

"I'll get all the pasture horses inside the indoor arena," Justin said.

"I'll help you," Cody said.

"Me and Billy will tend to the bulls." Roth unfolded the newspaper, handed the sports section to Nelson, and then snapped open the front page. Both men ate with faces hidden behind newsprint.

"Woman pulls gun in Chuck's parking lot," Roth read out loud. "What the hell?" His paper came down in a hurry and he looked wide-eyed at Cody.

"Let me see that," she said.

Roth passed it over. All faces turned to her. Justin stood and read over her shoulder. The article named names: Justin Powell, Katie and Sarah Sterling, all four McKinley men.

"Witnesses told police the men attacked Justin with no provocation," Cody read out loud. "Katie Sterling acted in self-defense."

Also mentioned was the allegation made by Jabe that Justin was a thief.

"No charges have been filed, and the incident is under investigation," she read.

Nothing about rape, thank God. She glanced up. Bear had quietly entered the room and stood at the end of the table, listening and watching with brooding eyes. He made the hair on her arms stand up. There was something creepy about a big man who moved with the stealth of a cat.

"Dad's got an investigator looking into this," Cody said. "Justin did nothing wrong."

Justin took his seat and listlessly resumed eating while the paper got passed around the table.

"The McKinleys are a rough lot. Never did like them," Roth said. "Specially Kenny. Something's off about that dude."

"All four of them attacked you?" Nelson asked Justin.

"Yeah."

"If me 'n Billy and Roth was there," Nelson said. "We'd have given 'em a fair fight."

"Beat the holy crap outta 'em," Billy said, dark eyes flashing. "Wish I coulda seen Cody whip out that Colt. Badass Cody! They should've known better than to mess with a Sterling."

The three hands laughed heartily.

Bear sat down with his food and studied the article when it came his way.

"Justin kicked the old man in the nuts," Cody said, still grinning. "You should've seen his face. Kenny was about to land a good one on Justin, but Sarah jumped him from behind like a starving orangutan on a banana." She shared more highlights, and everyone laughed out loud, except Bear, who kept a mirthless little smile on his face. The story eventually lost its steam, and everyone resumed talking about preparations for the storm.

Glad that the story raised no doubts about Justin, Cody caught his gaze for a moment, glanced away, and then irresistibly, was drawn back to his electric blues. A trace of a smile touched his mouth. Her lips tilted upwards of their own accord. Justin was having an effect on her—warm and pleasant, like sinking into a bath of hot water on a freezing cold night. She glanced at Bear, who sat quietly watching the exchange, his face giving away nothing. His eyes, open and sharp as a camera lens, clicked away, catching every nuance of what unfolded around him. God only knew what was at work in that reptilian brain. A chill touched Cody's spine at the thought of Sarah taking him back.

CHAPTER SIXTEEN

SULLY ARRIVED at Maggie's at 8:00 p.m. Lights blazed from the windows and cars lined both sides of the road. He dashed through a torrent of rain to her front door, then entered to find the great room packed with people balancing drinks and plates in both hands. The loud din of voices competed with throbbing background music. Men were dressed in slacks and golf shirts. Women wore summer dresses, or designer jeans and clingy tops. A lot of skin on display. Nice visuals.

Dressed in a blue chambray shirt, Wrangler's, and the only boots he owned that weren't scuffed to hell, Sully felt like a hound dog at a poodle convention. After hanging his hat on the coat rack, he waded through the crowd and spotted Maggie in the kitchen. She was talking to a middle-aged couple and the man who had chided her at the pub last week. Wearing a pinstriped shirt, silk tie, and navy blazer, the shrink looked as animated as a mannequin in a storefront window. Who even dresses like that in Bend?

Sully joined people circling the island piling food on paper plates. He helped himself to giant prawns, grilled chicken on a stick, stuffed mushrooms, and a slice of ham and cheddar quiche. After clinking ice cubes in a plastic glass and splashing them with tequila, he polished off his food, washed it down with tequila, and helped himself to seconds.

Finally, he heard Maggie call his name. The older couple had moved away but the shrink stood planted at her side. Maggie normally had an unfussy fashion style, or lack of style, as she claimed, and dressed in jeans and T-shirts. Tonight she wore a low-cut halter dress that accentuated her graceful curves and beautiful legs. Her hair fell across her shoulders, her eyes were outlined in smoky gray, and her lips were strawberry red. She looked mysterious, and kissable. "You look beautiful."

She smiled and gave him a hug. Hands full, he was helpless to hug back, though he liked the way she smelled, the way her body felt.

"Sully, meet Brennan." Turning a cool gaze to the shrink, he set his plate down and shook Brennan's hand, which felt smooth and soft, nails manicured. Sully wondered how he got his hair so perfect.

"Ah, Maggie's pool partner," Brennen said. "You let her win most of the games, I noticed."

"I won those fair and square!" she grinned.

"She's a natural," Sully said, finding it unsettling that Brennen had had them under his scrutiny.

"So, you work with horses."

"That I do. You ride?"

"No. Never been on a horse." He sniffed, his handsome features holding a hint of snobbishness. "Golf, chess, teaching, pursuits of the intellect are my passion."

Warmed by the tequila and happy to be near Maggie, Sully ignored Brennen's rudeness.

"Excuse us, Brennen." Maggie took Sully's arm and navigated him out of the kitchen. "Don't mind him. He comes off a little stiff, but he's a gifted psychiatrist. Well respected."

Maggie moved Sully expertly through the crowd, making fluid small talk and witty comments, impressing him with her social ease. A sharp-nosed woman named Rachel and her clique of friends peppered Sully with questions.

"How did you and Maggie meet?"

"Oooh, you knew Eric in Afghanistan?"

"Thank you for serving our country."

"You get wounded over there?"

"Sorry to hear that."

"Dangerous place … terrible war … bankrupting this country."

"Is the war for oil?"

War wasn't something he wanted to talk about, but he answered their questions politely. This was his debut as Maggie's date, and he didn't want to mess it up. Already, he looked forward to the end of the evening so he could be alone with her, away from curious eyes and questions about a world they didn't understand.

Tugging him away from Rachel, Maggie parked him in front of two young, pretty women from her health club, Noel and Allison. After stoking the conversation, she abruptly ditched him and slipped back into the kitchen, so smoothly he didn't see it coming. Disappointed, he tried to focus on Noel and Allison, who were talking about their teaching jobs at a local middle school. He inserted a mindless comment here and there, all the while stealing glances at Maggie, who was now huddled with two other couples, and the shrink, talking up a storm and laughing.

Noel wandered off to talk to a friend. Allison remained, seemingly in no hurry to mingle. She was a tall, willowy redhead with intelligent brown eyes and ivory skin. After downing more tequila, Sully started to relax, and he and Allison shared some laughs about local lore.

"Where do you work out?" she asked. "You're pretty buff."

"Just do ranch work," he said lazily, sipping his drink.

"I grew up in Tumalo."

"I'm in Wild Horse Creek. Dancing Horse Ranch."

"Dancing Horse? That's the Sullivan family."

"I'm Michael Sullivan. Everyone calls me Sully."

Her eyes widened. "Your dad's a rodeo legend."

Sully chuckled. "He's been called worse."

"I did barrel racing in high school. You and I were at rodeos together."

"That right?" His interest piqued.

"It's okay if you don't remember me. I was a scrawny kid, no talent. Didn't even register on the radar."

He didn't remember her, but still, he was impressed. She had to be a hell of a rider. "My rodeo days are long behind me."

"Not that long. You ranked second in World Bareback Riding." She narrowed her eyes. "Was it 2002?"

He laughed, flattered. "You've got a hell of a memory."

Allison told him her family owned Hollow Tree Ranch, and bred Morgans. He'd been three years ahead of her in high school, so they never partied in the same circles. As the evening wore on and the crowd got more juiced up, the music switched to eighties' disco, and people danced to music so loud the walls vibrated. Brennen and Maggie watched from the sideline. Sully tried several times to catch her eye, but she seemed to deliberately look away.

Allison asked Sully to dance. The tequila boosted his confidence and they joined other bodies writhing on the dance floor. Sully pulled out all his old dance moves, which he'd been told looked like calisthenics, but Allison didn't seem to care. Sensual and graceful, she swayed her hips in perfect sync to the music, not matching him, but definitely keeping him inspired. Gyrating to the beat, some dancers performed moves that might've looked illegal at the start of the evening.

Sully and Allison stayed on the floor for a half dozen tunes. A fast-paced country song came up, and he led Allison through a western swing with as many fancy turns as he could remember. She kept up like an ace and wasn't out of breath when the song ended. They both had been grinning for a good half hour. His shirt was damp, and he decided to sit one out and grab a cold drink. Maggie was walking off the dance floor in front of him as a slow song came on by Garth Brooks. "The Dance." A favorite.

"My turn," he said, pulling her into his arms. Without thinking, he started a two-step, but she couldn't follow. He switched to traditional slow dancing, pulling her close. She followed him smoothly, resting her head against his shoulder. "Feels like you've been avoiding me," he murmured.

"Just visiting friends."

Sully understood, but he didn't have to like it. He pulled her tight, and felt her heart beating against his own. This was how it was supposed to be when two people were right for each other. Just the two of them. Floating in a soft-edged universe. The music moved around him and through him and he sang softly with the lyrics. Maggie glanced up and smiled. She looked beautiful. Her mouth was close enough to kiss, and he wanted to kiss her. The pull was strong, but he got hold of himself, and enjoyed the smell of her hair, the feel of her in his arms. When the song ended, he spun her around. She turned gracefully, thanked him, and sauntered back to Brennen without a backward glance.

Sully blew out a breath. *What the hell?* This was supposed to be their night, not hers and Brennen's. He didn't understand what she was doing, but admittedly, he didn't understand women. Horses, he could deal with. Tonight Maggie seemed as spooked as a wild filly. He needed to take it slow, not frighten her off. It was late. He had to get up at dawn, and it didn't look like the party was going to end any time soon. Maggie was preoccupied. Frustrated, Sully decided to call it a night.

Brennen seemed to be standing guard when Sully said goodbye to Maggie. He spoke quietly, "See you Sunday night."

"Do you mind if we eat out for a change?" Maggie asked. "Brennen wants to join us."

"They have great seafood at McGees," Brennen said. With an air of ownership, he put his arm around Maggie's waist and pulled her close.

Sully didn't like him touching Maggie. It disturbed him more that she didn't pull away.

"Sully?" Maggie asked. "Dinner on Sunday?"

"Wanna walk me to the door?"

She nodded, and said to Brennen, "I'll be right back."

The room was pulsing. Barely able to hear his own thoughts, Sully placed a guiding hand to the small of her back, skirting dancers who marched across the floor waving their arms to "YMCA" by the Village People, grins plastered on their faces. He lifted his Stetson from the coat rack and stood holding it. "What's going on between you and Brennen?"

"Nothing."

He looked at her, hard.

"We're not dating, if that's what you mean." Her words came out slurred and he realized she'd had a lot to drink.

"You could've fooled me. Any idiot can see he's got a thing for you."

"He's a caring friend, that's all. He helped me realize … I need to get out more, and …." She hiccupped, put her fingers to her mouth. "Spend more time with people my own age."

Sully bristled. "Instead of me?"

"No, just other people, too."

"You blindsided me tonight."

She didn't meet his eyes.

"You invited me as your date, then you avoided me."

"We're not dating."

"We could be."

Her face clouded. She looked confused by his comment. "I'm sorry I've misled you, Sully. You just came home from war. You haven't had time to adjust." She hesitated, looked away, and then her soft gaze came back to his. "I've monopolized your time. Kept you from meeting women your own age."

"What?" Her words made no sense. Then it dawned on him that Brennen had planted doubts in her mind about him. "Those Brennen's words, or yours?"

Silence.

"Don't let him control your feelings, Maggie."

"I'm sorry," she slurred, seeming to be in a fog. "We've gotten very wrapped up in each other. We should take a break."

"That's bullshit."

She stood quietly for a long moment. "I want to do what's best in the long run. Neither of us wants a romance that's just a bump in the road. We've already been through so much."

"Stop talking like a therapist. Get out of your head. Listen to your feelings."

Maggie looked away, biting her lip.

Sully said sharply, "I'm gonna give your shrink friend a piece of my mind."

She put a hand on his chest. "It's best if you go."

"Now you're kicking me out?"

"You were leaving anyway." Her expression looked determined. Abruptly, she turned on her heel, and weaved her way back through the crowd.

He wanted to follow, reason with her, but he knew he was too angry. He'd cause a scene. Sully disliked the shrink intensely, his soft hands and perfect hair. He thought again about giving Brennen a piece of his mind.

Allison caught up to him before his avenger idea fully took shape.

"Hey, cowboy," she said cheerily. "You leaving?"

"Thinking about it," he said.

"No goodbye?"

"Sorry, I have to get up early." His gaze settled on the pretty face smiling up at him.

"Ranch work is never done. That's why I switched to teaching."

"Smart girl."

"Look, I think it'd be fun if we got together sometime. Maybe do a trail ride."

Her smile was contagious. He felt one corner of his mouth tilt up.

With an expression that was anything but tame, she pressed her lips against his, and gave him a sweet, sensual kiss. When she pulled away, she was perfectly composed, eyes steady. "Here's my number, Sully. Call me." She pressed a card into his palm, folded his fingers around it, and faded back into the crowd.

Wow. Sully stood flustered, his mind being pulled in one direction, his anatomy in another. Clearly, Allison was a woman who knew what she wanted, and wasn't afraid to show it. Right now, he needed bare-boned honesty in his life, not mind-wrangling therapeutic nonsense. He looked across the room, his eyes searching for Maggie. She stood with her back to him, indifferent, Brennen's arm wrapped around her shoulders. Sully fumed. If Maggie wanted to push him to the background while making Brennen her chief advisor, he'd give her all the space she wanted. That didn't mean he was going to sit on his thumbs waiting for her to get her head together. He tucked Allison's card into his shirt pocket and walked out the door. A cold, hard rain was blowing sideways. A hell of a storm was sweeping in.

CHAPTER SEVENTEEN

A STRONG WIND buffeted the house, branches scraped the windows and knocked against the eaves. Cody found it impossible to sleep. Since midnight, the tempo of the storm had increased steadily. She tossed fitfully. Felled trees would be strewn across the grounds tomorrow. Ditches would be flooded, with mud oozing over roads and pastures. Days of cleanup ahead. The clock on the nightstand read 3:15 a.m. She took little comfort knowing that even in this god-awful weather, one of the hands would be out patrolling. Livestock often spooked in these conditions, crashed into fences, suffered serious injuries.

Lightning illuminated the room, followed by a booming thunderclap. That did it. Sleep was out of the question. Cody tossed the covers aside and peered through the mottled glass at the storm-whipped landscape. Wind bent the tops of trees to the east and rain sliced through the blackness in horizontal sheets. Veins of lightning trembled in the distant sky, then vanished. Up the hill, the outdoor lights to the barn were out. She tried the bedside lamp, and light spilled over the nightstand. The power wasn't out, just a line to the barn. Why didn't the back-up generator switch on? Cursing under her breath, she decided to go and check the horses.

Dressed in jeans and a wool turtleneck, she hurried downstairs to the office, grabbed a twelve-gauge shotgun from the gun cabinet, slid cartridges into the magazine tube, and chambered the first round. It was irrational to think she needed to be armed, but she wasn't a rational person. Using the low beam of the Maglite to find her way down the hall, she paused outside Justin's door, which stood partly open. "Justin?" No answer. Baffled, she pushed the door open with the barrel of the gun and scanned the room with the low beam. The covers were strewn aside, and the room was empty.

No lights on anywhere downstairs. Where was he?

Right now she didn't have time to worry about Justin.

Cody's bare feet padded over the floorboards to the mudroom where she wrestled into a slicker and mud boots. When she opened the door, wind struck her with a force that stole her breath and nearly blew her backwards. The second she stepped off the porch, icy rain pelted her face and water streamed off the brim of her hat. The moaning and pounding of the storm was deafening. Tense before, now she was rigid.

With the shotgun in the crook of her arm and the high beam slicing through the darkness, she bent into the gale and made her way awkwardly up the hill. Taking slow, careful steps, she sometimes slid backwards as the mud shifted under her weight. It took some muscle to slide open the barn door against the wind. The lights were out inside, too. Above the howling storm, she heard the horses nickering and carrying on. Something wasn't right. Casting a beam towards the stalls, she stumbled into something heavy on the ground. Before her beam found it, she knew it was a body. Billy! Fresh blood gushed from a gash above his ear, eddied around the front of his earlobe, and ran down his jaw.

Her heart punched against her ribs. She knelt and felt for a pulse. Alive, but out cold. She fished her cell phone from her pocket and pressed Roth's number. Behind her, something moved. Reflexively, she struck out hard with the butt of the gun and heard a shriek as she landed a blow to someone's leg. A second figure flew at her from the side, slamming her to the ground. Her head hit the concrete hard. Stunned, she lay motionless. There was an ache in her optic nerve, and a steady throbbing at the base of her skull. Then the sound of thundering hooves came right at her. Horses were out of their stalls. Stampeding! Groaning through the pain, she rolled next to Billy as deadly hooves thundered past her out of the barn.

She felt a withering jolt of pain as she struggled to her feet and stumbled outside. Her high beam illuminated two mounted figures rustling the horses up the trail leading off the property. Cody sent seven explosive blasts above the heads of the riders, reloaded, fired again. The buckshot couldn't get anywhere near them, but it frightened the hell out of the horses. Half of them scattered. The two riders kept going, with a handful of Sterling horses running between them.

Cody whistled and a runaway horse galloped back to the barn. Thank God. Buster! Looking back down the hill, she saw lights on in the bunkhouse and two flashlights beams moving swiftly toward her. Wearing wide-brimmed hats and long slickers, Roth carried a rifle, Nelson gripped a revolver.

"Horse thieves," she yelled. "Billy's hurt in the barn. I'm going after them." Not waiting for a response, she grabbed a handful of Buster's mane, intending to mount and ride after the thieves.

Roth grabbed her arm, pulled her back. "You're not going alone. Get saddled."

Roth was right. In this weather, riding bareback was a damned fool thing to do. They hurriedly saddled Buster and Tahoe, and then trotted out of the barn. Nelson was walking Billy to the house, the two looking ghostly through the hazy curtain of rain.

"Call the sheriff!" she yelled after him.

He gave her a thumbs up.

Roth rode in the lead, his beam bouncing over the rutted trail. Rain churned the earth to mud. The landscape was unrecognizable, trees and grass heaving and thrashing, branches creaking.

Lightning cracked open the sky, followed by a rolling thunderclap, illuminating the trail bright as day. Cody caught a muzzle flash high on the ridge and heard the thwack of a bullet hit the ground below her.

Roth thumbed off his beam and they were engulfed in black. He dismounted, turned Tahoe around, slapped him on the rump, and sent him home.

Horses made a bigger target.

Roth grabbed Buster's reins, screamed up at her, "Go back!"

She slid out of the saddle, sent Buster home, too.

Roth's face tightened with anger. "Scat," he yelled above the storm. "Home!"

Lightning lit the sky. Two more muzzle flashes. Roth pushed her to the ground and fell on top of her. Bullets thudded into the mud inches from their heads.

"Christ!"

"Go home, Cody! Before you get us killed!"

She fought against him. "Let me up!"

"Will you go?"

"Yes, damn it!"

Roth rolled off her and lurched away into the darkness.

Cody drew in a whistling breath as she extracted herself from the icy, sucking mud. Her heart pounded against her ribcage. Shivering, she felt a deep sinking sensation in the pit of her stomach. It took a moment for her to realize it was fear. She and Roth had missed being murdered by a hair. With every intention of following him, she checked her weapon, fingers trembling. The shotgun was caked in mud. The cartridges in her pockets were wet, too, making the shotgun too dangerous to shoot. *Useless.* Her tears gave way, filling her eyes. Blinking them back, she realized she had no choice but to slog home, attend to Billy, and identify which horses were taken.

Bracing against wind that shoved her with muscular force, Cody slid and stumbled like a drunkard. Mud gripped her feet, water seeped inside her collar and raced along her spine. Visibility was poor. Switching on the Maglite wasn't an option. The occasional flash of lightning was her only compass home. She stopped to suck in oxygen, chest heaving, and imagined men materializing in the darkness from every direction. A blurry figure on horseback did come out of the black and was almost upon her before she raised her shotgun and clicked on the high beam.

The rider raised a forearm to his eyes. "Turn that off!"

Justin, riding Buster! Relief weakened her knees. "What're you doing out here?" she yelled as he dismounted.

"I could ask you the same thing," he yelled back. "I was out jogging. When I got back, I saw horses running loose. Buster came at me like a bat out of hell, saddled. I figured you were in trouble."

"You were out jogging?" she asked, incredulous.

"I couldn't sleep. That's what I do."

"In a thunderstorm?"

"It wasn't bad when I left. How about putting that gun down. It could go off. You're shaking."

"Sorry, I'm not thinking straight." She lowered the shotgun. "Some men tried to kill me and Roth. I caught them in the barn stealing horses."

"Holy hell! You okay?"

"Yeah."

"Where's Roth?"

"He went after them on foot."

"How many?"

"I saw two."

"Ride Buster home. Gimme your gun. I'll go help."

"It's too dark. Too dangerous. If Roth has any sense, he'll come home."

"I can't leave him out here alone."

"Roth can take care of himself. I can't risk having you both killed." She was now thinking more clearly. Justin showing up with a horse was a Godsend. "Mount up. Let's catch those loose horses. Check on Billy."

His face looked tense, but he shrugged his shoulders. "You're the boss."

She slung herself into the saddle. Justin heaved himself up behind her. With the wind whipping their slickers, they settled into the sway of the gelding's sure-footed gait. Buster's keen eyesight and inner GPS guided him steadily home. Cody had a good chill going on and looked forward to the heat of the house.

"What happened to Billy?" Justin asked, his mouth close to her ear.

"The thieves knocked him out. But I got one pretty good with the butt of my gun."

"Good job." He sounded impressed. "Calamity Jane."

They commenced to yelling back and forth and Cody became aware of his strong body moving rhythmically against hers. The circumstances had been horrific the last time a man had been this close. Buddy beat her unconscious, waited for her to come to, then knifed her slowly and savagely, his face a demonic mask. She shuddered, and forced back the memories. Justin wasn't Buddy. Justin was calm and reassuring. The closeness of his body felt protective and prompted a piercing yearning for intimacy. At the same time, her heart started to race with a touch of panic. Fear diluted her desire.

CHAPTER EIGHTEEN

WHEN CODY AND JUSTIN rounded the last loop of the trail, the thunder sounded further to the east, and the storm had downgraded to a hard driving rain. The windows of the house were beacons of light floating in the darkness. Justin was relieved to see Nelson mounted on Roth's big bay, herding mud-spattered, nervous horses into the barn. One horse reared up and had to be restrained by a lasso to keep it from bolting.

Nelson had gotten the backup generator going, the lights were on, and the air inside the barn felt warm and dry. The three of them hurriedly stalled the animals and took a tally. Six missing; four seasoned cutting horses, two leggy yearlings in training. The shock of it knocked the breath out of Justin and was mirrored on the faces of Cody and Nelson. Tension made the muscles of his shoulders and neck burn, but there was no time to brood. The animals needed to be brushed down and settled.

As he labored, Justin tried to calm his nerves. Since his attack by the McKinley clan, and his secrets slithering out of hiding, his anxiety had mounted steadily, disturbing his dreams, and erupting tonight in a panic attack. Everything became slow and hypnotic. He felt like he was suffocating, and his heart was being crushed in a vise. He leapt out of bed, threw on his gym clothes, and staggered out of the house. Out in the open, he pushed his body hard, slogging through rain and mud until sheer exhaustion calmed him down.

When he returned to the house, the storm was furious, his slicker billowed like a sail, the ranch was in chaos, and spooked horses were running wild. Buster came at him at a full gallop, stopped at the last second, then snorted and pawed the earth. Justin slung himself in the saddle and Buster forged through the storm, eventually finding Cody.

She looked dog-tired but determined, the shotgun aimed at his chest. Thank God she didn't shoot him!

After the horses were settled, Justin, Cody and Nelson hiked down to the house and stripped off their sodden shoes and slickers in the mudroom. Cody swept off her hat, releasing a tangle of blonde hair around her mud-flecked face. His eyes searched hers for recognition of the affection they'd come to share, but she responded with a cool, steady stare, and quickly looked away.

All packed muscle and barrel-chested, still wearing his hat, Nelson led the way into the kitchen in bare feet and muddy long johns. The rest of the household was assembled around the island wearing bathrobes and strained expressions. Wrapped in pink flannel, Maresol stood pressing a blood-soaked towel to Billy's scalp, her face creased with worry. Billy sat slumped in a chair, eyes downcast, his work shirt stained red.

Justin felt the nervous tension in the room. Calamity struck, and everyone was trying to sort out the details and figure out where to go from here. Carlos passed out hot coffee. Justin and Nelson readily accepted, wrapping cold fingers around hot mugs. Justin blew over the surface and took a sip, felt the warmth trail down to his stomach.

"Billy, you okay?" Cody asked.

He gave a slight shrug of his shoulders.

"Let's take a look."

Everyone leaned in as Maresol lifted the towel. A trickle of blood escaped from a gash a few inches long. He winced when she reapplied it.

Cody frowned, the hollows of her cheeks deepening. "How's your vision?"

"A little blurry."

"You need stitches. And an MRI."

Maresol looked stricken. "What is Em-Mar-Eye?"

"A brain scan. He may have a concussion." Although she was clearly exhausted, Cody managed to come across as collected and focused. "Hand me some of that coffee, Carlos. I'm cold as a corpse." Carlos passed over a mug. She nodded her thanks, and said, "You better get Billy to the ER."

"Sí, sí. I go geet dressed." Carlos hurried into the mudroom, the outside door shutting behind him.

Everyone stood mute. The roar of the storm rose and fell.

Poised on a barstool drinking coffee, wearing white chenille and fluffy slippers, Sarah looked as dazed as a sleepwalker.

Cody sipped her coffee. "Billy, tell me exactly what happened."

"Not much to tell." The young ranch hand brushed a sheaf of dark bangs from his eyes and met her gaze. "Nelson woke me at two and we traded shifts. It was bad out there. Never seen nothing like it. By three, it was like a hurricane. Everything blowing sideways. I saw the lights go off up the hill. Figured I'd go start the generator. I hiked up there, went inside." He frowned. "Don't remember nothing else."

"I must've gotten there right after they clobbered you," Cody said.

"God, he watching," Maresol sniffed, holding a tissue to her nostrils. "If you not come ... my poor boy ...."

Billy blushed to his hairline. "It's okay, Ma. I'm okay."

"That ain't the only thing to thank Cody for," Nelson said, rage smoldering in his deep brown eyes. "If she hadn't fired them shots and scattered them horses, the thieves woulda gotten more 'n six."

"Which horses did they take?" Billy asked.

"Four geldings," Nelson said bitterly. "And two yearlings, Buck and Shiloh."

"Dirty bastards!" Sarah hissed, now fully awake.

"Them animals can't be replaced," Nelson said. "Can't find no better cow horses nowhere. Nobody trains 'em better than us."

Cody's chin lifted with a sudden jerk, and she said fiercely, "We'll get them back."

Bundled in a thick parka and wool cap, Carlos rushed into the room jingling keys, and then he helped Billy into his jacket.

"Be careful," Cody said. "It's hell out there."

"Sí. I drive slow." Carlos ushered Billy out the door.

"Dad should get home from Boise this morning," Sarah said, nervously finger-combing her hair. Justin thought she looked softer and more appealing with her mask of makeup washed off.

Nelson straddled a stool and tugged the corner of his bushy mustache. "Hank ain't gonna be flying in this storm."

"Riding out this emergency will make him really pissed," Sarah said. "No one ever stole a horse from us before."

"No way they could. This storm was perfect cover," Cody said. "You can't see or hear yourself think out there. Where the hell is Bear?"

"He went to Dancing Horse Ranch early this evening," Sarah said. "Must've taken cover somewhere when this storm hit."

"What's he doing out there?"

"Picking up a new reining horse. Champion stock."

"What we need is a cow horse."

The door to the mudroom opened and slammed shut. Roth padded barefoot into the room, long johns muddy, hair sticking every which way, eyes hard as granite.

All faces turned to him expectantly.

He shook his head, his posture rigid. "No luck. When I got up to the ridge, the thieves were gone. No footprints, no nothing." He pounded a fist on the counter. "Wish I coulda gotten 'em in my crosshairs."

Silence hung heavy in the room. Justin knew everyone was wishing the same thing.

Roth filled a mug with coffee, caught his image in the window and smoothed down his hair, then sat gloomily next to Sarah. He picked a banana off the fruit bowl, peeled it, and ate it in three bites.

Sarah filled in the void. "Everyone must be starving. I'll help Maresol cook breakfast. No one can think straight on an empty stomach."

"Sí, sí. I geet dressed," Maresol said. "We eat in half a hour."

"Did you call the sheriff, Nelson?" Cody asked.

"Yeah. I called him," Nelson said. "He said he'd be here at first light."

Cody released a weary sigh. "Nothing left to do until he gets here. I'm heading for a hot shower."

Seemed everyone had the same idea. The kitchen emptied quickly, except for Roth, who sat drinking coffee with a dark cloud brewing over his head. Sarah was already getting out mixing bowls and skillets from the cupboards.

Feeling exhaustion in every limb, Justin headed for his room, anxious to wash off the cold chill and the mud.

CHAPTER NINETEEN

AFTER FINISHING BREAKFAST, everyone sat hunched over the table nursing mugs of coffee and taking comfort in each other's company. Carlos and Billy returned home and joined them. Billy's head was wrapped in a gauze bandage and pain pills were managing the pain. Cody was relieved that he had no concussion. Bear returned shortly after Billy, damp and windblown, but he appeared unfazed by his failed attempt to reach Wild Horse Creek.

Sarah immediately renewed her flirtations with Bear. The two sat together at the end of the table, fingers interwoven on the tabletop. Sarah was wearing her engagement ring and it occasionally caught the lamplight, sparkling like a firecracker. They exchanged steamy kisses a few times, forcing the ranch hands to avert their eyes. Nelson coughed with embarrassment.

Cody massaged her temples, warding off a headache.

Outside, black clouds darkened the sky and shook the timbers of the house. Wind moaned beneath the eaves. The blazing fire hissed and popped in the grate, doing little to ward off the collective feeling of gloom.

A sharp rap sounded at the front door and Carlos hurried to answer it.

"Sheriff here," Carlos called from the front room.

Boot heels scuffing hardwood in the hallway announced the arrival of Sheriff Jake Turner and a deputy. They followed Carlos into the dining room. Raindrops beaded the brims of their hats and water trickled down their khaki-colored slickers leaving a trail on the floor.

Sheriff Turner removed his hat and shook out of his slicker and Carlos hung them by the door. Beneath his close-cropped white hair, his ruddy face was shadowed with stubble. He'd had years of exposure to wind and sun, but he wore the damage remarkably well. The deputy that accompanied him was tall and thin with a sharp nose, long neck, and protruding Adam's apple. Standing stiffly, he made no effort to remove his rain gear. After nodding to everyone at the table, Turner focused on Cody. "Morning, Cody."

"Morning, Jake." Conveying gratitude for a debt she could never repay, Cody held his hand warmly, and smiled into his eyes. Responding to her 911 call the night Buddy stabbed her, Turner found her unconscious and covered in blood. His quick action, applying pressure dressings to her stab wounds, followed by his high-speed race to the hospital, saved her life.

"Good to see you looking so well, Cody." He smiled back, warmly, then his brow creased into deep furrows. "Sorry to hear about your horses. Your dad around?"

"He's in Idaho. Can't fly back until the storm passes. We can fill you in. Coffee?"

"No, thanks. I've had about a gallon already. Been up all night." Turner's pale blue eyes were red-rimmed behind his glasses and he stood a little stoop-shouldered, as though weighted by responsibility. "County's gone nuts. Pile-up on the highway, power lines down, trees crashing on roofs." His manner changed abruptly, all business. "We need to head back out, so let's get going here. We got the ATV in the truck. It's about the only thing that can get up these muddy trails. Deputy Conner's gonna go up to that ridge where the shots were fired. See if he can make sense of anything. Can you ride up there with him, Roth?"

"Sure thing." Roth scraped his chair back from the table.

"Let's be quick about it."

"Suits me." Roth shoved his arms into his slicker and followed Conner out into the storm.

The sheriff lowered his body heavily into Roth's empty chair. His gaze was scalpel-sharp as he went around the table drilling everyone with pointed questions. "So the lights were out in the barn. Billy, you went in first, got assaulted?"

"Yep. Didn't see nothing inside, it was so dark. But the horses were really spooked. Before I could check on them, I got clobbered, right here." Billy touched the bandage that concealed two-dozen stitches.

"Don't remember nothing after that."

Turner scribbled in his notepad. "Then you showed up, Cody?"

"Yeah. I found Billy around 3:15. It was really dark. Two men came at me, and one of them tackled me to the ground. My head hit the concrete and stunned me for a minute. Gave them just enough time to herd the horses out of the barn. If I hadn't moved at the last second, those stampeding horses would have killed me."

"She got one of 'em pretty good with the butt of her gun," Justin added.

Turner raised his brows. "That true?"

She nodded. "Instincts. Wish I shot them full of buckshot."

"Fast thinking, Cody."

"They're cold-blooded killers, Sheriff," Roth said. "They shot at Cody and me when we went after them. Missed us by a hair."

The sheriff's face tightened. He shook his head and exhaled sharply. "You two are lucky to be alive. Hope we can find some kind of evidence to ID them."

The room was silent as Turner's pen scratched his notebook. He finally looked up. "They specifically targeted the horses in the barn?"

"Don't know if that was their intention," Cody said. "But all the other horses were in the indoor arena. Nelson checked the bullpens. All accounted for."

"So six of your most valuable horses were snatched?"

"Yes."

"They insured?"

"Yes."

"Where were you during these events?" The sheriff shot the question at Bear.

"Outta town." Bear's voice sounded calm, but Cody noticed tightening around his eyes. "Been gone all day. Went to pick up a horse in Wild Horse Creek."

"When did you get back?"

"About an hour ago."

The sheriff's eyebrows rose above his glasses. "That's a two-hour drive. What took you so long?"

"Wind was bad. Started blowing the trailer around. I waited out the worst of the storm behind a gas station in Redmond.

"Didn't get the horse?"

"Never made it to Wild Horse Creek," Bear said without blinking. "I'll go back when the weather calms down."

Turner scribbled notes for a few seconds, then turned to Justin. "And you, what's your name?"

"Justin Powell. Been working here six weeks."

"Justin Powell. Sounds familiar." His eyes narrowed, and the corners of his mouth jacked up. "Hell, I remember you. You were on the track team with my boy, Jude."

"Yes, sir." Justin smiled back.

"Good athletes. The both of you. How do you fit in?"

"I was out jogging. When I got back to the house, I saw Buster racing down the trail. Figured Cody was in trouble, so I mounted him and went looking for her. Found her halfway up the ridge. She told me what happened."

"Customary for you to jog in the middle of the night?"

"No. I couldn't sleep. The storm wasn't bad when I left."

"Understand. Sometimes that's the only way my son can relieve stress." The sheriff lifted his glasses and rubbed his eyes before questioning Nelson. Afterwards, he sat quietly flipping through his notes. The door opened with a blast of wind and the deputy and Roth were half blown into the room. Roth hung up his slicker.

Conner stood dripping, looking tense. "Nothing up there but rain drilling mud. Slabs of rock and boulders scoured clean. But we did find a couple of shell casings."

"Good. That's something."

"I'd say it looks like an inside job," Conner said coldly.

The hair rose on Cody's arms. She saw the hands exchange startled glances. Both lawmen eyed the group closely. Dead quiet. A burning log broke into pieces in the fireplace.

"You think someone here worked with the thieves?" Cody asked.

"That's my take on it. Someone familiar with your ranch."

"That's bullshit!" Sarah said.

Turner leveled his gaze on her, said coolly, "These thieves knew the lay of the land, Sarah. They took a huge risk to get to your most valuable horses. Knew exactly where they were."

"They also knew about the trail leading off the back of the

property," Conner added. "Easy to disappear into the forest from up there."

Silence lingered as everyone digested the news. Wind whistled around the window frames and the glass shuddered in the panes.

The sheriff pulled back his sleeve and glanced at his watch, said crisply, "We need to head out. We'll turn in the shell casings, see if they have any prints, or match any guns in the system."

"That's all you're gonna do?" Sarah asked hotly. "What about getting a posse together? A helicopter? We need to move while the trail is hot."

"There is no trail," Conner said. "Rain washed out the tracks."

"Can't get a chopper up in this storm." The sheriff buttoned up the front of his slicker and pulled his Stetson low on his forehead. "Even if we had a budget for chasing horse thieves, all you could see from up there is forest. Men on horseback disappear."

"So that's it?" Cody asked. "We're supposed to kiss our animals goodbye?"

"Folks lost their lives last night, Cody. Bad car wrecks. A couple kids in ICU fighting to stay alive. I'd say you're lucky it's just horses you lost. We'll do what we can."

"Install cameras and a good security system," Conners advised. "If you had one, we'd have footage of these guys."

The officers left. Everyone sat speechless, still processing the traumatic events of the evening. In addition to wrung out emotions and a stunned sense of loss, an accusation of criminal activity now hung over their heads.

Cody broke the silence from her seat at the head of the table. "For what it's worth, we'll take security measures to prevent this from ever happening again." She read the sullen expressions around the table. A slow ache tightened her throat, which forced her to take a moment to compose herself. "I know it feels like we just lost members of our family. We were all very close to those stolen animals. We've all put in a lot of hours working with them. They know how we think. They know what needs to be done before we even ask for it. They did their jobs with loyalty and good nature. Nelson, you worked with those two colts like they were your own kids."

"They was my kids." Nelson clenched his jaw. Not one to show emotion, he looked down at his coffee cup, but not before Cody saw his eyes were glassy.

"We won't give up on them," she said adamantly. "We *will* get them back."

"In the meantime, we're down four good cow horses," Roth said soberly.

"We got the gelding coming in from Dancing Horse, soon as this storm clears," Bear said.

"That horse is champion stock," Roth said. "Too valuable for cow work."

Bear glared. Roth glared back.

Cody felt the tension bunch up in her shoulders. It'd been a long night. She hoped the hands wouldn't start looking at each other differently—with a hint of suspicion, wondering who the insider was. The traitor. She turned to practical matters. "Billy, no concussion thankfully, but you need to stay low. No work for a couple days. Maresol, keep an eye on him. The rest of you, storm or no storm, work needs to get done. Ride the property. See what damage the storm caused."

"Horses don't stop crapping. I'm heading to the barn." Justin pushed his chair back from the table, donned his coat and hat and walked out into the storm.

He was barely out the door before Bear started running off his mouth. "We need to talk about what the sheriff said. About someone here working with the thieves."

Cody felt a twist in her stomach. This was exactly what she wanted to avoid. Best to wait until Hank returned, see how he wanted to deal with the mess. But if the hands were going to talk, it was better they do it now, out in the open.

"I've been here two years," Bear said. "Nothing's ever been stolen."

"I've been here five," Nelson said, crossing his arms.

Roth said nothing, his face solemn, though he'd been here the longest. Nine years.

"My family don't steal," Billy said angrily. "We're good Catholics."

Maresol laid her hand on her son's shoulder and dabbed her eyes with a tissue.

Cody resented Bear for putting good people on the defensive.

"Now we got horses gone." Bear's eyes were dark and calculating, his tone forceful. "What's the common denominator?"

"Common what?" Nelson asked.

Looking puzzled, Billy traced a pattern of scratches on the worn tabletop with his index finger. Maresol fished in her pocket for a new tissue and blew her nose.

"What's different? We have a new man, that's what." Bear's mouth twisted into a sneer. "Everything was fine and dandy until Justin showed up."

Cody's anger came up fast and hot. "Don't start tossing accusations around, Bear."

"Face facts, Cody," Bear said. "Your dad helped him out of a tight bind in Arizona. He was mixed up with a bunch of criminals. Cheated them, what I heard. This week, he's in the paper, accused by Jabe McKinley of being a thief. Now our horses are stolen."

"Plus, he lied about who he was," Sarah said. "He keeps to himself. Damned anti-social." Something cold moved in Sarah's eyes and she leaned forward in a conspiratorial manner.

Oh shit. Cody thought. Here it comes.

"Jabe said Justin raped his wife and got her pregnant," she said with a ring of bitterness.

No one in the room moved.

Cody felt the sudden tension. Her back stiffened. She peered out the window at the furious energy of the storm and worked at keeping her voice calm before turning back to the table. "Either of you have a shred of evidence Justin did anything wrong?"

"Just saying," Bear continued. "His story about jogging in a thunderstorm is frigging nuts. Roth, you buy this crap? Nelson? Who the hell jogs at two in the morning? He was probably out there guiding the rustlers in."

Nelson stole a glance at Roth, as if to gauge his reaction. Roth's face tightened and the skin around his mouth paled. "Keep me outta this crap." He scraped his chair back and rose from the table. "I got work to do."

"Me, too," Nelson said, standing up. Looking damned uncomfortable, both men grabbed slickers off pegs and bent forward as they stepped out into the storm.

Faces pinched, Billy and Maresol stacked the dirty dishes on the table and disappeared into the kitchen.

"Nice work, Bear," Cody said.

"Don't pick on him," Sarah snapped. "He's got every right to speak his mind."

"You were off the property, too," Cody said to Bear. "Got any proof you were in Redmond? Maybe you led the thieves in."

"Bear's been here two years. He's proved his loyalty. Why are you defending Justin?" Her sister's eyes were full of venom. "He's a homeless, penniless rodeo bum!"

Yeah, the rodeo bum you've been hitting on until you snooped into his mail. It was difficult for Cody to keep the disgust from her face. She abruptly left the room, holding back the angry words burning her tongue. Roth and Nelson had the good sense not to get caught up in an internal squabble. Best way to get fired in the long run. Cody believed Justin had proven himself to be of good judgment and solid character, but Bear had planted nasty ideas in their heads. Like a splinter left under the skin, that kind of thing could fester, and turn poisonous. Cody wished her father were here. He'd know how to ease unsettled minds and put Bear in his proper place.

CHAPTER TWENTY

JUSTIN'S CLOTHES were almost completely soaked through, and he wished he'd put on a slicker before sprinting to the indoor arena. He and Cody had herded all the pasture horses into the spacious enclosure yesterday for protection. Huddled in groups on the dirt floor, twitching their tails and nervously eating hay, they jerked up their heads with each loud clatter of wind. Porter separated himself from the herd, trotted over, and placed his velvety muzzle in Justin's outstretched hand.

"Hey, boy. Wild night, huh?" Justin haltered the mustang, mounted bareback, and rode him through the downpour to the barn. As he led Porter up the walkway between the stalls, horses jutted their heads above the gates and whinnied pitifully for treats. He routinely gave each animal some grain when he cleaned their stalls, and now they viewed him as a treat ticket. A mix of anger and sadness brewed in his gut when he confronted the six empty stalls. He had gotten deeply attached to the six stolen animals, especially the two mischievous colts, who never failed to make him laugh. They had never been off the grounds before. He worried about them the most.

As he reached Buster's stall the gelding snorted and stamped his hooves, demanding attention. Justin was grateful Buster wasn't stolen. A tragedy Cody averted by her quick action last night. "You were a real hero," he said, stroking Buster's neck. The gelding's ears swiveled back and forth. He blew into Justin's hair and nibbled his collar. Justin fed him a small apple.

After tethering Porter in the grooming area, Justin tossed mineral pellets and grain into a big rubber bowl and left him alone to eat. He turned his attention to cleaning the stalls. The smell of pine shavings and oiled leather, and the gentle rustling of animals calmed the adrenaline fizzing through his veins. The Sterling barn was his cathedral, with its high ceiling and light streaming though the tall narrow windows. When he finished the last stall, Porter was dry enough to groom. The mustang dozed lazily, head bowed, one hind leg relaxed. He barely stirred as Justin groomed him.

The barn door opened and shut and boot heels clicked down the center aisle. Justin heard Cody murmuring to Buster as she took him out of his stall. He finished picking Porter's last hoof as she tethered the chestnut bay next to him. Her presence brightened the shadows in the barn.

She slipped out of her slicker and hung it on a peg. Her face was pale except for two spots of color on her cheeks, and he sensed her restless energy. "After nearly losing my boy last night, I couldn't wait to spend time with him."

"Getting your hands on a horse is good medicine," he said.

Emotion played over her features as she rubbed the white blaze on Buster's forehead. She scanned the six empty stalls, turned back to him, her eyes glassy. "Wish I could've saved them all. Thanks for rescuing me last night."

"Thanks for saving my ass in the parking lot at Chuck's."

She smiled. "We need to find better ways to spend our time."

He smiled back. "Yeah, something that isn't life threatening."

She started brushing Buster with long firm strokes. "Maybe we could take a trail ride when the weather clears. I could show you some beautiful places on the ranch."

"That'd be great."

Her eyes found his over Buster's withers. He never knew what he was going to get from her, but this morning, a grounded sense of trust came shining through.

She turned back to Buster and started rambling: a stream-of-consciousness, caffeine-charged monologue, ranging from ranch work to her college years when she majored in philosophy. She told him she dropped out when her marriage got too stressful. Whenever she paused to take a breath, Justin inserted a response just to keep her talking. He liked listening to the sound of her voice, the gentle rhythm rising and falling like a melody.

Mindlessly combing the snarls out of Porter's mane and tail, he stole glances at her, noticing how pretty she was when her guard was down. He admired the courage she showed last night, and the way she took charge this morning when the hands looked to her for leadership. Justin hungered for easy companionship with a woman, and the sense of community he'd found here at Sterling O. He wanted to trust Cody, to accept her friendship and return it in full, but life taught him to move cautiously, stay detached, and be prepared to pull up roots at a moment's notice. His instinct for self-preservation was cast in iron, and wouldn't melt easily.

The windows shuddered and they both peered outside at the rain-thrashed landscape.

"What do you think about what the sheriff said?" She said, the lines tightening around her mouth.

"The theft being an inside job?" He shrugged. "Seems logical."

She was quiet for a long moment. "Who'd do such a thing?"

"Any number of people. How many folks go through here every year?"

"A lot. We hire extra help during calving and haying season."

"Any disgruntled?"

She thought for a while, shook her head. "Dad pays well. Treats people fairly. I can't understand why anyone would do this to us."

"Don't take it personally, Cody. This was probably about money, not revenge."

"Guess the world is changing and we need to catch up. I feel so bad for the horses." Tears welled in her eyes and she wiped her eyes with her fingertips. "They're probably so scared."

Justin was at her side in an instant, pulling her into his arms. He said softly, "The horses will be okay. They have strong instincts for survival." He caressed her back as he would a child, but Cody felt every inch a woman under her baggy shirt—soft and warm and sweet-smelling. Her body relaxed into his, and they stood pressed together, listening to the rain drum the ceiling. His hands followed the lines of her small waist to the gentle swell of her hips. Justin could hardly breathe, he wanted to kiss her so badly. Reluctantly, he released her and stepped away.

"You're right," she said with a wobbly smile. "The horses will be okay. And we *will* get them back." Squaring her shoulders, she turned away from him and resumed brushing Buster in long lazy strokes.

CHAPTER TWENTY-ONE

MAGGIE HIT the gym early Monday morning, determined to get back on track with her exercise regimen. After twenty minutes of strength-training, she crossed the gym to join the people who were sweating it out on treadmills and exercycles. She stepped onto an elliptical machine and started moving. Her three month absence from the gym became quickly evident. After twenty minutes, her legs felt leaden, she was panting hard, and she was debating on whether to call it quits.

"Hey, Maggie." Piper Quinn flashed a high-wattage smile as she mounted the elliptical next to hers and punched in a workout code.

"Hey, Piper." Maggie smiled, dabbing her face with the hand towel around her neck. She and Piper had been friends for twenty years. Her friend was an accomplished architect who had worked for David for ten years. Her daughter McKenzie had dated Eric and had been a regular fixture at the house. The two families had vacationed together, and took turns hosting monthly dinners. Maggie had been a supportive friend when Piper's marriage went bust two years ago.

"Glad to see you back at the gym," Piper said, pulling her long blonde hair into a ponytail.

"My body's not too happy about it," Maggie panted

"But you look *maaahvalous*. Doesn't matter how you feel, right? It's how you look."

"If you say so."

Though Piper's tone was teasing, Maggie knew she was preaching gospel. Her friend was ten years older, but easily looked Maggie's age. Piper had a slightly artificial perfection to her beauty, thanks to years of nips, tucks, and injections. But men loved the Barbie look, and the money she'd invested in her packaging had reaped big rewards. Piper had been on the receiving end of lavish gifts and vacations by a slew of eligible men—sowing the wild oats she missed out on by marrying young. After meeting Harvey Bowman six months ago at a fundraiser, she and the oncologist had been inseparable. Maggie liked Harvey, and found him to be a witty, well-grounded man, who made no attempt to hide his affection for Piper.

"I was surprised to see you solo at my party," Maggie said. "Where was Harvey?"

"We're taking a break."

Maggie arched a brow. "Why?"

"He asked me to marry him."

"Ah, I see. Big step."

"I came close to saying yes, then I panicked."

"Marriage is a scary proposition."

"It is, but I'm not getting any younger, and he's the real deal."

"A great guy."

"I'm building up my courage."

"Harvey would make a wonderful husband," Maggie said earnestly.

Piper smiled her thanks. "That was some wild party, Maggie. I haven't danced liked that since I was the disco queen in the nineties."

"Ditto."

Piper's legs and arms were pumping fluidly, and fast, but outwardly it barely registered. She was in superb condition. "Those working stiffs really know how to let their hair down."

"Drinking helps," Maggie said.

"Got that right. You and I were knocking back those tequila shots like college girls on spring break."

"Don't remind me. I'm still getting over my hangover."

"Poor kid. You couldn't walk a straight line by the end of the night. You still managed some smoking hot moves on the dance floor."

Maggie groaned, not sure whether she should be proud or embarrassed.

"Life's short. Dance until your legs fall off. That's my motto. What's going on with you and Brennen, by the way?" She shot Maggie a curious look. "He looked like the Gestapo, hovering over you all night. I felt like clicking my heels and saluting every time I crossed his path. Little possessive, don't you think?"

"Just protective."

"Of what? Afraid you might get laid? He certainly kept the guys away."

Maggie chewed her bottom lip.

"You okay?" Piper managed to look concerned, even though the Botox in her brow kept it from creasing.

"He *was* keeping someone away."

"Who?"

"A guy named Sully."

"Sully?" Piper's hazel eyes lit up like a camera flash. "The gorgeous guy in cowboy boots? All muscle, blue eyes?"

Maggie nodded.

"He's into you?"

Before Maggie could respond, Piper's phone rang. She held up a finger and took the call.

Maggie drifted into her thoughts, conjuring memories of her party. From the moment Sully walked into her kitchen, all she wanted to do was move into his arms. Instead she treated him coolly, and stayed close to Brennen. Though she pretended indifference, laughing and visiting with friends, Maggie knew where he was at every moment. It distressed her that he spent most of the evening with the beautiful redhead, Allison. Maggie lost track of how many shots of Tequila she drank. The only bright spot was when Sully came up behind her on the dance floor and pulled her into his arms. While enveloped in the soft cloak of inebriation, he held her close, his voice warm in her ear. She buried her face in the cove of his neck, absorbed the heat of his body as he guided her over the dance floor, and wanted to stay there forever.

"Sorry I had to take that call." Piper's voice filtered into Maggie's thoughts. "Okay, so help me understand this colluding you and Brennan were doing against the cowboy."

"It wasn't colluding. I didn't want to encourage Sully, is all."

"Why not? I would've been all over him, if I didn't have Harvey."

Maggie admired her friend's audacity. Piper didn't care what people thought, and she wasn't afraid to do as she pleased, short of hurting someone. Harvey was eight years her junior.

"A half dozen other women would have, too," Piper continued, "But he was wrapped up in that hot little number."

"Allison."

"Right, Allison. She works out here."

"She's in my yoga class. I invited her and Noel, so Sully could meet them."

Piper slowed down almost to a stop and gave Maggie a look that clearly said she was certifiable. "Let's back up here. This drop-dead gorgeous guy is interested in you, but instead of having the time of your life, you throw him into the arms a hot babe, while Brennen guards your chastity like a pit bull?"

"Sounds like the worst soap opera ever written, but yeah, that pretty much sums it up."

"Help me understand your demented reasoning, Maggie. He's attracted to you, yes?"

"He was. I don't know anymore."

"Why'd you ditch him?"

"Ethics."

"What?"

"I wanted Sully to meet women his own age. I don't want to exploit his vulnerability." Even as Maggie recited the words she'd rehearsed in her head the last two days, they sounded disingenuous. Pathetic, really.

"What vulnerability?" Piper asked.

"He's recovering from trauma."

Piper snorted. "Shit. Who isn't? Trauma is the bedrock of the human psyche. That's why the world is such a fucked-up place. My opinion? You're over-thinking. Biology isn't ruled by logic. If it was, no one would get married."

"That's a rosy analysis."

"Realistic. You're manipulating this poor man's feelings, Maggie, and denying your own. Most therapists are freaking nuts, but you take the cake." Piper ramped up to full speed again, arms and legs working hard. "You're off the charts crazy. Where'd you meet him?"

"He was Eric's squad leader."

"A marine? Nice."

"He's fourteen years younger than me."

"Great," Piper said, not missing a beat. "He's handsome *and* young enough to keep up. When are you going to tell me something bad about this guy?"

"He doesn't have money. Works all the time. He's a cowboy. Our lives don't really blend. But he's also gentle, strong, sensitive, intelligent, and funny."

"That's a lot of adjectives." Piper was staring at her with a knowing expression.

"What?"

"I thought you were trained in matters of the heart, as well as the mind. But you're blind to your own feelings. You're in love, Maggie."

The words struck her as both unsettling and startlingly true. "I wouldn't go that far."

"Yeah, right. Whose bad idea was it to keep you away from Sully? Yours or Brennen's?"

"We discussed it together."

"Brennen's. He's not exactly the go-to guy for love advice. He's going through the world's shittiest divorce. Did it occur to you he may have a thing for you?"

Maggie shook off her words. "We're just friends."

"Take off the fuzzy lenses, girlfriend. Brennen's probably got a big motive for putting a wedge between you and the cowboy, and it's right between his legs."

Maggie chuckled, despite herself.

Piper shot her a naughty smile. "You could be getting your workouts at home, instead of this freaking gym."

"I don't want a few steamy nights, Piper. I want something that lasts. As a therapist, I've seen too many cases of self-made wreckage. If Sully goes for Allison, I'm diverting a disaster."

"I know you think you're being noble, but you're crossing into martyrdom. Don't dangle a jelly doughnut in front of a hungry man and expect him not to bite."

Maggie mulled this over, a queasy feeling in her stomach.

"Nothing's risk free. Men don't come with warranties." She looked at Maggie with sympathy. "Take a chance. After what you've been through, you deserve a little fun."

"Maybe you're right."

"I am right. No risk, no payoff." Piper's eyes drifted to the morning talk show on the TV screen above them. "Geez, look at that Julia Roberts. When's she gonna get a friggin' wrinkle?"

Maggie's code panel beeped. She stepped off the elliptical machine and toweled her face.

Piper tugged her attention away from the screen. "Let's go to happy hour sometime."

"Love to." Maggie gave her a sweaty hug. "I'll email you."

The locker room was warm and steamy and smelled of soap and shampoo. Maggie peeled off her workout clothes and showered. As she dressed and put on makeup, her thoughts spun in circles like a dragon chasing its tail, and she revisited the conversation she had with Brennan about Sully. Admittedly, he targeted her greatest vulnerability, and hit the bullseye—fear of loss. Maggie lost her husband, Ryan, and Eric. And when she thought of Sully, fear of loss crouched on the edge of her consciousness like a hammer, ready to bludgeon her. Falling headlong into a relationship with Sully meant accepting the risk of losing him. Unnerving. But taking the path of least resistance wasn't any easier. She already felt the pain of loss, like the sharp tines of a fork scraping her skin. Where was her courage? Piper's words echoed like a mantra. No risk. No pay off.

Maggie pulled her phone from her handbag, stared at Sully's number for a long moment, pressed the call button, and tried to think of something lighthearted to say.

"This is Sully. Please leave a message."

"Sully, this is Maggie. I'd love to talk to you. Call me back." Not brilliant or witty, but she did it, and it couldn't be taken back. She grabbed her gym bag and backtracked through the club to the front door, almost colliding with Allison, who was rushing in from the parking lot.

Allison folded her umbrella and shook off the rain. She looked willowy and fit in stretch pants and a flowing gold yoga shirt. "Can you believe this storm? I thought my roof was going to fly off last night."

"It's a holy terror," Maggie agreed.

Allison's face lit up. "Thank you for introducing me to Sully."

"Oh, how's that working out?"

Her smiled widened. "Great. We talked last night. We're going to go riding together."

"That's great, Allison. Really great."

"Gotta run. I'm late for yoga!"

After a hurried goodbye, Maggie crossed the parking lot in a daze, ignoring the wind and rain. It appeared Sully's feelings for her weren't strong enough after all, just as Brennen predicted. It only took him two days to make a date with Allison.

Suddenly feeling old and worn out, Maggie sat inside her Prius and watched the rain stream down the windshield. Last night would have been her weekly dinner and movie date with Sully. Instead, she went out with Brennen and endured a five-course meal in a stuffy, over-priced restaurant. She ate and drank too much, sitting in a clingy dress that got tighter as the evening wore on. Her feet swelled inside her heels and pinched her toes. She forced herself to make cheerful small talk but all the while she longed to be home lounging in her sweats, eating popcorn, laughing at some silly movie with Sully.

Looking back over the evening, the realization dawned on her that Brennen was indeed attracted to her. She had tried to go Dutch but he insisted on paying. Feeling bloated, she just wanted to get out of her dress and heels, but he stood rooted to her porch talking about mindless trivia, and he hinted at coming inside for a drink. She begged off, saying she was exhausted. They bumped heads when they hugged goodnight, his open mouth skimming hers. She pulled away and escaped into the house. *Damn.* How could she have been so blind?

Wipers swishing, Maggie drove out of the parking lot, her mind preoccupied with Sully. What was he doing right now? What was he thinking? Did he miss her? Was he reliving over and over the sweetness of their kisses, and imagining what might have been if they had kept their date last night? Or had his interest shifted completely to Allison? Maggie scolded herself. With cold premeditation, she had thrown a beautiful man into the arms of another woman.

CHAPTER TWENTY-TWO

THOUGH THE WIND had died down, a hard driving rain still pelted the grounds. Widening pools encircled the house and several of the pastures were half flooded. Though Justin knew the storm would pass overnight, he was impatient for everything to dry out. Bone tired, he stepped from the wild wooly world outside into the warmth of the dining room. The smells of dinner made his stomach clench, and the heat from the fire felt good on his back when he seated himself at the table. The others murmured greetings, already halfway through their minestrone soup. The tone at the table was noticeably subdued.

Maresol stepped out of the kitchen, placed a hot bowl of soup in front of him and quietly left. He buttered two thick slices of crusty bread and dove into his soup. Though busy eating, he was keenly aware of the somber mood. The gathering could have passed for a funeral wake. Sarah and Bear spoke in hushed tones at their end of the table. Cody caught his gaze a few times and smiled, but her eyes looked uneasy. Carlos and Maresol crept in and out, placing steaming platters of spaghetti and meatballs on the table. They dropped dessert off at the same time, tiramisu, and disappeared into the kitchen. There was nothing even remotely cheerful in their manner.

"Are Carlos and Maresol boycotting us?" Justin said as the platters were passed around.

"Everyone's burned out," Cody said, sprinkling grated Parmesan over her pasta.

Justin sensed something more, something menacing residing just below the surface. While twirling spaghetti around his fork, he made stabs at conversation, trying to get people talking. Maybe the hidden culprit would rear its head. He quizzed Roth with mundane questions.

How was the sick calf? Was the mama cow nursing yet? Were the antibiotics working on Jazz, the appaloosa?

Roth focused on his plate, never forming a whole sentence or meeting Justin's eye, just sifting through his pasta as though expecting to find a gold nugget. Nelson's fork and jaws were in constant motion. It was obvious he just wanted to be gone from the table.

"You gearing up for an eating contest?" Justin asked.

"Just hungry," Nelson mumbled.

"Where's Billy?" Justin asked.

Nelson grunted, nodded toward the kitchen, mouth packed with food.

"His head okay?"

"He's fine," Cody volunteered, sopping up sauce with bread.

"Why's he in there?"

"Eating with his parents," she said.

Sarah shot Justin a look of pure contempt that made the hair prick on his arms. He caught a hard glint of hatred in Bear's eyes.

"Someone wanna tell me what's going on?" Hostility was coming at him from half the table, nervous tension from the other.

Dead silence.

Maybe Billy, a true friend, would clue him in. Up until this storm, the young ranch hand was still getting Justin up every morning, luring him out of bed with a mug of strong coffee just the way he liked it. Regardless of weather, Billy was right there at his back, trotting on horseback, keeping him going with his light-hearted ribbing. Justin grabbed his empty glass, scraped back his chair, and pushed through the swinging door into the kitchen. Billy and his folks sat eating in the nook speaking rapid Spanish, their expressions animated. They looked up, surprised, when Justin barged in.

"I help you?" Maresol asked.

"No, don't get up. Just thought I'd grab some milk."

The three said nothing as he walked to the fridge. Their abrupt silence was unsettling. Feeling their eyes on him, Justin rummaged through the fridge taking his sweet time, though clearly the jug of milk was visible on the top shelf. He placed his glass on the counter and slowly filled it. The only sound was the ticking of the clock.

"I no like Bear say," Maresol volunteered.

"What's that?" Justin asked, turning and leaning against the counter.

"He say you bad man."

"What?" Justin's adrenaline spiked.

"He thinks you helped steal the horses," Billy piped up, dark eyes flashing. "I don't believe it. Neither do mama and papa."

"When did he say that?"

"After you left this morning. Sarah said Jabe thinks you raped his wife."

Justin's anger reached a flashpoint, white hot. He shot across the kitchen floor and burst through the swinging door back into the dining room.

The foreman's chair was empty.

"Where's Bear?" he asked, his tone vibrating.

Sarah glared, mouth tight.

"Just left," Roth said, rising from his chair. "Don't do anything stupid."

Roth's alarmed voice trailed behind as Justin charged across the room and out into the rain. In the murky half-light of dusk, he spotted Bear thirty yards up the hill, heading for the barn. Justin starting running, already hearing the shuffling of feet behind him on the porch, the door slamming shut.

"Bear!" Justin shouted.

The foreman turned as Justin caught up to him, a cocksure smile on his face, eyes blinking against the rain. Justin rammed into him with all his strength, shoulder first. Bear slipped on the sodden earth and hit the ground like an oak, eyes startled wide open. For a big man, he moved fast and was back on his feet in an instant. Darting, blurry figures surrounded them, yelling, voices indistinct.

Lips pulled back from his teeth, Bear popped Justin in the jaw, lightning quick, his fist the size of a shovel. It was a shuddering impact. Justin reeled backwards and fell to his knees. In a second, Bear had a knee on his back, pushing him flat on his stomach. He pushed harder and all the air rushed out of Justin lungs. One giant mitt pressed his head into the mud. He couldn't breathe. Wrenching to the side, he tipped Bear just enough to squeeze out of his hold, then he sprinted to his feet, spitting dirt and leaves and blood. Funneling in on the big man, his vision and hearing sharpened. Both men circled each other. Crouching beneath the powerful arms, Justin put all his force behind his fist and pummeled Bear's gut—once, twice, three times—heard Bear's guttural groans.

Bear got him again with an uppercut to the jaw. It rocked Justin backward. His mouth filled with blood, ran down his chin. Regaining his balance, he darted in and out of the massive arms, jabbing his fists again and again into the big man's torso. Bear stood unsteadily, rocking back and forth, swinging blindly with his massive arms. Justin threw himself into the swing and hit him in the throat with an elbow. He followed with another swinging left to the cheek. Bear fell backwards onto the seat of his pants.

Roth got an iron-like grip on Justin's arms from behind and pulled him away. Sarah moved into his line of fire, wild-eyed, screaming. "You bastard!" Her wet blouse clung to her heaving breasts, dark trails of mascara ran down her cheeks. "You could've killed him! You are so out of here!"

Covered in mud, Bear got to his feet, clutching his gut with a pained expression. Spitting blood, Justin pulled hard against Roth's arms but he couldn't break free, and he couldn't dodge Sarah's sudden blow. She slapped his face full force, snapping it to the left, then shook her hand as though in pain.

Cody was on Sarah like a coyote on a ground squirrel. "Stupid bitch!" The two began jostling and pushing, slipping in the mud, their fists balled in each other's hair. Nelson and Billy pulled them apart, prying fingers from tangled hair. Everyone stood in a loose circle, panting, pelted by rain.

"Chill, Justin," Roth warned, face tense and glistening.

Justin shook off his grip, balled and unballed his fists, then backtracked across the yard, stormed into the house to his room, and slammed the door so hard the frame shook.

CHAPTER TWENTY-THREE

CODY RAPPED on Justin's door.

"Go away!"

"I'm coming in." She opened the door and found him furiously packing his gear, slapping folded clothing into a scarred leather bag on the bed. He'd changed into dry clothes, while she was barefoot, soaked to the skin, shivering. "Why are you packing?"

He didn't answer. She crossed the room and touched his shoulder.

When he turned, she gasped. The left side of his face was fiery red, his eye swelling fast. A cut ran along his cheekbone, and his bottom lip was split. "I'm getting an ice pack. Take two Ibuprofen, now!" She rushed down the hallway to the kitchen, almost colliding with Maresol, who had dirty dishes stacked in both hands. "Sorry, Maresol."

"How eez Justeen?" Maresol looked stricken. "I should say nothing. Beeg mouth, me. Now he hurt."

"He deserved to know. It's not your fault." Cody grabbed a bag of frozen peas from the freezer and hurried back to Justin's room. With one hand, he was pressing down the top of the bag while the other tugged at the zipper. He glanced at her, then at the bag of peas.

"Sit," she commanded.

He sank onto the edge of the bed. She sat next to him and handed him the bag. He pressed it to his face, wincing.

"He did a good job messing up your pretty face."

Justin scowled.

"You did a good job on him, too. Got in some good punches."

"Did I break his ribs?"

"Doubt it. He's strong as an ox. Bruised his ego, is all. If you ask me, he got what was coming. He's been walking around here puffed up with his own importance for too long. Now Sarah's his evil twin. Sorry she slapped you so hard."

"Sorry you two got into a brawl. You okay?"

"Heck, what's a little hair pulling between sisters? Why are you packing?"

"You heard. Sarah fired me." There was an agitated edge to his voice.

"You're not fired. Sarah had no right to say that."

"You all think I'm a thief."

"Not true. I don't."

He looked at her and lowered the ice pack. "Don't know how much weight one person carries, but thanks."

"Keep that on your face, or you're gonna swell up like a sage grouse."

He reapplied the peas.

"So you're slinking away into the night?"

"No. At dawn."

She felt a piercing ache of sadness radiate through her chest. "Can I say anything to stop you?"

He studied her. "Why do you care?"

"I just do." They locked eyes. She realized their legs were pressed together, the heat of his body warming hers. His closeness felt comforting, and exciting.

"You're soaked," he said.

"I know." She made no attempt to leave.

"Wanna put on my sweats?"

"Okay."

He unzipped his bag and tugged out his gray sweats. "There's a comb on the counter in the bathroom."

She grabbed the sweats, went into the bathroom, and gasped when she saw her mud-flecked face and tangled hair. After peeling off her clothes and hanging them next to his over the shower, she yanked on the flannel bottom and top, washed her face, combed her hair, and reseated herself right up against him. He didn't move away.

"You look like a little kid in pajamas," he said.

"They're soft."

"For what it's worth, I'm not slinking away. I'm gonna hunt down the men who stole your horses. Clear my name."

"That's crazy." She shook her head. "You're outnumbered. It's not your fight."

His mouth hardened. "I've caused nothing but trouble since I arrived. I want to make amends."

"I'm going with you."

"That's not an option."

"But it's okay if you get killed?"

"It's my reputation on the line. I'm being accused of rape and colluding with horse thieves. I have the whole household worked up."

"I'm coming with you."

"No way. I won't put you in danger." His tone was determined, final. "I'd never do that to your dad."

She studied his stony expression, which told her he wouldn't budge. "I think it's a foolish thing to do, but I can't stop you." She paused a few beats, thinking. "You'll need a good packhorse. Take Juno. He's nimble-footed and has good endurance."

Justin nodded his gratitude. "Right nice of you."

"Let's see your face."

He lowered the ice pack. The swelling had gone down a little.

"Keep it on another ten minutes."

He reapplied it.

"You wanna tell me why you were out jogging in the storm last night?"

Blood rushed to his face. He swallowed. "I wake up with panic attacks sometimes. I get claustrophobic. Getting outta the house and moving fast helps."

"I get them, too. Bad marriage."

"Sorry," he said softly.

Some longing to connect with Justin at a deeper level drove her to open up to him. "Three years of hell. Buddy almost killed me five months ago."

His eyes widened. "I figured something terrible happened to you. Never imagined anything that bad. What happened?"

She felt her mouth curve downwards.

"It's okay," he said. "You don't have to tell me."

"Buddy stabbed me and carved up my breasts with a hunting knife."

"Christ almighty!"

A long silence. Justin looked speechless.

"He passed out before I bled to death. Luckily, I managed to call 911. Sheriff Turner saved my life." She looked down at her clasped hands, white-knuckled. "Buddy was a mean, violent drunk. He started beating me the second year of our marriage."

Anger ignited in Justin's eyes, "I would've killed him. People who hurt women and children are cowards. They should be shot."

"I wish I had shot him." She looked out the window, feeling tears sting the back of her eyes. The old fear vibrated through her.

"I don't know how anyone could hurt you. You're so beautiful." Justin's voice held a curious combination of something soft and rough. He brushed a strand of wet hair from her eyes.

"I bet you're wondering why I let him do it. Why I stayed."

"No, I understand."

"You do?"

"I had my share of abuse, too, Cody. From foster parents." He gave a dry laugh, no humor in it. "One of the worst was a crazy, wrinkled up old widow named Gretchen Bligh. Bone thin, frizzy gray hair. Half blind. She could hardly walk. Used a cane. They placed me at her ranch when I was seven. The place was really run down, but she had some nice horses. I did all the ranch work for her. To thank me, she called me maggot. She thought that was really funny. 'Get them stalls mucked up, Maggot.'" Justin imitated the woman using a tinny, high-pitched voice. "Get them horses fed, Maggot."

The hair stood up on Cody's arms.

"When Gretchen got herself worked up, she took it out on me, lashing me with a horse crop, calling me filthy maggot. I ran away most of the time and slept in the barn, but sometimes she caught me by surprise and got in some pretty good licks. I still have scars on my back." He looked away, jaw tight, as though reliving the experience. "That lasted a year. I came home from school and found her dead in the shower. The water was still running. She'd fallen and hit her head. Blood was everywhere. Lying there dead, all shriveled, she looked so small and harmless. I remember crying a lot. She was still the only mother I had. I never reported her, or any other foster parent. Never said a word to anyone. I didn't feel strong enough to stand up for myself." He paused, looked at Cody as though looking through her. "I didn't want to stand out as different from other kids. I tried to act normal. Though I never had a clue what normal looked like."

"I'm sorry for everything you've been through," Cody said softly. "That no one protected you."

"No one protected you, either."

"No one knew what I was going through, either. Buddy had everyone fooled. He was charming and funny in public. When we went out, he watched my every move. If I didn't put on a good show, I paid later." Cody felt herself sinking into dread, an awful gnawing in her gut, as she recalled living with a monster. Trying to intuit Buddy's mood. Trying to maintain the delicate balance between pacifying him and triggering vicious rage. The line disappeared. Buddy hit her for no reason, a routine as natural as changing his socks.

Justin reached over and folded her hand in his.

She forced herself to look at him, expecting to see contempt. His eyes were kind and had an almost hypnotic effect on her. She lost herself a little. Everything about Justin was warm; his hand, the tone of his voice, the feel of his body next to hers.

He put his arm around her and pulled her back against the pillows. They lay with legs intertwined, her head pillowed by his shoulder. What he was offering was comfort and shelter, not a request for sex.

"Would you consider not going tomorrow?" she asked.

"I have to go, Cody. I have to clear my name." The muscle tensed in his jaw. His voice sounded determined. "Most of my life, I pretended to be something I wasn't. Since I've been here at the ranch, I've started figuring out who I want to be, and that's not someone who runs from trouble."

"I see who you are, Justin. You're a good man."

His lips grazed her head, the warmth of his body seeped into hers, and the tremendous fatigue of the last twenty-four hours settled in. She lay quietly, listening to the rain outside shift its rhythm from high to low. After a while, the light from the window faded, and she had a hard time keeping her eyes open. Sleep pulled at her doggedly until she just let go and floated into a dream. She woke to a blackened room. The rain outside had stopped. Justin was asleep, still lying with his arm around her, lightly snoring. He roused when she moved, kissed the top of her head, pulled her closer.

Lying with her head tucked into the groove of his shoulder, her arm across his chest, she thought of the secrets they'd unearthed tonight. In the telling and the listening, the bondage of the past loosened its hold a little. Their friendship deepened, and it felt as though their souls were stitched together. She realized Justin was her closest friend, her most trusted confidante. At dawn, he would leave her and go on a dangerous journey. Fearing for his well-being, she started thinking of things she could do to keep him safe. "Do you have a gun?"

"My Ruger," he murmured, half asleep.

That gopher rifle? "You can take my .45. I'll go pack some food for you." She pulled away from the haven of his body and left his room.

***

Justin stood over the sink wolfing down a Danish and gulping strong black coffee. The silvery light of day filtered through the window and misted like smoke through the trees. The storm had passed, and his thoughts loomed vivid and large in the stark silence. The chain of events leading up to his decision to hunt down the rustlers had been dramatic and violent—the attack by the McKinleys, and the stinging accusation of horse theft and rape. He shuddered from the impact on his psyche. After the fight with Bear last night, he had wanted to climb out of his skin, hating the forces that shaped him, compelling him to ruin every opportunity that showed up in his life.

His thoughts shifted to Cody. She came to his aid when he desperately needed a friend. She stayed by his side, calming him down, switching off his self-hatred with a gentle hand. They had shared secrets, hidden like a cobra in a basket, waiting to strike when the lid was lifted. They watched the serpent glide into the room, and neither turned away from its scaled skin and hissing tongue. He felt safe in Cody's presence, and knew his confessions would remain private. Hank told him good relationships were built on trust. Without it, love could not exist. All his life, Justin had nothing to build on, but now he and Cody shared a sacred covenant, steadied by pillars of trust.

He heard the soft pad of footsteps behind him.

"Morning, Justin." Barefoot, wearing some kind of silky nightgown, Cody sauntered in, sleepy-eyed, blonde hair limp around her shoulders, skin pale as milk in the morning light.

"Morning." He'd never seen her in anything but baggy clothes, and now his eyes appraised her graceful curves, the soft outline of her breasts against the fabric. He thought of the disfiguring scars left by Buddy's knife, and how he would touch her gently if he ever got the chance.

She poured coffee into a mug, stirred in cream and honey. "You taking off?"

"You just caught me. Juno's packed, ready to go."

The tenderness he felt for her embarrassed him. He said gruffly. "Thanks for all your help, and the supplies." He didn't know what was in the pack of food she left on the counter, but it was substantial. If left to his own resources, he would've gotten by on jerky and water.

"It'll get you through a few days. Dad's old cell phone is in there, too. Will you call me when you can?"

"Count on it."

She pulled her Colt .45 from a pocket on the pack and two boxes of shells. "Protection. She shoved them back in and turned to face him. "Please come back safe."

There was a lump in his throat as hard as a stone. "I will. Just for you."

"How's your face?" She stood very close and her fingers touched his cheek.

"I'll live."

He took her hand in his and kissed her palm. He pulled her close, felt her body softly mold to his. Breathing in the smell of her, he slid his hands down her back, felt the curve of her spine, the roundness of her hips. He brushed her forehead with his lips.

She lifted her face, offering her mouth.

He kissed her sweet and slow, touched her nipples with the tips of his thumbs and felt the weight of her breasts in his palms. He felt an urgent need to lift her in his arms, carry her down the hall to his room and love every inch of her. Fighting every instinct, he pulled away, grabbed the pack, and strode out of the kitchen into the startling brightness of the morning. The face of the sun skimmed the treetops and blasted the morning with bright summer light. Every nerve in his body was on fire.

CHAPTER TWENTY-FOUR

BENT OVER ONE of Diego's front hoofs, Sully sang loudly to a western tune blaring from the radio. He drove in the last nail on the horseshoe, cut off the sharp point, and cinched it down. It wasn't until he straightened up that he noticed Sheriff Matterson standing behind him, watching, an amused expression on his face.

"Hey, Carl." Sully wiped his hands on his leather apron, reached out and turned the music down.

"Good farrier skills," Matterson said. "The singing, not so much."

"That's why I sing in the barn."

"Nice day." Matterson nodded toward the barn door, wide open today.

Sully followed his gaze, thankful to see starched white clouds in a clear blue sky after the grey tumult of the storm.

"Glad that damn storm's done," Matterson said gruffly. "My deputies and I were wet for two days straight. I was getting ready to build an ark. Never seen so many trees down, blocking roads, knocking out power lines. Everything's still mud out there."

Matterson looked beat. Sully felt for him. "Yeah, forced me to get caught up on inside work." Sully arched his back and stretched. He'd been bent over all morning and was feeling it. "All my horses are trimmed and shod."

"Wish I could say the same. My horses need attention, bad. Mateo did all my shoeing. Don't know who to call anymore."

"Ask Mateo's brother. He's taking over the business."

"Good idea." Matterson trailed behind as Sully ushered the gelding down the aisle to his stall and shut the gate behind him.

"Coffee?" Sully asked.

"Just had a quart at the station."

Sully started shoveling fresh pine shavings into an empty stall from a wheelbarrow, wondering when Carl was going to get to the point.

Matterson cleared his throat. The lines around his mouth tightened. "Got a call from Sheriff Turner in Beaverhead this morning. Night before last, the horse thieves who killed Monty and Mateo struck again. Thought I'd swing by before you heard it on the news."

Sully put down his shovel, his temper rising. "How do they know it's the same men?"

"Found shell casings. The lab matched them to the ones collected on Monty's property. Must be from one of the rifles they stole from him."

"Who'd they hit?"

Matterson tipped his hat back, frowning. "Folks out at Sterling O."

Sully felt a jolt of surprise. "Hell. That spread's surrounded by hundreds of acres of Hank's own land. You could see thieves coming for miles."

"True, under normal conditions, but with the storm, they couldn't hear or see a thing. Just rain and wind thrashing everything to hell."

Sully stood leaning on the shovel. "Anyone hurt?"

"Came close. The rustlers were making off with a herd of horses, but they were interrupted by Hank's daughter. They shot at her and Roth, and clobbered a hand."

"Holy shit." Sully's pulse started to race. "They're lucky to be alive. They get any horses?"

"Half a dozen good cow horses."

Recalling his sense of loss when Gunner was stolen, anger spilled into Sully's voice. "Glad Chico wasn't there."

"Whaddya mean?"

"Hank bought him. His foreman tried to pick him up the night of the storm. Had to turn back. He's coming out today."

"Big guy, size of a house?"

Sully nodded.

"I've seen him around. Not a guy you forget." Matterson lifted his hat, ran a hand through his thinning hair, and replaced his hat. "Hank can sure use Chico right now."

"I imagine so. Anyone get a look at the rustlers?"

Matterson's face darkened. "Only from the back."

"How many?"

"Two. They knew how to get to the best horses, Sully, and how to get them off the property fast. Sound familiar?"

Their eyes locked for a moment.

"Mateo's gone. Who else is working with them?" Sully asked. "Who knows Sterling O that well?"

"Good question."

"What's being done about it?"

"Now that the theft is linked to two murders, Beaverhead cops are taking it seriously. Their going in with dogs and covering the area by air. The back of Sterling O borders BLM land. Dense forest. A couple fire roads run through there that lead to highways. Those horses could be out of state by now." Matterson shifted his weight, hooked his thumbs in his holster belt. "They don't expect to find anything. The storm washed out all the tracks."

Sully heard an indignant voice behind them, spewing curses in Paiute.

He and Matterson turned as Travis joined them.

"Do I even wanna know what you said?" Matterson asked.

"No, you don't," Sully said.

"How much did you hear?" the sheriff asked Travis, crossing his arms over his chest.

"Enough." Travis's dark eyes flashed angrily. "No way eight horses can disappear without a trace."

"Law enforcement is using the tools they got," Matterson said. "Dogs."

"Dogs don't pick up scent washed out by rain. Can't see what a tracker sees," Travis said.

"No police force in Oregon has a good tracker on the payroll," Matterson said.

"I'm growing gray hair waiting for the law to find these guys," Sully said tersely. "Two men are dead. This is our first lead. I think Travis and I should go out there, take a look. Monty would be out there in a heartbeat if one of us got killed."

Matterson arched a brow. "I don't advise it."

"It's public land," Sully said, setting his jaw. "No one can stop us."

"I don't like it," Matterson said.

"You game, Travis?" Sully asked.

"Hell, yeah," Travis growled, his eyes hardening.

"Christ, have a go at it," the sheriff said, his voice resigned. "You can haul your horses over to Sterling O. Leave your truck and trailer there."

"We'll leave at dawn," Sully said. He removed his leather apron and started putting his tools away.

"You'll be looking for a needle in a haystack," Matterson said. "There're thousands of acres of forest back there. If these rustlers are holed up someplace, it's off the radar."

"If they're there, we'll find them," Sully clipped.

The sheriff's voice turned serious. "Don't play vigilante, Sully. These men are dangerous. They won't hesitate to kill you."

"Sounds a lot like Afghanistan."

"Kinda reminds me of Nam, too," Travis said.

"If you find anything, call for backup," Matterson said stubbornly. "Shoot only in self-defense."

"We know the drill, Carl." Sully stretched the stiff muscles that had bunched up in his shoulders and neck.

"Damn, no use talking to you two." Matterson added in a wistful tone, "Wish I was going."

"Better you stay here and fight crime in the big city," Sully smiled.

"Fuck you." Matterson smiled back. "That being said, I better get at it. Criminals don't arrest themselves."

He put on his shades and Sully saw himself reflected in the polarized lenses.

As Travis walked the sheriff out to his truck, Sully started planning the mission. Tonight he'd load and unload his magazines and weapons in the dark in the event he had to protect himself at night. At the sound of clopping hoofs, he looked out the barn door and saw Joe riding Whistler up to the squad car. He dismounted and leaned into the sheriff's open window, wearing his holstered Glock. Sully could hear their muffled voices. Joe looked up sharply as Sully joined them. "You n' Travis going after them murderers?"

"That's the plan."

"I'm coming."

"No way, Dad."

Joe started right in, insisting on going. Sully didn't want to point out the obvious, that he could hardly walk, and that he and Travis could make better time alone. "This isn't a camping trip. It's gonna be hard riding through rugged country."

"I'm coming!"

Matterson cast Sully a sympathetic look. With a little salute, he backed up his truck and drove out of the yard.

"Who's gonna watch over the ranch?"

Joe stared back but didn't have an answer. "I'll figure something out."

"No time. If you wanna help, go see Shankel. He'll have to come over to help you with the livestock."

Joe's jaw jutted forward in a silent gesture of willfulness, but he didn't say anything.

Sully figured reasonableness was settling into his stubborn brain.

CHAPTER TWENTY-FIVE

HANK LIFTED his phone to his ear, pulling his attention away from Cody. She sat on the edge of a sofa chair looking annoyed by the interruption. "Hank Sterling, here."

"Hank, it's Jake Turner."

Hank felt the muscles tighten in his jaw. Furious and worn out with worry, he'd finally gotten skies clear enough to make the flight back from Idaho. Despite the rugged construction of the Cessna 206 and its powerful engine, forty knots of headwind coming right at the nose had made the flight bumpy and challenging. Only home for twenty minutes, he'd just been updated about Justin's foolhardy decision to go after the thieves. A dull pain was building behind his eyes. "What's up, Jake?"

"You remember those horse thefts in Tumalo a few weeks back?"

"Hell yeah, I remember. They murdered Monty Blanchert. Old friend of mine."

"Ballistics came in. The shell casings found on your property match those found at his ranch. They weren't kidding around when they shot at Roth and Cody."

Hank felt a sharp stab of alarm as he looked at his daughter.

"You guys okay up there?" the sheriff asked.

"Not entirely. A big concern came up. One of our hands got it into his head to go after these guys on his own. He's just a kid."

"Justin?"

"Yeah."

"Hell. That's all we need, him getting his fool head blown off. I'll tell my men to watch out for him. They'll be scanning the area behind your ranch from the air today. I've got men and dogs heading out there, too." He hesitated. "A note of warning. Now that the two crimes have been connected, expect reporters to start calling, maybe even showing up at your place."

"Thanks for the heads up." Christ almighty! Valuable horses stolen, his daughter nearly murdered, Billy clobbered, now reporters showing up on his property. The ranch had gone to shit while he was in Idaho. He was angrier than hell with Justin. Pressing his fingertips to his throbbing temples, he paced the floor between his desk and Cody's chair. "How could Justin have used such poor judgment?"

"He felt he owed us, Dad. He says he's caused nothing but trouble since he's been here. Bear accused him of colluding with the thieves."

"Colluding?" Hank stopped, gave her his full attention. "That's ridiculous."

"They got into a fistfight."

"What?"

"Yeah, pretty nasty." Cody detailed the drama of the evening, explaining how Bear and Sarah tried to turn everyone against Justin, which led to the fight outside.

"Bear should know better! He's twice Justin's size, and he's got the strength of an ox."

"Justin held his own, Dad. You would've been proud. He got in some good punches. But his face didn't look too good this morning."

Hank stopped pacing and sharply exhaled his frustration. "Justin's about to do big time rodeo. We don't need him all busted up."

"You should fire Bear," Cody said, eyes flashing. "He's an instigator."

Hank hadn't seen Cody this riled up since she came home from the hospital. He looked at her exhausted face. "Come here." He wrapped his arms around his youngest daughter and murmured words of comfort. "Justin will be okay. The sheriff's sending out dogs today. They'll be searching from the air. They'll find him."

Hank knew he was trying to convince himself, as well. He had formed a strong attachment to Justin. The young man's tenacity reminded him of himself at that age. He knew what it was like to be young and naive, adrift without an anchor, struggling through life without the steadying hand of loving parents, not a single good role model in sight, and temptations beckoning from every alleyway. Already a big rodeo star at Justin's age, Hank didn't deal well with adulation. He couldn't reconcile the fact that just because he knew how to ride a bull meant he was better than anyone else, and that he should be treated like he was special. He fell in with a hard crowd, did a lot of drinking, fighting, and whoring, and got himself into a few scrapes with the law. A six-week stint in county jail detoxing from bad company persuaded him to go straight.

Hank had hoped to steer Justin clear of the minefields he stumbled into. He didn't believe in coincidence. The timing of Justin's appearance at the ranch seemed predestined, and the benefit of their relationship worked both ways. Justin sorely needed a home, good people, and solid career training. His natural athleticism was a gift, but it needed to be honed and polished. Hank could provide all that. In return, Justin gave Hank a newfound sense of purpose, and mentoring the young man helped fill the painful void left by Olivia. Hank felt sick at the thought of something violent happening to Justin. The pain behind his eyes was now pulsing down the right side of the head, turning into a migraine.

CHAPTER TWENTY-SIX

IT HAD BEEN a long, wasted day. Justin was exhausted. Juno's hooves plodded aimlessly over trails that meandered and crisscrossed one another with no rhyme or reason. The silver coils of the Chawtaukee River sliced through the forested landscape, emerging and hiding, the roar of water never ceasing. The trail opened to meadows, narrowed to footpaths, or disappeared altogether in tangled undergrowth. Countless times Justin backtracked and searched until he found it again. The forest teemed with small rustling creatures. Twittering birds flitted through the trees. Animal tracks carved a maze on the ground, but there was no sign of humans or horses.

Mid-afternoon, Justin dismounted in a flowered meadow and let the big chestnut roam free to graze on clover. He sat with his back against a mossy log, his legs stretched out in front of him, and sorted through Cody's pack. He found a loaf of Maresol's thick brown bread, a chunk of cheddar cheese, two blueberry muffins, and a dozen packets of freeze-dried meals. He wolfed down some of the bread and cheese and drank cold water from his canteen. The sun warmed his body and the buzzing of insects dulled his brain. He drifted off. The sun had moved lower in the sky when he awoke, and long shadows stretched across the meadow darkening the grass.

Feeling anxious about lost time, Justin mounted Juno and plowed onward. As he rode further east, grassy meadows and leafy trees gave way to conifer forest and carpets of pine needles. The air was sharp with pinesap and a living halo of insects traveled with him. Listening to the steady rhythm of Juno's hoofs, Justin sometimes was lulled into a trance. Then his predicament would rush back and hit him with a startling sense of urgency.

After a full day of riding, the trail curled out of the forest onto the grassy basin forty miles east of Sterling O. He realized riding straight through the grassland would have saved him half the time. After following an elk trail through fields of bluebunch wheatgrass, he reached a heel of corrugated granite that jutted from the base of Dead Horse Peak. His path intersected a trail that came out of the grassland from the west, and to his astonishment, it was pocked with the tracks of shod horses. He had stumbled upon the path of the horse thieves! He felt a thrumming of fear in his chest, but also excitement. He yanked Hank's old phone out of his pocket and dialed nine-one-one.

No reception.

Justin sat for a long minute, trying to decide his next course of action. A tightness in his gut warned him of danger. But he decided to push onward nonetheless and follow the tracks up into the mountains. He climbed in elevation for a couple of hours but when the sky turned the color of salmon, he was forced to set up camp. He picked a site surrounded by clumps of sagebrush and a few scrappy juniper trees. After unpacking Juno, he gathered a big pile of deadwood and got a good fire blazing. Leaning against his saddle, he waited for water to boil in his old blackened coffee pot, ripped open one of the freeze-dried packets, and added steaming water. The smell of reconstituted pasta and chicken in cream sauce clawed at his stomach. He ate quickly, also consuming a chunk of brown bread and cheese, and washing it all down with coffee.

The red sky bled into indigo and the temperature dropped quickly with approaching darkness. The stars above were so thick and close he felt he could walk right into them. Cold wind gusted down from the peak and shook the branches of nearby trees and sagebrush. The fire stuttered and he felt his ears going numb. Somewhere in the distance, Coyotes nipped, and an owl hooted. There wasn't much to do but try to stay warm. Justin threw more wood on the fire, burrowed into his down bag, and watched flames shoot embers into the night. His thoughts drifted to Cody. Reliving their intimate moments in the kitchen warmed him.

A twig snapped some distance from the fire, pulling him from his reverie. Juno heard it, too, and stood frozen, ears thrust forward, eyes staring into the darkness. Coyote? Cougar? Justin thumbed on his flashlight and sent a cone of light into the darkness, moving slowly from left to right. Sagebrush shivered in the wind. Juno relaxed, but Justin lay awake for a long while, his gun close by, analyzing every whisper of sound, until he drifted to sleep.

***

Justin was jolted awake by the metallic sound of a gun being cocked an inch from his head.

"Pull yer arms out real slow." Male voice. Harsh.

Justin obeyed. His arms were barely exposed before he was yanked roughly out of the bag. He bucked, pulled, and struggled, but two strong men flipped him belly down and a sharp knee was placed on his back, holding him down. Justin tried to roll over but the knee ground deeper into his spine. Air rushed from his lungs and he could barely breathe.

"Move again, and I'll spray yer brains all over this campsite."

Justin went limp. His hands were bound behind him and the pressure on his back let up. He gasped for breath and turned on his side to face his attackers. Two figures loomed above him, faces in the shadows, firelight reflecting off a revolver and a rifle barrel.

"Looky here. Ain't it a small world?" The voice was raspy, arrogant.

A chill touched Justin's spine. A voice Justin would never forget. Porky! And there was no mistaking his bow-legged companion. Waters.

With something resembling a chuckle, Porky stepped into the firelight wearing the hat and boots he'd stolen from Justin. The faces of both men were dark with stubble, their clothes crusty with dirt.

"Nice hat, nice boots," Justin said, forcing a calm tone.

"He won 'em in a fight," Waters sneered.

"See what else the kid's got," Porky said, his eyes hidden in the shadow of his hat.

Waters started ransacking the campsite. Porky squatted and picked up Cody's Colt .45, checked the safety and shoved it into his belt. Then he rifled through Justin's saddlebags, his gaunt face cruel in the flickering light. A hand-rolled cigarette dangled from the corner of his mouth sending up a curl of smoke. He pulled out Hank's cell phone and touched the keypad and it dimly lit up his face. He tossed it in the dirt, smashed it with the butt of his rifle, and then rammed the barrel of the gun into Justin's ribs. "Why the fuck are you tailing us, asshole?"

"Just out hunting."

"Huntin' us." He pushed the barrel deeper. "Cut the crap. Why're you up here?"

"Looking for Hank's horses."

Porky squinted at him.

"What horses?" Waters snarled.

"The ones you stole from Sterling O."

"You hear this shit?" Waters said.

Porky looked amused. "You got nothing but a .45. What was yer plan? Think we were gonna line up and let you shoot us one by one?"

Justin held his tongue.

"You got some big balls for such a little shit."

"Let's gut 'im right now," Waters sneered. "Save a bullet. Let the vultures eat 'im."

Justin didn't breathe.

Porky ignored him, and said, "Taco, git over here. Tie his feet."

A wiry Mexican, barely five-feet tall including his hat, stepped into the firelight holding a lariat. He squatted and made quick work of hogtying Justin's wrists to his ankles.

Justin lay in painful silence, every cell on high alert. He took a deep breath, fighting against his spreading anxiety, telling himself to go along, stay quiet, watch for a way to escape. He knew he'd cross paths with these men again, but not in the wilderness where he was isolated and helpless. They could kill him and bury his body, and no one would be the wiser.

"Keep your eye on 'im," Porky said.

"*Sí, sí. Vete al carojo,*" Taco nodded.

Justin wasn't sure he heard right. It sounded like Taco told Porky to go to hell. Justin's high school Spanish was rusty, but he'd picked up a fair amount of swear words from Spanish ranch hands over the years.

Waters dumped Justin's belongings in a pile on his bedroll. Eyes gleaming in the firelight, he fingered a jackknife, pulling out the blades one by one. He snapped the knife shut and shoved it in his pocket.

"Who said you could take that?" Porky pinched his cigarette between his thumb and forefinger and flicked it into the fire. "Put it back."

Waters hesitated, then reluctantly obeyed.

Porky crossed the campsite with a limp. Justin figured he must be the thief Cody clobbered. In a crouch, he sorted through Justin's belongings and picked up a metal box Cody packed. He pulled a hunting knife with a nine-inch blade from a leather sheath and jimmied open the box. A dozen chocolate bars fell into the dirt. With a surprised gasp, he ripped off the wrapper of a Snickers bar, shoved most of it into his mouth, and chewed ravenously.

Waters dove for a Milky Way. Like Porky, he couldn't eat it fast enough. Taco joined in. In the orange glow of the campfire, the men shoved each other, and clawed the dirt for chocolate bars.

Justin watched them anxiously. He figured they'd been out in the wild too long, sugar-starved, their ties to normal behavior dulled by rough living conditions. With the gang distracted, he tugged at his restraints. The rope gave a few inches, allowing his cramped legs to stretch a bit, but there'd be no escape tonight. He was bound good and tight.

"How many you got?" Porky asked, sitting back on his haunches.

Taco held up three Hershey bars.

"Two Milky Ways," Water's said.

"Including the one you ate?" Porky asked.

"How many you got? You ate one, too."

"I got me four Snickers," Porky said. "So we's even."

"How's that even?" Waters lips curled back.

"I ain't got time for this shit." Porky picked up the jackknife. "You want this?"

"Yeah," Waters said.

"Gimme your chocolate bars."

"Hell no!"

"Taco, want this knife?"

With a sly look, the Mexican held out one bar. "I geeve one. You geeve knife."

"Here, shithead. Take it."

"I'm taking the flashlight," Waters growled. "And the compass."

Justin watched the negotiations continue until his small pile of goods was divided three ways. The candy bars, as valuable as gold, swapped hands several times, in Porky's favor. Porky shed his sheep-lined jacket and pulled Justin's blue-plaid Pendleton over his dirty T-shirt. His gangly wrists stuck out of the sleeves a couple of inches, but he looked deeply pleased.

Taco strutted back and forth, preening in Justin's slicker, which hung on him like a pup tent, the hem stirring up dust. The Mexican then started looking over Juno. The gelding tossed his head and reared back.

"Git away from that horse," Porky growled. "The horse 'n saddle are mine."

Taco sneered back. "*Eres más feo que un apo de mono.*"

You're uglier than a monkey's ass, Justin silently translated.

With a sour look, Taco joined the other men and settled in close to the fire. Porky added wood and stoked the embers to a hot crackling blaze, then he sat rolling cigarettes while Waters made a pot of Justin's coffee. The men drank the hot brew, ate tiny morsels of chocolate, and squirreled the rest away. Porky elevated his injured leg on Juno's saddle and chain-smoked, lighting a new smoke with the butt of the old one before tossing it into the flames.

With the others distracted, Taco started fingering the down bag. To Justin's dismay, he spread it out by the fire and sprawled on top of it. Justin lay close enough to the fire to keep one side of his body warm while the other froze. Periodically, he rolled to the other side. His senses wide open, he watched, and listened. The men's scruffy beards told him they'd been living in the wild for some time, and clearly, they hated each other. Porky pulled rank. Taco and Waters obeyed, grudgingly. Porky had some mysterious hold on them. Justin hoped it was enough to prevent a mutiny. His fragile existence seemed to fall squarely in Porky's hands.

"What're we gonna do with the bull rider?" Waters asked, as though reading Justin's thoughts.

"Ain't figured that out. I hear tell he's good at shoveling shit." Porky turned to Justin with a sinister grin.

"He can dig his own grave when we get back," Waters said.

Justin clenched his jaw so tight he thought it might crack, a realization crystallizing in his mind. Porky wouldn't have known Justin shoveled shit unless he talked to someone at the ranch. These low-life cowpokes *were* working with an insider, like the sheriff surmised. But who? A migrant worker, veterinarian, farrier, one of the ranch hands? Anger simmered in his gut as he listened to their empty-headed conversation about gambling at rodeos. Picturing bullet holes in their foreheads helped keep his mind occupied as the minutes of agony crept into hours. The temperature felt like it was dipping into the thirties.

The fire sputtered and crackled. There was nothing for Justin to do but lay there in misery, holding his breath when the smoke blew his way, turning over periodically to keep from freezing. He didn't feel like the person he'd been when the day began and he was holding Cody in the kitchen. That world existed light years away. Here his survival was tenuous. Moment to moment. Dependent on the whim of a murderer.

The cowpokes eventually drifted off to sleep, their snorts and deep-throated gurgles blending into a harmony from Hell. Justin weaved in and out of a tortured sleep, awakened frequently by missiles of pain shooting through his body. His joints and muscles ached, rocks bit into his flesh, his ass was freezing. After rotating his backside to the fire, he submerged and reemerged from nightmarish dreams.

Eons passed. The night shifted to dawn. The crimson sky bled into the landscape. The pungent odor of sagebrush mixed with the smell of coffee. A sheath of red frost coated everything.

CHAPTER TWENTY-SEVEN

MAGGIE FOLLOWED her GPS directions closely once she turned off the highway. The street signs on the narrow country roads were posted miles apart, the words bleached and worn, some riddled with bullet holes. Hemmed in by forest, the road occasionally opened up to sprawling hay fields and stunning vistas of the Cascades. Weathered barns, old ranch houses, and grazing livestock swept past the window— horses, cattle, goats, and sheep. A few ostriches shared a pasture with alpacas.

"In one half mile, turn right on Alfalfa Market Road."

Maggie swerved right onto the narrow road. The ferocious rainstorm had scrubbed the landscape clean and deepened the colors of green and gold. Billowy white clouds drifted in a clear blue sky.

"In one quarter mile, turn left. You have reached your destination."

Maggie turned onto an unpaved road and drove under an arched, weathered sign that read Dancing Horse Ranch. She continued west toward the house and barn, past tall arcs of water that irrigated hay fields on both sides of the driveway. She heard gravel hitting the wheel wells and saw a plume of dust rise behind the Prius. It was 7:00 PM. The sharp evening sun glared through the windshield until it was eclipsed by the roof of a handsome gable-roofed barn.

She parked facing a corral occupied by long legged horses with shimmering coats and muscled haunches. Several lined up along the fence and watched her with large, curious eyes. She was tempted to walk over and stroke their beautiful heads, but stopped herself. She wasn't here by invitation. Feeling like a trespasser, she walked toward the solidly built two-story house that featured river rock trim and a wide covered porch. The windows facing due west reflected the evening sun.

The paint was faded, and she recalled Sully saying he wanted to paint the house before inviting her over. Clearly her visit was premature, and probably an intrusion.

Dressed simply in a blue T-shirt and jeans, she walked up a paving stone pathway. Bordering each side were flowering shrubs and a profusion of flowers. The scent of honeysuckle infused the air and butterflies and bees darted among the blossoms. Maggie found the whole setting charming and lovely, even though the garden looked overgrown and was in need of pruning. The neglect, she knew, was due to the absence of Sully's mother, an avid gardener.

She mounted the stairs, stepped into the cool, deep shadow of the porch, and spotted three pairs of dirty work boots lined outside the door. Her knuckles barely touched the door before it opened wide and Sully stood facing her, his eyes blinking in surprise. She'd never seen him like this, unsmiling, dressed in dirty work clothes, his hair matted from his hat and sweat. His shirt was unbuttoned, revealing a long rectangle of muscled torso. Eric's St. Christopher medal dangled from his neck. As their eyes met, it was an intensely intimate moment. Then he retreated to some interior place, cold and remote.

"Who is it?" A gravelly voice called out behind him.

She gazed past him into the dark kitchen and made out two seated men silhouetted against the window.

"A friend."

"Invite her in," the gravelly voice said, now insistent.

"Come in, Maggie."

Breathing in his musky scent, she stepped past Sully into the spacious kitchen—a room designed for a cook. An assortment of pots and pans hung over a big work island, and there were plenty of cabinets to store all the accoutrements of a chef. The room smelled of grilled chicken and something sweet and freshly baked. Her eyes adjusted to the dim interior while Sully made introductions in a toneless voice. From his past descriptions, she immediately recognized the two men pushing back their chairs and getting to their feet.

Sully's father, Joe, stepped forward with a limp. At once, she was captivated by his brilliant blue eyes. His chiseled face was weathered and deeply creased, but his thick silver hair gave him a youthful allure. She felt as though she was seeing a future projection of Sully. Unlike his son, who exuded a sense of unquenchable energy, Joe's slouching posture suggested a man overworked and worn out. She thought it odd that he wore a holstered gun at the dinner table. His big-knuckled hand enveloped hers.

"So, you're Maggie." Though one side of Joe's mouth was a little slack, his smile was transformative. Out of the exhausted face came the charm of a man who was still strikingly handsome, though it was more character than perfect features. A man who knew his way around women and expected a certain response.

She smiled, taken in. "Sully's told me wonderful things about you, Joe."

"All true." Joe gave a gruff laugh. Despite the charm, she detected a hard glint in his eye, a steel toughness to his character.

She turned to Travis, who had a broad forehead, strong nose, and intelligent brown eyes. Neatly braided gray hair fell past his shoulders. The crevices of suffering and compassion were carved on his face, and his manner was respectful, even gentle. His hand was dry and callused, the fingers bony and strong.

"So nice to meet you, Travis."

"Same here, Maggie."

All three men looked rumpled and dusty, and the heat from the sun seemed to linger on their skin.

"You gonna ask her to sit down?" Joe asked. Before Sully replied, Joe pulled out a chair. "Sit, Maggie. We're about to carve up some peach pie. It's store bought, but tasty. How 'bout some coffee? Sully, get her a cup."

"Please, don't bother," she said, catching Sully's stern expression. "I only stopped by for a minute."

Sully took his cue. "Let's talk outside." He grabbed his hat, opened the door for her, pulled on his boots on the porch, and followed her into the startling sunlight. "What're you doing here, Maggie?" he said as he buttoned his shirt, his eyes in the shadow of his hat.

"I'm sorry to catch you off guard like this. But you didn't return my call. I didn't know if you were going to. I just want to talk. Can we go for a walk? It's beautiful here. I've wanted to come out for so long, see what you do." She had a case of nerves and knew she was rambling, but she was determined to speak her mind. "Your horses are beautiful. Can you show me a little of your property?"

A muscle ticked in his left jaw. "You made it pretty clear Friday night where we stand. What's the point of a walk?"

"I'm sorry for the way I treated you. It was unforgiveable." Feeling awkward, she stuck her thumbs into the pockets of her low-cut jeans. "I don't always see things clearly, or make good decisions. My brain's been in a muddle lately." She paused, biting her bottom lip. "I had to come out. I couldn't leave things the way they were. And you didn't return my call. Can we walk?"

His voice warmed minutely. "Let's go out by the creek. It's shady. We can get out of this heat."

They walked up a trail that overlooked the hay fields, and in the distance, a stack of clouds blossomed above the Cascades like smoke signals.

"Your father and Travis are just as I pictured them," she said.

"You're seeing us at our worst. Dirty. In our work clothes. The ranch is a mess."

"The ranch is stunning. You all look pretty good to me. I respect men who work with their hands as well as their brains."

"We do a lot of that." He gave her a sidelong glance, a quick blaze of blue, the muscles still tight around his jaw.

The path leading into the woods curved around columns of lodgepole and ponderosa pine. Maggie inhaled the scent of pinesap and wet earth and heard the clattering rush of water before Wild Horse Creek swept into view. This vigorous channel, Sully once told her, was fed by two prominent rivers and was the lifeline that irrigated the local ranches and gave the town its name. As they continued walking, the character of the creek changed at every turn; opening wide and running wild as a river, narrowing again to a mossy passage shrouded with ferns, and cascading over polished rocks. A fallen log occasionally served as a footbridge to the other side. Along the way, Sully pointed out the tracks of rabbit, deer, raccoon, and skunk. Maggie identified wildflowers and birdcalls.

They came to a big grassy meadow colored with columbine and Indian paint bush. Here the water was mirror-calm and reflected the towering trees. Sunlight fingered the branches, and cool air moved up from the creek. A pair of mallards rippled the surface, ushering ducklings across the creek to disappear into tall reeds. They followed the creek deeper into the forest, their shoes sinking slightly into wet earth. There was a long lapse in conversation and Maggie became keenly aware of Sully's unyielding presence. She glanced at his unreadable expression and wondered if he was enduring her company out of politeness.

Abruptly, he asked in a blunt tone, "Did you have a nice date with Brennen Sunday night?"

She saw the glint of hurt in his eyes. "It wasn't a date. And no, I didn't have fun." Hell, she was just going to be honest, speak her mind. "I thought about you the whole time, and I thought what an ass I was to you at my party. I would rather have been at home watching a movie with you."

His eyes narrowed for a moment and he showed the hint of a smile. "Are you trying to say you missed me?"

"Yes, I missed you."

He looked away, chewing on her words. His eyes returned and watched her closely. "More than a friend?"

"Much more than a friend."

His face relaxed, and he smiled.

It melted her heart.

"I missed you, too."

"More than a friend?"

His smile deepened.

She felt as awkward as an adolescent exploring intimate feelings for the first time. Shy, wary. It was a delicate moment, their first admission of mutual attraction, after a disastrous couple of days. They continued walking, quietly reflecting, taking care not to touch. Up ahead, she saw a copse of aspen trees backlit by the sun, with the roofline of a small house peeking through. "Is that the cottage your mom's moving into?"

"Yes. It was my parent's first house, built thirty-years ago."

"It's been empty since then?"

"After my folks built the big house, Travis lived here with his wife. When Chenoah died, he moved to the rez. I didn't see him for a year. Then suddenly, with no fanfare, he was back. He moved into the bunkhouse next to the barn. The cottage held too many memories. It's sat empty ever since."

"That's very sad, losing a lifelong spouse. How did she die?"

"Driving home in a snowstorm. A semi crossed the highway and hit her head on."

Maggie shuddered. "Horrible. Poor Travis. How old were you?"

"Thirteen. It was a hard year. After he left, I didn't know if he was ever coming back." Sully was quiet for a moment. "He'd been a second father to me. The good father."

"Joe was the bad father?" she asked. Sully had never talked about his conflicts with Joe, just skimmed over them.

He looked away.

She knew he was recalling hurtful memories. No doubt, Joe had been abusive. "With Travis gone, you probably felt abandoned. You lost your protection."

"That just about sums it up." He looked at her with appreciation. "It forced me to stand up for myself. Dad and I worked things out his way. With our fists. I broke his nose, blackened his eye. I didn't look too good either, but he never laid a hand on me again."

"Hard way for a boy to become a man," she said gently.

He shrugged. "Needed to be done."

"Travis came back to you."

"True. He belongs here."

In the diminishing light, they stood in front of the little house his parents built long ago, before Sully was born—painted sage green with white trim, storm shutters on the windows, and a covered porch big enough for two Adirondack chairs. The house looked sturdy, built to last.

"Wanna see the inside?" he asked. "We've started fixing it up for Mom."

"I'd love to."

They mounted the stairs and entered. The interior smelled of fresh paint. Paint cans and spattered tarps lay across the living room floor. Two walls were faded blue with lighter rectangles where pictures once hung. The other two walls were painted a warm, buttery yellow. The spaciousness of the kitchen surprised her, again designed for a cook, with a large island and windows that overlooked the creek. The appliances were decades old and Maggie had the illusion of stepping back in time. Down a hallway were two bedrooms and a bath, freshly painted and ready to live in.

"Like the color?" he asked.

"Love it. It's warm and cheerful. This house is incredibly charming. Your mom will be happy here. Your first home?"

Smiling warmly, he nodding toward the smaller room. "My room until I was five. It seemed enormous when I was little."

For a moment she pictured him as a fair-haired little boy with high energy.

They backtracked to the porch, sat on the worn wooden steps, and watched the colors of the sunset deepen above the trees. She could feel the heat and sharpness in the air.

He sat close to her, his arm against hers, and she inhaled his musky scent, a faint mix of earth, sweat, and soap.

"So, what's going on with you, Maggie?" The shadows softened his expression, but she heard confusion in his voice. "You just said you like me more than a friend. What does that mean? The other night, you said all I could give you was an affair. That really rubbed me the wrong way."

Maggie swallowed. "I had a lot to drink. I wasn't thinking clearly."

"You mean you were coached by Brennen."

"Sorry to say, I let him influence me."

"What are your true feelings, Maggie? You didn't come here on a lark."

"I came because I wanted to tell you …." She paused, trying to put her feelings into words. "I care about you, Sully. Very much." She met his eyes. "A part of me wants to rush headlong into a relationship with you. Another part of me is saying, move slowly. I don't want to hurt you. I don't want to be hurt, either. I need to make sure we're on the same page."

He said nothing, just listened.

Maggie heaved out a breath and spoke frankly. "Sometimes I feel the need to stand back from my life and assess what I'm doing. Look at all possible consequences."

He nodded.

"We have a wonderful friendship," she said. "I don't want to ruin it."

"We're way past friendship, Maggie." He gazed at her hard and long. "We can't go back. There's only one way to go from here."

"Then there's something we need to talk about." She chewed her lip, afraid to broach a subject that might wedge them apart, not closer.

"What? I'm too young?"

"Yes." She felt him stiffen beside her.

He shoved his hat back, and his eyes filled with concern. "I've done more and seen more in my life than men twice my age."

"It's not a matter of maturity, Sully. It's expectations. I've been married. I raised a son. You're just starting out in life. You're going to want kids. I'm forty-two." She looked down at her hands, tightly interlocked. "My child-bearing years may be behind me."

"You've really thought all this all out, haven't you?"

"I'm a therapist. That's what I do."

"This is a lot of serious discussion, considering we haven't even been out on a date."

"I know, Sully. But it needs to be talked about."

"I definitely want kids." His voice softened and she saw tenderness in his eyes. "If we end up together, and you decide you can deal with raising another child, and you can't get pregnant, we can always adopt. There're plenty of kids who need good homes. Do you want kids?"

"Yes." She felt the hot sting of tears in her eyes. "Another child would be a gift, after losing Eric."

"Hey, don't cry." He wrapped his arm around her and pulled her close. "We can make this work."

"You sound so confident."

"I am. I know how I feel about you. We can face anything together."

Resting her head on his shoulder, Maggie smiled in the darkness, comforted by the warmth of Sully's body, the sturdiness of his character. The sounds of the night enveloped them; the shrilling of insects, the wind rustling leaves. Somewhere in the darkness a frog croaked. Another answered. And another. A frog ditty ensued.

Sully put his hand under her chin and tilted her face. His mouth found hers and they tenderly kissed. Maggie's world evaporated. When their lips parted, he placed her hand flat against his chest, covered by his own. She felt the beating of his heart, which matched the rhythm of her own. Her feelings for Sully deepened, expanded, enveloped her. She allowed herself to believe this union could endure.

His lips grazed her forehead, and he said gently, "I better walk you back. I have a lot to do tonight. I have to pack. Travis and I are leaving at daybreak."

Holding hands, they retraced their steps through the forest. All around them, nature pulsed with life. Details appeared more intricate, colors more sumptuous. Wind, water, and living creatures harmonized in an ebullient melody. There was a lightness to her body. Maggie knew she had been possessed by the psychotic malady of lovesickness.

When they reached the open meadow, the colors of the wildflowers were muted in the dimming light. An untroubled band of sandy beach sloped gently down to the water's edge.

"This is my favorite place on the ranch," Sully said. "I want to build my house here."

"It's a perfect spot," she said, taken in by the serene beauty.

He proceeded to describe the design in detail, the back porch facing west toward the creek and the mountains, the front facing the hay fields. "I'll build the garage and machine shop over there." He gestured with his hand.

"I can picture it completed."

"Just waiting to get this ranch right side up again." He draped an arm around her shoulder and they stood listening to the night. "We better head back while we can still see the path."

"Where are you going tomorrow?"

"A horse trip."

"Fishing? Hunting?"

"Did you hear on the news about the horse theft in Beaverhead two nights ago?"

"No. I haven't watched the news lately."

"The men that took Gunner and killed Monty and Mateo stole some horses from a ranch out there. Lawmen are looking for them, but they aren't very hopeful. The tracks were washed out by the storm. Travis and I are going to lend a hand."

"You'll be with a bunch of officers?"

He hesitated. "Travis and I can do a better job on our own."

"You're going after murderers alone?" She stared up at him. His features were barely discernable in the darkness.

"You sound worried. Don't be."

"I am worried. Two rangers were murdered on Mt. Hood last year. They were after just one bad guy. You're going after two."

"Those rangers confronted the suspect. A cornered animal fights back." He squeezed her hand. "Travis and I are good at what we do. We're quiet in the woods. If we come across the rustlers, we'll call for backup. They won't even know we're there."

Still, Maggie felt uneasy. Until Sully was safely home, she would be living on a razor's edge. "Will you call me, let me know you're all right?"

"Yes. As soon as we get within range."

They had reached the vista overlooking the hay fields. Stars began to prick through the black canvas of night, and further down the trail, she saw the lights of the house glowing in the dark.

Sully's mouth curved into a slow, sexy smile, and he pulled her close. "You and I are an item now, right? Exclusive?"

"Yes. Absolutely."

His lowered his head and his mouth found hers. They kissed softly, then deeply and with urgency. She felt an irresistible yearning, a rush of feeling, like a stream racing to merge with a wild, roiling river.

"Whew. You have a gift for kissing." His voice was husky as he pulled away. "I thought you wanted to take it slow. You're not making it easy."

Breathless, she didn't trust herself to speak.

"I better get you to your car." He took her hand and they continued down the trail, past the house, and across the clearing to her Prius. They kissed again. When his mouth lifted away, she placed a hand behind his neck, drew it gently back to hers. They kissed hungrily, bodies pressed tightly together. Eventually they needed air.

"You're one wild little filly," he said, his forehead pressed to hers.

She heard the door of the house open and footsteps crossed the porch. Someone was standing there, watching.

Sully opened her door and smiled. "Get yourself home, woman. I'll call when I get back."

She sank into the driver's seat, knees like jelly, body humming with desire, and watched him fade into the darkness.

CHAPTER TWENTY-EIGHT

HAULING TWO HORSES and a mule behind his truck, Sully and Travis drove east into the fiery sunrise. By the time they reached the Chawtaukee river basin, the landscape had brightened, and clouds as thin as gauze stretched across a brilliant blue sky. The air was sucked dry of moisture, and the desert was so still it felt like traveling into a photograph. Sully drove through the immense stone gates of Sterling O Ranch and followed the meandering road through forested land and grassy meadows dotted with grazing cattle. They passed sculpted basalt outcroppings jutting from granite hills. Beautiful country.

The road rose steadily in elevation. After another couple of miles, Sully parked in front of a sprawling ranch house perched on a ridge overlooking Hank's vast property. They climbed out of the truck as two men hurried down the porch steps to greet them. Sully immediately recognized the lean, handsome man with silver hair. Hank Sterling hadn't changed much since Sully's rodeo days. His companion pushed up the brim of a dark hat and revealed the face of a pretty young woman.

"My daughter, Cody," Hank said. Cody's face was thin with high cheekbones, a full mouth, and intelligent gray-blue eyes. There was a tension to her manner, and she didn't smile or say hello, but shook hands with an inscrutable expression.

"We're having breakfast," Hank said. "Please, come join us."

"If it's all the same to you, we'd like to get saddled and head out," Sully said. "The rustlers have a big jump on us."

"Of course. We appreciate you coming. The sheriff said you were ace trackers. Every pair of eyes helps."

"Monty and Mateo were close friends," Travis said.

"I knew them well." Hank's expression looked sympathetic as he draped his arm around Cody's shoulder. "Could've lost my daughter. Stunned the hell out of us. Murderers coming onto our property in the night, stealing our horses. Roth said they stole Gunner from your property a few months back. Sire to the gelding we just bought."

"My best stallion," Sully said.

"We're getting him back," Travis said tersely.

Two deep vertical creases appeared between Hank's brows. "Hope we all get our horses back." He added in a lighter tone, "Chico's a fine animal. Cody's already claimed him as her own."

Cody missed her cue to comment. Lines tightened around her mouth and Sully sensed her impatience.

"I've got a satellite phone you can take," Hank said. "You find anything, call the sheriff. He'll send help straight away. Cody can show you where to park."

Cody hastily climbed into the back of the cab and directed Sully up the hill to a dirt lot opposite the barn.

"Want to walk us through what happened?" Sully asked.

"Follow me."

He and Travis trailed her into a spacious barn that smelled of fresh pine shavings and oiled leather. He took in the high-beam ceilings, stained concrete floors, polished knotty pine paneling, and custom wrought iron trim. In the spacious tack room, he saw steel and brass sparkle, and numerous glowing saddles on racks. Top-notch quarter horses peered out above the stall doors, their luminous eyes watching them closely. The light slanting through the tall rectangular windows reminded Sully of a cathedral. Nice what money could buy.

Blending in with the elegant surroundings, Chico stood tethered to a nearby post. He whinnied when he spotted Sully and stuck out his velvety muzzle. Sully sauntered over and stroked his glossy neck. "How ya doing, buddy?"

Chico lifted his head high and pulled his lips back in his version of a happy face. He whiffled pitifully when Sully rejoined Travis and Cody.

"They knocked out the power," Cody was saying. "I couldn't see anything. I stumbled over Billy who was lying right here, out cold. I got one of the rustlers with the butt of my shotgun pretty good, but the other one slammed me to the floor. I heard the horses coming right at me, and I barely got out of the way before they stampeded out of the barn. Two mounted men were herding them up the trail."

"Sounds rough," Sully said.

"It was. They shot at me and Roth when we went after them. Missed us by inches."

Brave woman, Sully thought, removing his shades. As he tucked them into his breast pocket, a curious expression came over Cody's face. She glanced away, then her eyes locked on his again. "Sorry to stare, but your eyes remind me of one of our ranch hands. Same intense blue." She cleared her throat and her voice came back stronger. "He took off after the rustlers."

"Alone?" Sully asked.

"Yes."

"When?"

"Yesterday, at dawn." Her sorrowful expression told Sully he must be her boyfriend.

"Armed?" he asked.

"Colt .45."

"Semi?"

"Single-action."

"That it?"

"Yes."

Ignorant kid. Sully tried to hide his alarm, but he saw she picked up on it.

Fear played on her face and her delicate mouth trembled. "I should never have let him go."

"What's his name?"

"Justin Powell." Her eyes welled with eyes. She colored, squared her shoulders, knuckled away the tears. "Sorry. I'm worried about him."

With good reason, Sully thought. Her vulnerability pierced his tough-guy armor and he said in a gentle tone, "We'll find him, Cody."

She regarded him with uncertainty, then she visibly relaxed and her eyes lost some of their anxiety. He hoped he wasn't making a false promise. He glanced at Travis who stood light on his feet, poised to go, face creased with concern.

"Wanna direct us to where the shots were fired?" Sully asked.

"I'll get saddled." Cody hurried toward Chico.

While he and Travis led Diego, Taba, and Pistol out of the trailer, a two-ton flatbed truck pulled up next to them and parked. Hank's hulk of a foreman got out of the cab and placed a sable-colored Stetson on his head. "Hey, Sully." His smile didn't reach his eyes.

Preoccupied, Sully nodded, positioning his saddle over the pad on Diego's back.

Bear's gaze turned to Travis and gave him the once over.

"That's Travis," Sully said. "Travis, Bear."

"I'm Hank's livestock foreman," Bear said with an air of authority.

Travis grunted, busy with Taba.

"Hank told me to drop off this satellite phone," Bear said. "Know how to use it?"

"Yeah, we know how to use it," Sully said coldly.

Travis took the phone and slipped it into his saddlebag.

Tightlipped, with his hands on his hips, the big man stood rooted to the ground, watching.

"Help you with something?" Sully asked.

"You guys think it's smart to go after those murderers?"

"You worried about us?" Sully said.

"You're not lawmen," Bear said. "You could get shot."

Sully didn't respond. He didn't feel the need to justify his actions.

Bear stood a minute longer, shifting his weight, rocking back and forth on the balls of his feet. There was something menacing in his tense expression. "You hear we got some knuckle-headed kid who went off on his own yesterday?"

"Yeah, we heard," Travis said.

"Decided to be a hero." Bear chuckled. "Dead's more like it."

Sully missed the humor.

"A word of warning," Bear said, crossing his arms. "The sheriff thinks an insider is working with the thieves. My guess, it's this kid, Justin. I figure he left to join them."

After tightening his cinch, Sully focused on Bear. "That your opinion, or the sheriff's?"

"Mine. Justin's been suspicious since day one. Came up from Arizona all beat up, involved in a con job with some bad people. A neighboring rancher just accused him of rape and theft. The night our horses were stolen, he was nowhere to be found. I think he was directing the thieves in. If you run into him, watch your back."

Sully and Travis exchanged their dislike of the foreman in a glance. Accusations made behind another man's back rubbed Sully the wrong way. He trusted the instincts of Hank's daughter. Despite her privileged lifestyle, she wasn't all twisted up with self-importance. Cody found enough good in Justin to fall in love with him. Guilty or not, Sully wanted to save his life.

Cody clopped out of the barn on Chico, her skill in the saddle immediately apparent. Chico was a lot of horse—spirited, agile, quick. But Cody was in full control, handling him with a light rein and firm lower body commands.

Sully watched as her eyes made contact with the foreman's. The hostility exchanged seemed to charge the air. Bear's face darkened. He strode heavily to his truck and spun out of the lot like a cocky schoolboy, sending up a huge plume of dust.

"Asshole," Sully muttered, hoisting himself into the saddle.

***

The three dismounted up on the ridge. Cody watched Sully and Travis canvas the area around the boulders. Travis knelt and brushed the dirt with his fingers here and there, and then the two men stood talking as they surveyed the valley floor lunging away from them. Dun-colored grassland that looked as soft as suede stretched across the basin. Thirty or forty miles out, the land began to buckle into the steep barren crags of Dead Horse Peak.

Cody thought the two men made an impressive pair. Lean, rugged, with an air of toughness that didn't come from ranching alone. Though decades apart in age, they shared a purposeful manner and focus. She felt certain they were ex-military.

Their horses looked rock-solid strong. Necessary for the rough country ahead. Travis rode an ebony-patched paint with striking markings, one side of his face black, the other white. Sully's mount was a bay roan gelding with black socks, and a dark mane and tail. The only gear visible on their mounts were saddlebags, rifle scabbards, and canteens. A sturdy-looking mule was packed with spare supplies. In addition to the rifles, both men were armed with holstered handguns. They had the good sense to travel light, which meant a faster pace and less stress on the animals. She felt a keen longing, an ache, to go with them, but she knew that wasn't an option. Like Justin, they would view her as a liability.

With an air of business about them, they mounted their horses, said thanks to Cody, and tipped their hats in farewell. For a long while, she sat stiffly in the saddle watching their cautious descent, bodies swaying, the horses sure-footed on the steep terrain.

Beneath her, Chico was on high alert, almost vibrating with anticipation, anxious to follow along on the adventure. Cody turned the reluctant quarter horse back toward the ranch, feeling his anxiety keenly as his former owners and barn mates left without him.

Back in the barn, dust motes floated in the shafts of light slanting through the windows. The horses ambled into their stalls from the paddocks, whinnying, looking for Justin. Without a word, she had assumed his chores, mucking stalls and dropping hay. She didn't want his absence to be a burden to the other hands. She took comfort in the fact that Sully and Travis were following in his footsteps, but she hated that he was out there alone, and she hadn't insisted on going with him.

CHAPTER TWENTY-NINE

FROM THE TOP of the ridge, Sully could see a good distance in all directions. To the south, the hills were covered in conifer forest. Across the basin to the east, the grassland looked as crumpled and creased as an unmade bed. To the north, the land was well timbered with ponderosa and lodgepole pine. The Chawtaukee River, a slithering silver ribbon, carved canyons through the landscape and disappeared into the forest.

Sully and Travis followed the impressions in the wet earth left by the lawmen and their dogs, their tracks weaving back and forth through those of a lone rider, Justin. All the tracks headed north into the forest.

During his childhood, Sully and Travis had explored much of this backcountry on hunting and fishing trips. He recalled most of the forest floor was tangled in underbrush, making travel by horse almost impossible. For the most part, columns of basalt and steep granite cliffs hemmed in the river on both sides, with little shoreline fit for crossing. Turning his attention back to the collage of prints in the mud, he said to Travis, "Looks like the sheriff's dogs are tracking the kid, not the thieves."

"You're right. Pretty much a wasted effort. They'll find there's no way to get across the river. My guess, Justin probably rode around in circles, then made his way back out into the basin somewhere near the foot of Dead Horse Peak."

"Probably lost the better part of a day."

"Wish he'd given up and gone home. Nothing good will come of him if he happens upon those rustlers."

A plane from the sheriff's department buzzed overhead, momentarily swooping low to scout them out before flying north.

"There's taxpayer money down the toilet," Sully said. He heard a ping from his phone, a reminder he'd received a message while in the barn. "Hold on Travis, we're about to run out of coverage."

He pulled the phone from his saddlebag and listened to a message from Maggie. After telling him to be safe, she added, "I miss you already. Come home soon. I can't wait to spend a whole evening with you." Her voice warmed him and brought up a piercing sense of longing. He recalled her expression last night when they parted, her soft eyes gazing up at him, filled with trust and hope. When they kissed, he could barely muster the strength to pull away from her sweet, sexy mouth. He had wanted to lay her down in the cool night grass under the swell of stars and ....

Sully felt a pair of eyes burning into his face like cattle prongs. Travis sat watching him, his face tight with impatience. He turned off the phone and tucked it into his saddlebag. Goodbye, Maggie.

CHAPTER THIRTY

IT WAS A FRIGID MORNING. Frost coated everything. In a state of raw misery, Justin lay shivering on the ground until Porky stoked up the flames of the campfire. The parched wood ignited quickly, crackling and popping and sending clotted smoke into the air. The heat slowly encompassed him. The rustlers moved around the campsite stiffly, breath steaming from their mouths, scratching body parts, relieving themselves in the brush. In the early morning light they looked like flea-bitten, starving mongrels—greasy-hair, scruffy beards, dirt embedded in their skin and under fingernails. Porky sucked on a cigarette and started wheezing. He hacked up phlegm and spit it into the fire.

From his ant level vantage point, Justin saw Taco disappear by foot into the sagebrush. A short while later the clopping of hooves announced his return, sitting astride a stunning appaloosa. Another cowboy accompanied him, riding a bay quarter horse and leading a saddled buckskin. None were Hank's horses, but all were fine looking animals from quality stock. Not the kind of animals these rangy cowhands could afford. This fourth man must've been camped a good way down the trail tending to the horses, allowing the other three to creep up on him last night.

The two Mexicans dismounted and tethered their mounts. When the newcomer pushed back his sombrero, Justin realized he was just a kid, around ten or eleven, skinny as a twig, resembling Taco like a "mini-me." His son. The boy reached into a pack on his big bay, brought out a bag of jerky and made the rounds, passing out stiff ribbons of beef to each man.

"*Gracias, Poncho,*" Porky said with a nod.

The men sat in the haze of shifting smoke, hugging the fire, gnawing on jerky, washing it down with coffee. Justin lay in pain-filled silence, his full bladder nearing critical mass.

"Taco, git the bull rider up," Porky said, as though reading Justin's thoughts. "Take 'im out in the bushes before he pisses his pants. Keep yer eye on 'im."

"*Sí, sí, pendejo*," Taco said.

Justin translated. *Yes, yes, asshole.*

Taco kept a shotgun trained on Justin's chest while Poncho untied him. When the rope was released, his arms and legs fell to the ground like dead weight—numb, useless. He pumped his limbs to get the blood flowing, clenched and unclenched his fists, and then thousands of sharp little needles stabbed him all at once. Gritting his teeth, he pulled on his hat, staggered to his feet like a drunkard, and limped painfully to the nearest cluster of sagebrush. The cold wind scoured his skin as he hurriedly unzipped his jeans and whizzed. Never had peeing been more pleasurable. The two Mexicans provided an attentive audience. When he finished, Justin swept off his hat and bowed.

Poncho laughed. His father shot him a stern warning, and nudged Justin with the rifle, motioning him back to camp. Though it was a great relief to stand, stretch, piss, and move, anxiety twisted Justin's gut tighter than barbed wire.

Porky surprised the hell out of Justin by handing him a tin cup of hot coffee and two sticks of jerky. Justin met his squinty-eyed gaze, nodded his thanks, and got a second surprise. Porky half smiled, showing yellow teeth with molars missing top and bottom.

"Whatcha wastin' our grub on him fer?" Waters asked, his one good eye trained on Porky, the other quivering and looking off in the distance.

"Shut your hole," Porky said. He lit a cigarette, sucked in smoke, coughed it out.

Watching both men with a wary eye, Justin chewed on the tough strip of beef and drained his cup of strong black coffee. He slipped the other stick into his pocket, not knowing when generosity would show up again.

Waters fidgeted, pacing the campsite. He couldn't stay quiet for long. "You plan on taking this asshole with us? He probably planned on ambushing us."

Porky eyed him coldly.

"We don't need no bull rider slowing us down," Waters said. "If he could find us, lawmen can't be far behind. Time to clear out, fast."

Porky chewed his jerky.

"I say we shoot 'im," Waters said.

Justin coughed, and felt a stab of fear in his chest.

"Whatchu think, Taco?" Porky asked.

Squatting near the fire, Taco lifted his grizzled face and locked eyes with Waters. "No kill."

Porky tossed his last swallow of coffee into the fire. It hissed and sent up a tendril of smoke. "You're an ignorant fool, Waters. That's why I call the shots."

Waters flushed darkly, his reddened neck taut against his collar.

"The bull rider stays alive. We might need 'im fer insurance if we get cornered."

Waters cast Justin a scorching look that held the promise of violence.

The men proceeded to pack up camp and Porky kicked dirt over the fire. It wasn't lost on Justin that there were four horses to five men. Porky's solution became clear soon enough.

"Better keep up, kid, 'cause you're walking." Porky's right eye squinted against the smoke curling up from his stub of a cigarette. "We'll drag you, if we have to."

His twinge of kindness had sputtered out with the campfire.

Taco tied one end of his lariat around Justin's wrists and the other around his saddle horn, all the while giving stern instructions to his son in Spanish. Justin understood enough to know that he was warning Poncho to stay at the rear of the gang, and if trouble broke loose, he should ride away, fast. Clearly, he feared for his son's safety. Justin wondered how the two Mexicans got mixed up with the likes of Porky and Waters.

The men mounted up with Porky taking the lead on Juno. Waters nudged his buckskin behind Juno, and Taco fell into third place on the appaloosa with Justin following on foot. Poncho brought up the rear on the bay. Moving at an easy clip, they started traversing the peak on a narrow elk trail. Justin tightened the chinstrap on his hat and pulled his bandana over his nose to cut down on the dust being kicked up from the horses up ahead. To prevent his wrists from chaffing, he kept a lag in the rope, walking close to the rear of Taco's appaloosa. On occasion, he glanced back at Poncho, hoping for a friendly sign, but the boy avoided eye contact and kept a stony expression.

The sun rose high in the sky and bore down on their backs with increasing ferocity. Faces dripped sweat, wet stains blossomed across shirts, and the horses shimmered. Cobbled with loose stones and grainy sand, the trail got increasingly steep and difficult to negotiate, with a sheer vertical drop of hundreds of feet on the west side. When it narrowed to the double width of a horse, Porky signaled for the men to dismount. They forged ahead on foot, leading their animals, accompanied by grunts, heavy breathing, and hooves grinding stone. Hearing Poncho panting just a few feet behind, Justin turned and quietly asked the boy his real name.

Surprised by Justin's Spanish, the boy answered hesitantly. "Juaquín Humberto Ramirez Gonzales."

"*Hola, Juaquín. Me llamo Justin.*"

"Joosteen." The boy smiled shyly.

In halting Spanish, Justin asked why he'd only brought three horses to the camp. The boy glanced ahead to make sure no one was watching, then told him Porky's horse had broken a leg yesterday.

"Porky shot him?"

"*Sí,*" Poncho looked past him up the trail and Justin saw stark fear wash over his face. Justin followed his gaze.

The caravan had halted. Up ahead, the trail funneled into a narrow strip barely one and a half horses wide and spanned a length of about fifty yards before widening again. Justin's anger surged to the surface, instant and hot. What the hell was Porky thinking? He was a lunatic to bring horses up on this treacherous trail. With stunned expressions, the men waited to see what Porky would do. The horses stood frozen, blowing, and nervously flicking their tails.

Leading Juno, Porky hugged the rock wall and advanced fifteen feet on the narrow lip of the trail. He paused, apparently allowing Juno to get his bearings, then crept forward again. Rocks and gravel skidded off the edge in a continuous shower. Sure-footed and fearless, Juno plodded ahead until both horse and rider were safely anchored on the wider end of the trail.

Justin expelled a ragged breath. Nervous sweat ran down his back.

Waters advanced next. Wild-eyed and huffing, his buckskin stopped every few feet, his ribs heaving in and out, expelling manure, then the animal froze up. It took quite a bit of coaxing by Waters and gentle tugging on the reins before the buckskin stepped forward again.

Every muscle in Justin's body went rigid until the animal completed the journey.

Now it was Taco's turn. Before proceeding, he turned to Poncho and asked if he was okay.

"Sí, Papa."

"Bueno." Taco stepped forward cautiously, talking all the while in gentle undertones to the appaloosa. Wet with sweat, Justin stumbled behind, praying there'd be no misstep. If the appaloosa went over, he went with it. He avoided looking down, his tethered hands clasped tightly together. Every small cascade of rocks sent a shockwave through his nervous system. Justin imagined himself falling off the edge of the world, bouncing off jutting boulders, his body twisted and broken at the bottom of Dead Horse Peak. Lost forever. The appaloosa plodded onward, hoofs clipping stone, the Mexican's confident tone a lifeline edging him to safety.

Poncho and his bay followed right behind. Justin heard the horse's snorts of fear and the constant skidding of rocks over the edge. The bay whinnied pitifully and let out a piercing shriek.

Justin turned, expecting to see it toppling over the side.

Instead, the horse retreated, backing up steadily until it reached the wider perch, yanking the boy along with him. The gelding stiffened its legs, planted its hoofs, unyielding, eyes bulging with fear.

Poncho gave little tugs to the reins. The gelding squealed, bucked, backed up several more feet.

The men froze. Taco's expression collapsed.

"Don't pull!" Justin yelled.

The boy ignored him and yanked on the reins. His inexperience triggered wild behavior from the animal. A hind leg missed the ledge and slipped over the side up to his rump. The animal teetered, shrieking its terror. Justin braced himself for its fall. The bay corrected its balance and jockeyed onto the rim, convulsively shaking, wild-eyed, pressed to the granite wall like Velcro.

"Let me help him," Justin yelled to Porky.

Porky's rifle came out of its scabbard and trained on him. "Untie him, Taco."

Taco unwound the rope from his saddle horn, pulled out his pistol and trained it, too, on Justin.

Dragging the length of rope behind him, Justin backtracked to Poncho, who untied Justin's hands. Justin took hold of the reins.

The bay was young, spirited, terrified. Speaking in a soothing tone, Justin stroked the gelding's muscular neck, moving slowly, taking his time, his hands gliding over the animal's shoulders, back, haunches, down his legs. In time, the animal visibly relaxed. Justin backed him up a few feet, led him forward a few feet. He repeated the pattern a dozen times, gradually expanding the distance to ten feet. The animal obeyed, head slightly bowed in a submissive posture. Justin removed his shirt, and after letting the animal smell his odor, tied it over the bay's eyes like a blindfold. Justin proceeded to guide the horse through the same paces, keeping the reins short and controlled. With no hesitation, the animal plodded forward, covering the full length of narrow trail without incident.

Justin removed the shirt and handed the reins back to Poncho.

Tension melted on the faces of father and son. Taco said *'gracias'* under his breath.

Without comment, Porky lowered his rifle.

With a hint of a smile, Taco bound Justin to his saddle horn, and the party continued as though no interruption had occurred.

CHAPTER THIRTY-ONE

WITH THE SUN BLAZING hot on their backs. Sully and Travis rode through bluebunch wheatgrass that moved in waves with the morning wind. The horses carved pathways through the grass like the bows of boats. They passed pockets of red Manzanita and gray boulders that jutted from the earth like the skulls of buried giants.

Nature did a good job of concealing the rustler's tracks, but not a perfect job. Though hoof prints in the earth had been erased by the storm, the damage done to bunchgrass by eight large animals could not be hidden. On occasion, Sully and Travis dismounted and walked in circles through thigh-high blades until they relocated the route. Slowly but steadily, they were trailing the rustlers.

"They sure know this country," Sully said, when they paused to take a break. "Riding through a blinding storm with no visible landmarks." He gazed across the grassland to the distant dun-colored mountains. The only movement on the horizon was a red-tailed hawk lazily riding a thermal. "Why are they headed for Dead Horse Peak? Sheer granite, most of it. Rocky and steep."

"Can't be climbed as far as I know," Travis said. "Beats the hell out of me what men like this would do."

The sun blazed down from a sky so blue it looked like an inverted sea. Sully's face was beaded with sweat and his wet shirt clung to his back. He removed his hat, wiped his forehead with his sleeve, and replaced his hat. Before continuing, he took out his canteen and took a long pull of cool water. Travis did the same.

The climate became more arid as they rode east. The land was rugged and barren, dotted with tufts of gray-green sagebrush and juniper scrub trees. Signs of kangaroo rats, snakes, and lizards were scratched into the ground.

The storm hadn't dropped much rain out here. The tracks of the rustlers could be seen clear as day, heading straight for a dilapidated homesteader's cabin. The shack was propped up by a rotting wood frame and part of the sagging roof opened to the sky. Windows stared outward like blank eyes, and the doorway slanted at an angle like a mouth opened in agony. They dismounted and followed the boot prints to the door. Several nesting birds flew out when they entered, barely missing their heads. The place smelled of smoke and old wood. A fire had recently burned in what was left of the lava rock fireplace.

"Must've been nice to hole up here from the rain," Sully said.

Travis grunted, already heading back to Taba. Not wasting a minute.

CHAPTER THIRTY-TWO

WITH JUSTIN GONE, life on the ranch was mundane and eerily quiet. Cody cycled through her chores, her body feeling listless, hard to move. She had no appetite. Walking around in a lovesick haze, she kept replaying fragments of her last conversation with Justin. Some deep longing had driven her to open up and share intensely personal secrets. She wanted him to understand her in a way no one else could. She wanted to understand him in a way no one else could. She relived the memory of his kisses, the feel of his hands on her skin, his hard body pressed against hers. Those memories stayed with her, lingering like a ghostly presence, no matter what she was doing. Justin had stirred something within in her that felt raw and unquenchable.

At times, imagining the danger he might be in, her emotions shifted to near panic. Anger flared when she thought of all the trouble Bear had caused. The last two days, the foreman had made a point of keeping out of her away, but he strutted around with a cocky expression on his face. Now that he was back with Princess Sarah, he felt on top of his game again.

This morning Sarah, Bear, and Hank had driven to the Willamette Valley, looking to buy new cows. The other hands were out in the lower pastures with packed lunches, clearing debris caused by the storm.

Maresol put out a solitary lunch for Cody; a hot meatball sandwich with melted mozzarella cheese and tomato basil soup. It smelled delicious, but Cody barely touched it, her stomach tightly knotted. She heard the business phone ring in the office and rushed to pick it up. Justin?

"Sterling O," she answered.

"Who's this?" A gruff voice asked.

"Cody Sterling. Who's this?"

"I'm looking for Sully and Travis."

"What do you want with them?" Cody asked, suspecting he might be a reporter. After making the front page of the paper this morning, and a segment aired on the six o'clock news last night, she'd had enough of their personal business offered for public consumption.

"Sully's my boy," he said. "I need to know he's all right."

"Oh, he's all right. He and Travis passed through here just after sunrise."

"I'm coming out there to lend 'em a hand."

"They're long gone, mister. My guess, they can handle themselves just fine without you."

"Don't get smart with me, girl. Just tell me how to get to your place. I've got my horse trailer loaded up, ready to go."

From his stubborn tone, she knew the man would not be swayed. "There're lots of streets. What's your email address? I'll send directions."

"Hell girl, I got me a pen and paper. Shoot."

Cody barely finished giving directions before he brusquely clicked off, foregoing a thank you or goodbye.

***

Pulling a horse trailer behind his Dodge Ram pickup, Joe arrived at Sterling O two hours later. Cody directed him up to the barn and he parked next to Sully's Ford. Though half hidden by his wide brimmed hat, his creased skin told her he was older than her father, maybe sixty. He got out and limped to the back of the trailer, and she noticed his left arm didn't work too well, either. Somewhere along the line he'd had a stroke. How was he supposed to help Sully? He couldn't shoot a rifle with his disability, though he did wear a holstered pistol. Looked like a Glock.

Wasting no time, Joe led a saddled palomino out of the trailer. The horse was in decent enough shape, but like Joe, he was an old timer, his better years behind him. What brand of stupid was this old man? Had his brain been affected by his stroke? The sound of high-pitched barking turned her attention to the cab of the truck where a small, tawny-colored poodle was pawing the window.

"One of my barn rats must've gotten into your cab," she said dryly.

The old man shot her a look.

"He can't stay in your truck while you're gone, and I sure ain't taking care of him."

"He's coming with me. Name's Butch. I'm Joe." As he talked, Joe hung a sling around his neck. He scooped up the dog and eased him inside the sling. Butch's face peered out, brown eyes big as checkers. Cody loved dogs, but one the size of a cat that needed to be carted around, and couldn't protect itself from varmints was useless, especially on the trail. Vulture bait. Stupid just got more stupid. This man wasn't right in the head. He obviously needed her help, which reinforced the decision she had made.

Cody hustled to the barn where Buster stood packed and ready to go. She mounted and rode out of the barn and sat watching Joe tighten the cinch strap under the palomino. He shoved a rifle into its scabbard and heaved himself into the saddle. She had to admit, he moved fast and seemed pretty strong. As Cody nudged the gelding alongside him, the old man's gaze swept over her, Buster, and the provisions she'd packed. He stared her down with a stern expression. "Whatever you think you're up to, the answer's no."

"No way you can stop me."

"We'll see 'bout that. Your dad around?"

"Out of town. I'm an adult. Dad doesn't tell me what to do." She thought of Hank's shocked reaction when he discovered the letter she'd hastily written and left on his desk. In truth, her father would move heaven and hell to keep her from going after the rustlers. But she'd already missed two chances to help Justin. One, by not going with him in the first place, and two, by not trailing Sully and Travis. "You can let me ride along with you mister, or I'll just follow behind. Either way, I'm coming. You sure can't outrun me on that old plow horse of yours."

"Whistler's tougher than he looks," Joe said harshly. "Ain't no place for a female out in the woods chasing murderers. If they start shooting—"

"I'll return fire," she interrupted hotly. "I'm no helpless female. I can ride and shoot better than most men. Certainly better than you, in your current condition."

"I ain't got no condition," he snorted. He pushed his hat back and stared at her with intense blue eyes, his face flushed with anger.

They stared at each other, silent, and she watched the jaw muscles twitch under his skin. Something glinted in his eyes, hard as granite, that frightened her. She realized at once she'd underestimated him. There was more barbed wire in his character than she'd given him credit for.

With a look of impatience, he adjusted himself in the saddle, leather creaking.

She was expecting him to give her hell, but his tightened mouth relaxed, and he suddenly laughed, and looked at her with something like respect.

"Okay, Missy. We'll see whatcha got. But you'll probably be turning 'round and heading home before nightfall."

"You've got a lot to learn about women."

"So I've been told," he said dryly. He pulled the brim of his hat down against the sun. "Show me which way they went."

Cody touched Buster's side with her heels, maneuvered into lead position, and started up the trail toward the ridge, the clopping of the old man's horse right behind her.

It was easy going following the collage of tracks left by Justin, the sheriff's men, and Sully and Travis. At the bottom of the steep ridge all tracks headed north toward the forest and river. Cody and Joe followed mindlessly for a couple of miles until the prints made by Sully and Travis veered away from the trail and headed east into the grasslands. What on earth signaled them to do that? She reined in Buster, took out her binoculars and scanned the basin, seeing endless waves of yellowed grass with little interruption. Dead Horse Peak soared on the horizon, jagged and formidable. Slow moving clouds hung in a deep blue bowl of sky, casting massive shadows on the earth. The air was dry and sharp with the smell of sagebrush.

The ring of Cody's cell phone erupted from her coat pocket, startling her. She fished it out, read the name of the caller, and silently cursed. "Hi, Dad."

"What the hell do you think you're doing?" Hank's voice bellowed into the quiet afternoon. "Maresol just called. She said you took off after the thieves with some old man."

Cody's stomach tightened like knotted rope.

"Turn around right now and head home! Do you hear me?"

Long silence.

"Answer me, Cody!"

She said nothing, but glanced at the old man as he rode up alongside her. His hat shadowed his eyes, but his mouth was clearly visible, turned down in disapproval.

"Cody? Come home now!" Hank's tone held a note of desperation.

"Sorry, Dad. No can do. Love you, too." A little stunned by her own willfulness, she hung up and waited for her nerves to calm down. At age twenty-two, she still found her father's disapproval hard to handle.

She felt the old man's icy stare on her face, but all he said was, "What's the hold up?"

She forced an even tone. "Need to make a call? This is your last chance."

Joe sat almost motionless for a long moment and then he heaved out a sigh. "Yeah. There's somebody I need to call. Dial a number for me, girl."

"My name's Cody."

"Cody, pretty please dial the number for me," he said, in a singsong voice.

Jerk. She punched in the number he recited and handed him the phone.

Joe grabbed it and inadvertently pressed the speaker button. He held the phone to his ear, and she heard it ring three times before a woman's voice answered. Joe's eyes lit up like two candle flames and he broke into a wide-toothed grin.

A dazzling smile for such an old buzzard, Cody thought. He must've been a real lady-killer in his day.

"Ronnie? That you?"

Silence.

"Can you hear me? It's Joe. Can you hear me? Dammit!" He studied the cell phone with a look of perplexity, shook it hard, put it back to his ear. "Can you hear me?"

"Hello?" The woman said. "Joe?"

"Yeah, it's me." He shouted into the receiver. "I just wanna say …."
He rode Whistler a dozen feet away and turned away from Cody, his voice low and passionate. "I been meaning to call … just didn't know if you'd talk to me. You there? Shit. Can you hear me, Ronnie?" After a long, painful silence, he mumbled, "I love you, babe." Looking dejected,

he rode back over to Cody, handed her the phone. "My wife. Don't know if she heard me."

"I think she heard you just fine," Cody said, with a touch of sympathy.

Immediately, the phone rang again.

Joe looked hopeful.

"It's my dad."

His face clouded.

She pressed the off button and shoved the phone into a saddlebag.

"He don't approve of what yer doing," Joe said, with a sharp sting to his words. "As a father, I don't neither. You should turn that pony of yours around and go home."

Undaunted, Cody ignored him and rode on ahead. She and Joe had gotten a late start and needed to make up for lost time. Justin was out there somewhere. Cody meant to make sure he came home safe.

Though Sully's party had left behind a good trail, several times she and Joe dismounted to scan large swaths of grass before getting back on course. Though limping and slow moving, Joe had an uncanny gift for rediscovering it every time. "How did they know the rustlers came this way?" Cody asked. "Are they plugged into satellite surveillance, or some kind of voodoo witchcraft?"

"Travis has a sixth sense," Joe said. "Like a thirsty animal smelling water miles away. What little I know about tracking, I learnt from him."

Joe was a tough old buzzard, she came to recognize, and so was that old horse of his. The occasional squeak of leather and a jingle of the Palomino's bit stayed right behind her as she urged Buster through the tall grass. He allowed her to stay in the lead as the hours ticked by and never complained about the pace she set, stopping only to water the horses and let his mutt do his business.

As the sun melted into a sea of gold and crimson, the grassland fell away and the landscape became sparse and sandy. The tracks became as readable as traffic signs on Main Street. Cody felt a surge of excitement when the prints from Sully's animals caught up to those of eight other shod horses. As Joe rode up alongside her, she said, "They found the rustlers and my horses."

"They're locked on the scent. It's just a matter of time." He pushed up the brim of his hat. "Light's getting too poor to travel."

Despite her exhaustion, Cody wanted to keep going, close the gap between herself and Justin. But the old man was right. The waning light made it impossible, and Joe was looking worn around the edges.

"There's a shack up ahead," Joe said. "Tracks lead right to it."

They approached a lopsided dwelling surrounded by rabbit brush and a few scrappy juniper trees. The desert was dead quiet, with no wind. The spicy smell of juniper seasoned the desert air and sunset tinged everything with gold. Multiple horse tracks and four distinct sets of boot prints came and went from the hovel, then continued east toward Dead Horse Peak.

They dismounted and Joe crouched over some of the boot prints. "They've all been here," he said. "Sully and Travis didn't stay long. Their tracks are fresh. We're five, maybe six hours behind."

The sky was darkening rapidly and there was a noticeable drop in temperature. The poodle yapped loudly as they entered the shack. Panicked birds circled the room and flew into walls before finding their way out through the ceiling. Ashes in the fireplace and scattered cigarette butts told Cody the rustlers had spent a length of time here. "Must've stayed the night after stealing our horses," she said.

"Timing seems right."

"Let's get settled and eat."

"Suits me. We'll head out first light."

They unpacked and tended to the horses while Butch scoured the ground feasting on the scent of lizards and ground squirrels. After collecting a good amount of dead wood, they nested inside with their saddles and provisions, and a roaring fire quickly took the chill out of the room.

Cody set a pot of water to boil on a rusty grill.

Joe spread his bandana on the ground and dumped a handful of kibble on it. The poodle tore into it like a coyote on a carcass, crunching loudly, little tail wagging.

Famished, Cody leafed through her bag of assorted meals, fished out a foil pouch of dried chili, slit it open, and added boiling water. Her stomach rumbled as the smell of spicy beef filled the air. It wouldn't be ready for three minutes. While she waited, she found herself trying to coax the poodle into her lap. She had to admit, the dog was low maintenance and had an easy disposition, but he was having none of her enticement, and stuck by the old man like peanut butter to bread.

She handed her bag of food packets to Joe. "Which one do you want?"

With an amused look, Joe picked through the meals, squinting as he read the names. "Beef stew with peas and carrots, turkey casserole, sweet n' sour chicken." He glanced at her. "Blueberry cheesecake?"

"Yeah. We'll have that for dessert."

"Fancy fixings," he snorted. "You camp like a girl. A rich girl."

"I am a rich girl," she said, matching his surly tone. "Nobody's forcing you to eat it."

"Hell, I'll eat it. Been camping out in the desert my whole life. Never ate this fancy before."

"This may be a new trend." She scooped a spoonful of chili into her mouth. "What do you normally eat?"

"I hunt."

"Around here, you'd be eating ants."

"Seen plenty of ground squirrel burrows. Got me some dried biscuits, too, and jerky. Easy to eat while you're in the saddle."

"Sounds appetizing. Glad I'm not relying on you."

Joe poured water into a foil pouch of chicken stew. "Smells pretty tasty." After waiting the required three minutes, he ate heartily. Dipping his dried biscuits into his stew and talking out of the side of his mouth, he kept up a steady stream of conversation. He related stories of his days as a bare back rider, and later traveling the rodeo circuit for almost two decades with Sully.

Joe was an engrossing storyteller. Cody listened attentively, and she came to admire the hardworking ethic of the Sullivan family, and Travis, and how they built up Dancing Horse Ranch from scratch and came to breed quality horses like Chico. The old man seemed hungry for conversation. Cody figured living with two men was lonely for him, and he desperately missed his wife.

As Joe spoke, his big knuckled hands gently stroked the poodle stretched out at his feet. Butch occasionally twitched in his sleep and his legs started running. She wondered if he was chasing a rabbit in his dreams. Though Joe was a grumpy old coot on the outside, Cody saw he had a tender, sensitive side, but he didn't seem to know how to show it, except to his dog and his horse.

After a while, they both crawled into their sleeping bags and lay in the glow of the dying fire. The wood caved in on itself, sending up a shower of sparks. The silence of the desert enveloped them, punctuated by a popping ember or a bird rustling its nest. Cody had waited all day to be alone in the dark with her thoughts of Justin, and she was warmed by the memory of his kisses.

Joe interrupted her thoughts. "Why're you out here chasing them outlaws, anyway? You think them horses are worth getting killed for?"

Cody answered without opening her eyes. "Yeah, I care about my horses. I also care about someone who's out here looking for them. He left yesterday."

"You sweet on him?"

She smiled. "Yeah. I'm sweet on him."

"He work at your ranch?"

"Yeah. Dad's training him. Justin's a bull rider. A damn good one. Dad thinks he can go all the way to the top." She peered suddenly into the shadows of the ceiling. "Funny thing. His eyes are the same intense blue as yours and Sully's."

There was a long silence, and Cody thought he drifted to sleep.

"What's his last name?" Joe asked in a strained voice.

"Powell."

Another long silence stretched between them. She rolled over and peered at him. Joe was sitting straight up and the look on his face frightened her.

CHAPTER THIRTY-THREE

WITH THE TRACKS easier to follow in the dry earth, Sully and Travis made quick time, reaching the base of Dead Horse Peak by twilight. Soaring high above them, the summit eclipsed the sun, casting the front of the mountain in purple and blue shadows. They set up camp in a niche of boulders sheltered against the wind. A natural spring trickled out of the granite, providing clean water for the horses. Falling into the pattern of past hunting trips, Travis built a fire pit, gathered dead wood and got a good fire blazing. Sully unpacked the animals, placed the saddles and provisions around the pit, and turned out the horses on a picket line to graze on blue wild rye.

Once they were settled in for the night, Travis set a pot of water into the embers. When it boiled, he dropped in a handful of herbs, and unwrapped the dense Paiute bread he baked for horse trips, made of grain, crushed seeds, and dried fruit. Using his antler-handled hunting knife, he quartered apples and cut cheese and thick slices of bread and arranged them on their plates. The scent of sage and cedar filled the air as Sully poured the brew into tin cups. They leaned against their saddles in the shifting smoke, eating and talking, watching the fire spew sparks into the starry night. The two were of the same mindset, and they avoided the dour subject of the murderers they pursued. The conversation veered toward Maggie's surprise appearance in the kitchen last night.

"Maggie's sure easy on the eyes," Travis said with a grin. "You've been seeing her a while now."

"Couple of months. Sorry you had to meet her like that."

"Yeah, you seemed pretty stressed when she showed up."

"She caught me off guard. We had a falling out."

"At a stalemate?"

"Yeah."

"Were you gonna make a move?"

Sully shrugged. "Dunno."

Travis looked amused. "You'd let a woman like that walk away?"

"She wanted space. I was giving it to her."

"Looks like you might've given her too much."

"What's too much?"

"Beats the hell out of me. Women can be tough to figure out."

"Damn tough." Sully chewed on his bread and cheese and washed it down with a gulp of tea. He recalled the hurt and confusion he felt after Maggie dumped him at the party. It reinforced his belief that he wasn't good enough for her. Maggie was rich, educated, and refined, while he was none of those things. Not to mention he was wrestling big financial problems. He had thought seriously about walking away from her for good, licking his wounds, and not looking back. "Guess I've got dad's stubborn pride."

"Yep. That you do."

"Worthless trait."

"She's got backbone," Travis said. "She came to you."

"Yeah. Lucky for me." He was quiet for a few beats. "Maggie's more than I deserve."

"Don't sell yourself short, son." Travis refilled his cup from the blackened pot. "You're a good match for Maggie. She knows it."

Sully was grateful for his old friend's encouragement. "We agreed to be a couple last night."

Travis nodded, his eyes reflecting the dancing flames. "Bring her home for dinner. We want to get to know her."

"Yeah, well … what about Dad?"

"She's a shrink. She can handle Joe."

Sully chewed thoughtfully. "She loved the ranch. Thought the horses were beautiful."

"She ride?"

"Never been on a horse."

"Give her lessons."

"She'd like that."

They finished eating and sat in comfortable silence, lost in their own thoughts. Sully leaned forward, laid more wood on the fire, and stoked the embers with a stick. Sparks shot out like little missiles and he brushed a few embers from his jeans. The heat of the fire grew warm. Travis shook out of his sheepskin jacket. Sully saw he wore his string of agate stones over his flannel shirt. Stones of blue lace, onyx, moss, and ochre, polished smooth, glimmering in the firelight. Chenoah gave them to Travis on their wedding day, after having them blessed by a medicine man. They brimmed with puha. Travis always wore them on hunting trips.

Exhaustion was etched on the old Paiute's face, and he had a slouch to his shoulders. Travis had always been a ready companion no matter what was asked of him, and he wasn't one to complain, but still, Sully worried. This was a tough mission, long days in the saddle over rugged terrain. "We're gonna catch up to the rustlers tomorrow, Travis. Then anything can happen. I'm glad you have your magic stones."

Travis smiled, his face road-mapped with wrinkles. "Wouldn't be without them. Just like the puha in that medal you're wearing. It brought you home from Afghanistan."

Sully fingered the St. Christopher medal, given by a mother to protect her son, and then given to him. He prayed the puha would keep them both safe tomorrow. "I'm calling it a night."

"Sleep good."

"You, too." Sully pulled off his boots and crawled into his sleeping bag with his jacket rolled under his head as a pillow. Lying on his back, he peered at the wide band of the Milky Way arching across the blackened sky. He marveled at the fiery stars hurtling through space, held together by their own gravity, following their designated flight paths as they had for eons, irrespective of ant-sized men and their Everest-sized problems. There were more mysteries in the universe than a man could ever hope to understand.

Sully closed his heavy lids and drifted to sleep. At some point he woke, not sure if he was dreaming. He saw Travis sitting cross-legged, drenched in the fire's glow, half humming, half chanting, rocking a little in the smoky light. Chenoah's beads were clasped in his hands, his fingers moving from one stone to the next, releasing puha.

CHAPTER THIRTY-FOUR

THE GOING WAS STEEP and slippery as the gang descended the north side of Dead Horse Peak, and then mercifully, the cool arms of the forest reached out and enclosed them. They proceeded on a trail no wider than the antlers of a bull elk, curling through the underbrush under a thick canopy of trees. The air was sweet, the vegetation lush and green, the trees and bushes alive with the sounds of animals and birds.

After a few miles of easy riding, the men dismounted at a shallow stream and the horses stepped into the cool water to drink. The air was moist and shrilling with insects. Wildflowers and ferns grew densely along the banks. After scooping water into his mouth with his bound hands, Justin filled his hat and poured water over his flushed face and neck. He sprawled like dead weight on a thick carpet of prickly needles, the muscles in his legs twitching with fatigue.

Something like a pebble fell on his chest. He opened his eyes and found two squares of chocolate sitting on his shirt. Taco stood over him, facing away. With his eyes closed, Justin popped the chocolate into his mouth and let it dissolve slowly. The burst of intense pleasure momentarily overrode his tortuous situation. Considering how precious the chocolate was to the rustlers, he knew this was a generous gesture from Taco—no doubt in appreciation for helping Poncho.

Taco caught Justin's gaze, gave him a subtle nod, and walked away.

After the break, the men mounted up and drove the horses into the shallow stream, and to Justin's surprise, they began using it as a trail, heading north. Justin's hopes sank. Their scent would vanish in the water, so no one could track them. Shuffling through the water was slow going as the horses cautiously searched for firm footing.

Long tortuous miles passed. Several times, Justin slipped on mossy rocks, skinning elbows and knees, and the wet rope tightened and burned his wrists.

An eternity later, Porky abruptly led the way out of the stream onto a deer trail camouflaged by low-hanging branches. How the man knew of these obscure pathways, Justin had no idea. Porky had the instincts of a wild animal. Justin climbed the bank and sloshed onto the trail, his clothes and boots sodden.

The sun hung low in the sky. After trekking another few miles, Justin's boots tightened into vise-like grips, and with each step his foot felt like it was being squeezed into raw meat. The men drank water from their canteens, but no one offered him a drink. His tongue seemed to swell in his mouth every time he watched water dribble down their chins. His stomach rumbled with hunger and the jerky in his pocket called out like a cruel joke. He didn't have enough spit to chew and swallow. He was taking a beating, for sure, but no one was going to save him from it. He had long ago lost track of time. For all he knew, it could have been twenty, thirty miles since sunup at the camp. Stumbling in a pain-filled haze, he tottered a little when he walked. Sheer will pushed him onward.

Darkness was descending, but the men on horseback didn't slow down. Justin tried to lift his mind away from his suffering. He focused on the rhythm of plodding hooves and the wind rustling leaves. He thought he imagined the distant roar of water mingling with the symphony of the forest. Steadily, it grew louder, until it was a crescendo, and the deer trail intersected a wide turbulent band of river. Stepping out from the forest onto the thin band of sandy beach, Justin had no sense of direction. Could this be the Chawtaukee? The river meandered out of sight two hundred yards to the left, and the same distance to the right. The water was liquid pewter in the darkening light.

Justin thought Porky was crazy when he spurred his horse into the water. There was nothing on the other side but a few pine trees hugging a basalt cliff. Waters followed right behind, his horse plunging into the river. Justin was relieved to see that midstream the water was only shoulder high on the horses. Taco's appaloosa splashed into the river next. Justin waded behind into the icy water and was immediately swept downstream by the muscular current. He had little strength to fight it. The rope tightened. Justin was pulled behind the appaloosa by his wrists. He fought to keep his head above water, but he was submerged several times and came up choking and spitting, the force of the rope dragging him steadily to the opposite bank. His feet hit a sandy bank and he stumbled out of the water onto a sliver of shoreline. Waters stood holding tree branches to one side like curtains on a stage, revealing a vertical slit in the granite, barely large enough for a man leading his horse to pass through. Drunkenly, Justin followed the appaloosa through the opening.

Flashlight beams darted along the walls. The tunnel smelled damp and he felt the deep chill coming from the frozen walls. The tunnel opened to a large, cavernous chamber, black with shadows, with several tunnels branching off into the darkness. As light filtered into the room, Justin took in the gang's makeshift homestead, their sore lack of supplies stacked against the walls, dirty blankets hanging on ropes marking off individual sleeping areas.

Poncho untied Justin's raw and swollen wrists, then the boy disappeared with his father, herding the horses down one of the passageways. Soaked to the bone, shivering, leg muscles twitching, Justin collapsed on the ground, emotions numb, and yet he sensed a menacing presence crouching over him. It was Waters, his walleye quivering in its socket.

He hissed through long yellow teeth, "Why ain't you dead, boy? That walk shoulda kilt you. Looks like I'm gonna have to help make that happen."

"Git them lamps going, Waters," Porky said sharply.

Waters glared at Justin.

"Now!" Porky said.

Waters shot Porky a scathing look, got to his feet, and gave Justin a sharp kick to the tailbone. Justin gasped as pain shuddered along his spine.

Waters shot him a vengeful smile, then got to work lighting a half dozen kerosene lanterns.

Refusing to give Waters the pleasure of witnessing his suffering, Justin gritted his teeth and kept his face blank as he surveyed his surroundings. Flickering light shot up the walls and darted across the ceiling. A crevice opened in the vaulted ceiling above a big fire pit. From the amount of soot on the walls, he figured native people must've been using the cave for decades. Two large tree trunks provided seating around the pit, and strips of dried rabbit and venison hung on a crude wooden frame. Justin stared at the meat hungrily.

Puffing on a cigarette, Porky set to work building a fire. When he had a good blaze snapping and popping, he set a blackened coffee pot on the edge of the grill. "Git over here, kid."

Justin peeled himself off the ground and sloshed over to the welcoming fire.

"You're a tough little shit, bull rider. I'll give you that. I figured we'd be leaving ya along the road somewhere."

Justin detected a note of respect in the weathered cowboy's raspy voice.

Porky ripped a soiled blanket off a line and tossed it to him. "Git them wet duds off."

Justin pulled off his hat, which was hanging down his back by the chinstrap, followed by his shirt. His feet were embedded in his boots like concrete blocks. Try as he might, he had no strength to pull them off.

"Git them boots off 'im," Porky said to Waters.

Waters balked. "Hell, no."

Porky said nothing, just gave Waters a withering stare.

"Shit," Waters growled. He grabbed hold of one boot after the other, and with considerable effort, ripped them off Justin's feet while dragging him across the floor.

Justin pushed his wet jeans down over raw, blistery feet. His swollen toes looked inflated with helium. One big toenail was bruised black. Wearing only his skivvies, he wrung out his clothes and laid them on the big rocks encircling the fire, and wrapped himself in the scratchy, smelly blanket close to the heat.

Waters busied himself sorting through Cody's dry meals.

"Whatcha got there?" Porky asked.

"Tuna 'n noodles, spaghetti 'n meatballs, rice 'n chicken, meatloaf 'n taters …."

"Gimme the meatloaf," Porky said.

"I'll have me the tuna," Waters said.

"Give the kid some mush."

With a scowl, Waters uncovered a blackened pot sitting against the rocks, told Justin to put out his hands, and plopped a gluey mass into his cupped palms. Maybe rice. Maybe oats. Justin gulped it down like a starving dog. The sharp howling in his stomach quieted a bit.

Porky passed him a tin cup of water, which he accepted with keen appreciation. After a day of tortuous thirst, it was the cleanest, freshest liquid he'd ever tasted. He held out his cup and Porky refilled it. He drank slowly, relishing the cool, delicious water slipping down his parched throat.

Taco and Poncho rejoined them and spared little time picking out their own meal packets. As the men poured water over their dried food, the cave filled with tantalizing aromas. The smell clawed at Justin's stomach. Feeling wretched and invisible, he watched the men wolf down their grub in obvious bliss.

After dinner, the men sat around the fire belching and making mindless small talk while cleaning their guns and tack. Between them they had a good arsenal of pistols and rifles, and plenty of ammunition. Porky pulled his long-bladed Bowie knife from its sheath and made a display of sharpening it. He worked both sides of the glinting steel against the whetstone, then demonstrated its razor fine edge by slicing through deer bones as though they were butter.

The fire burned low. The men yawned and stretched. To Justin's dismay, Porky surprised him with yet another torment. He encircled Justin's neck with a chain the width of a dog leash and fastened it in place with a small padlock. After locking the other end around the base of one of the tree trunks, he slipped the key into a pocket of his crusty jeans.

"We should leave 'im here tied like a dog when we leave," Waters said with a cruel twist to his mouth. "Let him die real slow. Save us the trouble of burying 'im."

The two Mexicans and Porky ignored him. One by one, the men disappeared behind their partitions.

Justin shuddered at the prospect of slowly dying of starvation in this God forsaken cave, lost to the world. He pondered the motives of the rustlers for being holed up here. None had mentioned future plans. Where were the stolen horses? Lying on the cold, stony ground, wrapped in his smelly blanket, Justin tried to conjure memories of Cody, but the concept of a soft, sweet-smelling woman eluded him. Beset by misery and his grim prospects for escape, he remembered the jerky in the pocket of his jeans, now folded over a boulder at the pit. Lying flat on his back with the chain drawn tight against his neck, he managed to snag the hem of a pant leg between his toes. He dragged his jeans close enough to grab. Still wet, the jerky was tender and delicious. He ate it slowly, savoring every morsel. Then he set to work examining the chain wrapped around the trunk, testing the weakness of each link and the locks, but nothing gave. Resignation set in. He was trapped.

The fire burned itself out and an icy chill settled over the cave. Shivering, Justin floated in a limbo of pain and exhaustion. In a faraway dream, he felt a heavy blanket drop over his body. He stirred, and realized it wasn't a dream. Peering into the blackness, hearing no footsteps pad away, he couldn't identify his benefactor. Wrapping the two blankets around him, he formed a warm cocoon, and experienced a measure of comfort in his pain-racked existence. One of the bastards had a sliver of decency. No doubt, Taco.

CHAPTER THIRTY-FIVE

IT HAD BEEN a long while since Sully had slept outside on the ground, and the experience triggered disturbing memories of Afghanistan. He slept fitfully, explosions thundering all around him, the smell of cordite and sulfur strong in his nostrils. At dawn, he woke thinking he was camped out in the field with fellow Marines, then he saw Travis crouched over the smoky fire brewing coffee. A silvery sheen of frost muted the colors of the landscape and golden morning light crept down from the boulders.

"Morning, Travis."

"Morning."

Shaking off the dark residue of dreams, Sully pulled on his boots and jacket, rolled up his sleeping bag, and joined the old Paiute back at the fire pit.

"Fucking cold up here."

"This'll warm you up." Travis handed Sully coffee in a dented tin cup.

"Thanks." He took a sip of the strong brew and felt heat travel down to his stomach.

They hovered near the fire filling their bellies with bread and cheese and more coffee, then they broke camp, saddled the horses, and packed the mule. Combat memories lingered in Sully's mind as he hoisted himself into the saddle, his muscles stiff with cold.

They rode bulked up in sheepskin coats, hats pulled low, gloved hands on the reins, faces shadowed with stubble. The morning was dead quiet except for hooves clipping stone and the squeak of leather when the men shifted in the saddle. After a few miles through rabbit brush and scrub weed, Sully and Travis encountered a puzzling occurrence. The prints from the thieves were overridden by horse tracks coming down the slope from another trail.

He and Travis dismounted and sat back on their haunches studying the new tracks.

"Hank's stolen horses are being herded up the hill on the north side of the peak," Travis said. "These new tracks are fresher, made by four riders heading south. See the arrow symbol? These new horses belonged to Monty."

"What the hell? Are there more than two thieves?"

"Or the tracks were made by the same two men, going back and forth with different horses."

"Why do they still have four of Monty's horses after six weeks?"

Travis scratched the back of his neck. "Hard to say."

"Must have them holed up somewhere around here."

"If that's the case, maybe they still have Gunner."

"I was thinking the same thing. Let's keep moving. See what's up ahead."

They followed the new tracks about two hundred yards. The new prints turned onto a narrow trail heading up the mountain.

Sully rubbed his chin. "Two sets of tracks. Both heading up the peak on different trails." "Which do we follow?"

"Flip a coin?" Travis half smiled.

Sully smiled back. "Let's stick with the fresh tracks. Better chance of catching up to them."

Travis nodded.

They continued riding, single-file. Sully's gut tightened when he spotted vultures circling the sky a half-mile ahead. Vultures meant only one thing. Something was dead. They came upon a grisly scene. The carcass of a horse was half eaten by animals and birds of prey. They dismounted to inspect the remains.

"Front leg's broken," Sully said. "They had to shoot him."

Swatting flies, Travis examined one of the horse's shoes. "It has the arrow mark. One of Monty's."

Anger rippled in Sully's voice. "What a waste of a fine animal."

"Damn stupid to bring good animals into rugged terrain like this. This carcass is about two days old."

Travis walked around the area studying the pattern of boot prints.

"Two of these men are the same ones we've been following from Hank's ranch. They must've stashed Hank's horses somewhere. They came back out here with fresh horses and two extra men. After shooting this animal, they were down to three horses. The impressions made by one of the horses is deeper. Two men doubled up."

"Why would they come back?" Sully asked.

"Maybe to meet their buyer."

"Makes sense. If we follow their tracks back, we'd probably find evidence of a meeting."

"Right now, we need to stay on their trail, not backtrack."

"Let's roll."

They continued, climbing steadily in elevation. Within an hour they came upon an abandoned campsite. The ground was a maze of tracks and the story told was plain as day. The rustlers had come across the ranch hand, Justin. They had camped here overnight and left the next morning.

Travis's dark eyes flashed. "They took the kid captive."

Sully's anger surged. "Hope to hell they don't take it in their minds to kill him."

"The only reason he's still alive is they think they can use him."

Travis found a few hand-rolled cigarette butts and lifted them to his nose. "I recognize this tobacco. These are the same men who killed Monty and stole Gunner." He crouched over the fire pit and sifted ashes between his fingers. "Campsite's a day old."

Leading their horses and the mule, they followed the tracks out of the campsite.

"One of them is riding Justin's horse," Travis said. "He's on foot."

"We're lighter, and can move faster," Sully said with a new note of urgency. "With luck, we'll catch up to them tonight." Two rustlers had grown into a gang of four, and now they had a hostage. Everything had gotten a lot more dangerous. The old edge of anxiety crept into his stomach that he felt when on patrol in Kunar Province. The potential now existed for an innocent kid to get caught in the middle of a shootout. Sully thought of Eric, who was about the same age as Justin when he was killed. Sully would do everything in his power to bring Justin home alive.

He and Travis followed the tracks to a well-worn elk trail. Sully tilted his head back and surveyed the steep climb up to the peak. "You've gotta be kidding," he said, grateful they had horses. "Hope to hell Justin's in decent shape."

CHAPTER THIRTY-SIX

CHAINED AND HUDDLED in blankets that smelled like moldy dog, Justin sat wide-awake as the gang made sleepy appearances around the fire pit. Porky peeled Justin's clothes off the rocks and tossed them at him.

They were icy, damp, and smelled of smoke. Justin struggled into them, wincing as he squeezed his socks and boots over blisters and swollen toes. Light streaming through the ceiling crevice illuminated the corrugated walls of the volcanic cavern, and Justin recognized the tunnels as lava tubes. The tubes once actively drained molten lava away from the active epicenter of the volcano.

A blazing fire slowly took the chill out of the cave. The smell of coffee blended with Porky's cigarette smoke and the odor of unwashed bodies. Poncho passed strips of dried venison around, along with scoops of glop from the blackened pot. Expressions looked sour all around, eyes crusty, beards scraggly. The men ignored Justin until they finished eating. Seemingly, as an afterthought, Porky told Waters to feed him. With a look of open hostility, Waters dropped a ball of mush on the ground at Justin's feet, then he stepped on it, flattening it to a patty.

Justin kept his eyes lowered. An angry reaction was exactly what Waters wanted.

Waters viciously jerked the leash.

Justin's eyes shut tight as a wave of pain shuddered into his shoulders. Still, he ignored Waters, who stood over him with his hands balled into fists, clearly itching to beat the crap out of him.

The other men watched but no one acted in his defense.

Though trembling from the effort, Justin kept his mouth shut and calmly picked tiny rocks out of his mush. He ate it in small bites, all the while pummeling Waters into a bloody pulp in his imagination.

Slinging curses, Waters grabbed his rifle and strode off down one of the tunnels.

"Taco, take the bull rider outside and put 'im to work." Porky tossed Taco the key to the padlock and limped out of the cavern.

Taco unlocked the chain from Justin's neck and let it clink to the ground. He gestured for Justin to accompany them.

The prospect of seeing daylight again gave Justin a twinge of hope for escape. With a handgun trained on him, Taco and Poncho walked him through the tunnel into the sunlight. Blinking at the brightness, Justin pulled his hat low on his forehead and surveyed his surroundings. The tunnel emerged from a rugged, cone-shaped butte, once an active volcano. Jagged tentacles of hardened lava streamed down the slopes and disappeared into the forest. One arm of lava curled back on itself and formed an enclosure the size of a large arena.

Within this arena a herd of sixteen horses grazed on wild grass. Justin's heart raced as he identified Hank's six quarter horses. Several of the other horses were warm bloods, dressage, and show jumpers, and four had the graceful musculature of thoroughbred racehorses. Judging from the size of the half dozen manure piles stacked outside the enclosure, Justin guessed the animals had been here for weeks. The place stank of shit and the air buzzed with flies. It pained him to see horses kept in such unsanitary conditions. A well-run black-market organization should have had these horses moved out of state weeks ago. Something went wrong in the supply and distribution chain. Judging from their sore lack of supplies, the men had not expected to be camped out this long; unbathed, improperly fed, ready to murder each other.

The squealing of a horse brought Justin's attention to Waters. The scrawny cowboy was mounted on a nervous-looking stallion that was bucking a little, and walking at an angle. Showing a total lack of patience and horse savvy, Waters tried to control the animal with force, digging his spurs into the animal's hide and lashing him with a crop. Welts were visible on the stallion's hindquarters, some old, some fresh. Bristling, Justin stepped forward to intervene. A sharp jab in his side from a pistol made him freeze.

Taco shook his head. A warning.

With effort, Justin fought down his anger. Giving Waters a reason to shoot him on the spot wouldn't help the horse and would only get Justin dead in a hurry.

Porky signaled for Poncho to open a crudely constructed gate and then he and Waters herded the horses out of the corral.

"Where're they going?" Justin asked Poncho in Spanish.

"To find fresh grass," the boy said, swatting flies.

Justin felt relieved. They weren't going to the buyers yet. Once the horses were delivered, he figured he'd be good as dead. These hardened men weren't about to leave a witness alive who could identify them.

After pointing out the manure piles and two rickety wheelbarrows, Taco picked up a shovel and pantomimed shoveling shit. He handed Justin a shovel and said in Spanish. *"Comprende?"*

"Sí. Comprendo."

Justin and Taco got to work pitching manure from the piles into the wheelbarrows. Poncho watched at full attention, the gun trained on Justin, never wavering. When the barrows were full, the men wheeled them out of the corral, pushing them several hundred feet down a deer path and dumping them in the woods. The process was repeated all morning. Though it was mindless, crude labor, something a tractor could do in minutes, it was easy work, a job Justin did every day at Sterling O. Just not by the ton. He stopped periodically to wipe the sweat streaming down his face with the back of his sleeve. It felt good to slip into the coolness of the trees for a few minutes before hiking back.

CHAPTER THIRTY-SEVEN

PANTING HEAVILY after leading the horses up the last few hundred feet, Sully and Travis paused at the summit of Dead Horse Peak to catch their breath. The sun was straight up in the sky and men and animals were slick with sweat. From up here, Sully could see in every direction. Below, the Chawtaukee River slithered through the forest, reflecting the turquoise sky. The path they had just traveled had been narrow and arduous. One stretch had been particularly treacherous, and a frightening challenge for the equines. If their animals weren't as confident and trusting as they were, Sully would never have attempted it. A man had to be a lunatic to drive horses into the high country on a trail suited for mountain goats. Sully's anxiety festered as he considered the fearlessness of the men they were following. They were irrational, unpredictable, cold blooded killers. As smart as any predator in the wild.

The descent was steep, slippery, and sweltering until they trekked off the shoulder of the mountain into the thick canopy of lush forest. The immediate drop in temperature was a welcome relief from the brunt force of the sun. The interior of the forest was a collage of trees and shrubs in cool shades of green and gold. The narrow, smooth deer tail wove around moss-covered rocks and gnarled root systems. Sully and Travis made good time, riding for miles without incident, often sweeping low hanging tree branches and bushes out of their way. An occasional jackrabbit crossed their path, and lizards scurried into the brush. They spotted a herd of mule deer frozen in a shaft of light, their curious eyes watching them pass. By mid-afternoon they came to a wide, cascading stream twisting through the underbrush, the water blinking in the dappled light.

Sully and Travis dismounted and the equines lowered their heads to drink. The maze of tracks told them the gang had stopped here to rest. At its widest point, the streambed stretched thirty feet across and the clear current moved quickly over the sandy bottom. The air was cool and moist, and clouds of insects swarmed around their heads. While the horses drank their fill, Sully and Travis trudged along the bank which was obscured by thick, lush foliage. A decaying tree trunk straddled the water, serving as a footbridge, worn down by the use of wildlife. Crossing to the opposite shore, Sully saw no sign of prints. He crossed back over to Travis. "Seems they're traveling in the water."

"Figures. They're not gonna make it easy for trackers. Which direction is the question."

They walked in opposite directions along the stream. For a hundred yards going south, Sully saw no sign of man or horse. He headed back, catching up to Travis.

"See anything?"

"They came this way." Travis pointed out moss-covered rocks that had been tilted into unnatural positions, something Sully would have missed completely.

They continued riding north, cautiously maneuvering through the stream.

CHAPTER THIRTY-EIGHT

DRIPPING SWEAT, Justin and his jailers stripped off their shirts and worked bare-chested in the sun. Justin's feet felt like raw meat inside his boots. Over the years he'd learned to ignore pain, but still, he gasped from time to time when leather swiped the blisters. He'd kept a close eye on Taco and Poncho all day, looking for a chance to run, but none appeared. Keeping his pistol close, Taco maintained a coiled tension, ever alert. Though he barely reached five feet in height, Taco was as wiry as a Billy goat. Justin judged him to be in his mid-thirties. His weathered skin and calloused hands told Justin he'd spent many years laboring in the sun. His hair and beard were black, and his eyes were as dark as onyx with little delineation between pupil and iris.

Away from Porky and Waters, Taco was a more relaxed man. He spoke rapid Spanish to his son, sharing laughs, gold fillings flashing in his mouth. He and Poncho spoke too fast for Justin to translate, but their good-natured conversation steadied his nerves. Taco was a decent jailer, too, sharing their canteens of water freely. Justin drank deeply and often, rehydrating his parched body.

Once the manure piles were scraped clean, the three rested in the shade, letting the sweat dry on their skin. Taco pulled a faded neck scarf from his pack and unwrapped strips of dried venison. Justin looked the other way, expecting to be excluded, but Poncho poked him in the ribs, and shared their meager meal three ways.

"*Muchas gracias,*" Justin said. They sat eating in the quiet of the woods and after a while, Justin dozed. He awoke to an insistent tap on his boot. Taco stood over him, the ever-present gun aimed at his chest.

"Get up. We need firewood," he said.

Justin looked at him. "You speak English?"

Taco grinned, flashing gold. Poncho laughed gleefully, slapping his knee, as though his father's secret was the funniest damn prank he'd ever seen.

"You speak English, too?" Justin asked Poncho.

"More better than you shitty Spanish." Poncho eyes watered with humor.

"You no tell." Taco's grin disappeared. "Or I keel you."

His cold expression sent a chill down Justin's spine.

After haltering a couple of horses, Taco shouldered two axes and they headed off into the woods. They severed branches from dead trees and hacked them into logs. Sweating and dusty, they finished at dusk. After stacking the wood outside the mouth of the cave, they marched over the rim of the butte and down the other side. Shaded by cottonwood trees, a calm sliver of shoreline hugged the river, large enough for the three of them to sit and stretch their legs. In this protected inlet, the water was clear and smooth, and lapped gently onto the shore. Long shadows stretched across the stony beach into the water.

Poncho shed his clothes and waded out into the cove, his joints knobby on his pencil thin limbs. After sinking up to his neck, he smacked water back at his dad and Justin, laughing, just a regular kid.

Taco surprised Justin by motioning with his gun in the direction of the river. "You go."

Justin didn't hesitate, quickly shedding his clothes. After the first shock of cold, he sank up to his neck and then ducked under the surface, vigorously washing sweat and dust off his skin and hair. After a few minutes, Taco pointed the gun at him, looking nervous. "Come out."

Dripping and cold, Justin slogged onto shore and reseated himself on the prickly sand. Poncho took over as jailer. The boy released the safety, cocked the gun, and aimed the barrel right at Justin's head, his hand rock steady. Justin sat frozen, barely moving his eyes.

Stripped of clothing, Taco's body was all sinewy muscle rippling beneath taut brown skin. He, too, looked thin. Justin wondered how long they'd been living on a crap diet of dried meat and mush. Taco took his time, scrubbing his hair and skin, and then he floated on his back for a while, arms outstretched, eyes closed. He climbed back on shore, running his hands through his shaggy mane, dripping water on his son, who shrieked, then squealed with laughter. The mood between father and son was relaxed and playful, encouraging Justin to take a stab at conversation. "How long you two been here?"

Taco's face immediately darkened. "Too long."

"Six weeks," Poncho said. He and Taco exchanged a look. Clearly, they hated their current situation. Poncho continued, "Papa know Porky from rodeo, long ago. He call Papa. Say come help. Papa needs money, so he say okay. He not know the horses are stolen."

"Waters and Porky did all the stealing?"

"*Sí*. And two men more."

"Who?"

Poncho glanced warily at his father and continued. "Men from ranches."

"Close by?"

"*Sí*. They tell Porky, steal this horse, steal that horse. Then other men come. Take away many horses. They say to Porky they come again and get all the horses. They no come. Porky geeve Papa no monies. He say wait. We wait and wait. Two weeks. Six weeks. Men no come. We geet no monies."

"Who are these men?"

Taco's features tightened and he spoke in Spanish to his son.

"Papa say they *muy peligrosos*."

"Dangerous," Justin said.

Poncho nodded. "*Los Matónes.*"

Adrenalin shot through Justin like a bolt of electricity. "*Los Matónes?*"

"*Sí.*"

Holy Shit! *Los Matónes* was the most vicious drug cartel in Mexico. When Justin was in Arizona they were all over the news. They butchered people. They lopped off heads and limbs and dumped body parts along the Mexican / US border. How the hell did a lowlife like Porky get mixed up with Mexico's most savage crime organization? Justin tried to fit the pieces together. Apparently, Porky and his gang stole horses for two middlemen who were local ranchers. The two ranchers, in turn, sold the horses to the cartel. At the bottom of the totem pole, Porky was the moneyman dishing out their cut to Taco and Waters. Now he understood what kept them in line. Fear of being butchered by the *Matónes*. The cartel would hunt down anyone who swindled their associates. Justin ran his tongue over his dry lips. "When will the *Matónes* come for the rest of the horses?"

"Porky say one day, two days, three days." Poncho shrugged. "Soon."

Fear tightened Justin's gut.

"Basta." Expelling a heavy breath, Taco motioned with the gun, bringing the conversation to an abrupt end. "Clothes on."

Justin wormed into his clothes and yanked his boots over his bloody feet, which were now puffed up like dinner rolls. They trekked back over the butte in the deepening twilight. The horses were back in the corral and flies immediately landed on Justin's bared flesh. Swatting as he walked, he cut a path to the stallion that Waters had been riding, a stunning sorrel with white socks and a star-shaped blaze on his forehead. As Justin approached, the stallion stood motionless with every muscle taut, ears back, ready to bolt. "Easy boy. Easy now."

Guarded, the stallion stretched out his long neck to smell Justin's hand, then jerked away as though electrified.

"It's okay, fella. I wouldn't trust anything with two legs, either."

Other than being frightened the animal seemed to be in good condition. The wounds weren't deep, and the blood had congealed into scabs. Justin felt a gentle nudge on his back and turned to find Juno standing behind him. The big bay nibbled his shirtsleeve, seeking treats. Justin swallowed hard, guilt-stricken. "Sorry I got you into this, buddy." He stroked Juno's muscular neck and took solace from his gentle company.

Taco indulged him, then motioned toward the cave with the rifle.

Back to the pit of hell.

Juno clopped behind him right up to the opening of the lava tube and was still watching when Justin glanced over his shoulder. With a sinking heart he thought of his carefree days at Sterling O, grooming horses in the sweet-smelling barn, eating Maresol's cooking, sleeping in a clean bed. He clung to the hope of seeing Cody again, though she seemed like a fading memory.

Before entering the cavern, Taco nudged him and handed him two strips of venison.

"Gracias. Mucho gracias." Justin's sense of indebtedness to the wiry little Mexican had deepened. He and his son, in their own way,

were as much prisoners of Porky as he was. What might have been an alliance with Taco under other circumstances, even friendship, was severely curtailed. Even if Taco was willing to risk his own personal safety to help Justin, he would never jeopardize his son. Nor would Justin want him to. The boy's welfare came first.

CHAPTER THIRTY-NINE

TRAVIS AND SULLY spent a fruitless hour scanning both sides of the streambed. The forest was darkening, and Sully was giving up hope of finding the gang's exit point. He worried they'd have to repeat the effort tomorrow and lose an entire night. Abruptly, in one fluid movement, Travis turned Taba toward the southern embankment and brought the horse to a halt. "This is it."

Sully positioned Diego next to Taba, squinting in the fading light. "You sure?"

"Look closely. What do you see?"

Sully groaned inwardly. Travis was in teaching mode. From experience, Sully knew they would sit there until he figured it out. "The texture's different," he finally said, even though the light was dim, and he couldn't be certain. "The soil has horizontal markings, but it should be smooth."

Travis nodded. "They used branches to wipe off their tracks. See the bottom branches of the trees?"

Now he saw it. "Yeah, they're bent. Their horses stepped on them while climbing out of the water." He felt deep admiration for his old friend's innate ability. "You've got the eagle eye, Travis."

Following behind Travis and the mule, Sully urged Diego out of the stream and pushed through the bushes. Sully discerned another deer trail burrowing through the undergrowth. They followed the path for some time with night closing in like a heavy blanket. Sully strained to delineate shapes in the shadows. Trees turned into dark pillars that evaporated into velvety black. Sully had to rely entirely on the keen eyesight of his horse. He cursed as a branch scraped his cheek like a whiplash and he wiped away a smear of blood. Stiff-shouldered, feeling his exhaustion in every muscle, he heard the distant sound of rushing water. The resonance grew louder and then the ceiling of the forest opened, and they emerged onto the grainy shoreline of the Chawtaukee River. Moonlight played on the fast moving surface. Trees were etched in silver. Stars were so bright and thick overhead he felt he could reach up and touch them.

He rode alongside Travis. "Their tracks go right into the water." Directly across the river sheer, vertical cliffs loomed above them.

Travis too was staring at the cliffs. Sully watched his eyes narrow, then widen. "I remember this place. My father brought me here when I was a boy." Travis fell silent, as though lost in memories.

Sully tried to wait him out but finally had to ask, "Where are we?"

"Hidden Cave is what my dad called it. I was around eight or nine. We were on a hunting trip and got caught in a lightning storm. We spent the night inside those cliffs."

"There's a cave in there?"

"A helluva cave."

"Let's take a break and eat, figure out what to do from here." Sully turned his horse back toward the cover of trees and Travis followed. They sat on the forest floor on a blanket of pine needles, their empty bellies urging them to eat quickly. Sully poured coffee from the thermos into their cups. "Tell me about this cave."

Travis spoke between bites of bread and cheese. "There's a slit in the rocks behind those trees, right at the water's edge. The river's not deep here. I remember our horses walked across. My dad led me down a long passageway barely wider than a horse. It opened into a huge volcanic cavern. My people camped there for decades during hunting trips. White men used it, too. Outlaws, mostly." He drank coffee, swallowed. "If the gang is in there, we don't have a chance of getting them out."

Sully thought about that. From a tactical standpoint, he knew it would be suicide to go down a passageway that provided no cover. With the positions of the gunmen unknown, Justin could get caught in the crossfire. He chewed his food and washed it down with a second cup of coffee, lukewarm, but black and strong. He started feeling a caffeine rush. "We need to find out if they're in there. Is there another entrance?"

"Yeah," Travis said. "On the other side of that cliff. One of us will have to climb over it. See if the horses are there. I'll go."

"No way."

"Piece of cake," Travis retorted, screwing the top back on the thermos.

"I'm going. End of discussion." Sully knew that Travis was tough as nails and could do anything he put his mind to, but it wasn't a question of strength. The old Paiute looked exhausted, and Sully preferred to be the one placed in a dangerous position. He was younger, stronger, had faster reflexes.

Travis grunted his consent. "I remember something else. There's a smoke hole up on top. You might be able to hear them down below. If they're in there, come right back. We've done our job. Then it's time to call the sheriff." Travis looked tense, reflecting Sully's feelings exactly.

The two began checking their weapons, putting magazines and extra rounds in their pockets. Sully holstered his 92FS and strapped his semi-automatic carbine over his shoulder. Both his Berettas, pistol and rifle, shared the same 9mm magazines and were the civilian version of weapons he used in Afghanistan. He felt as natural carrying them as a schoolboy with a backpack. Sully liked his semi-automatics, but Travis was old school, still using the single action revolver and rifle passed down from his father.

Sully tried to check his impatience as he watched Travis insert six rounds, one at a time, into the cylinder of his bad-ass .357 Magnum with the seven-inch barrel. The thing was a canon. Next he inserted ten rounds into the lever-action rifle. Sully could clip in a whole magazine in the time it took Travis to insert one bullet. But Travis's aim was dead on. In Sully's mind, that made up for the loss of speed. A good man to have watching his back.

CHAPTER FORTY

COLLARED AND CHAINED, Justin did his best to hide his mounting anxiety. He quietly watched the men perform their nightly ritual, eating, cleaning their guns and tack, making mindless conversation.

"We're moving these horses outta here tomorrow," Porky announced without ceremony while sharpening the blade of his bowie knife.

Justin's attention went into high alert.

"We're meeting the buyers tomorrow?" Waters asked excitedly.

"Yeah."

"I geet monies?" Taco asked.

"We all get money," he said, his cigarette quivering between his lips. "And we get the hell outta this fucking cave. We leave at sun up. They're meeting us on a fire road about an hour's ride from here. They get all the horses except the ones we're riding. Once we git paid, we all go our own way." He looked at Poncho and spread his arms out like wings. "Vamoose."

"*Vamoose, sí, sí.*" Taco grinned broadly, flashing gold.

"I'm gittin' outta the horse business," Waters said cheerily. "Gonna buy me a lil' spread in Nevada. Raise cattle. Where you going, Porky?"

"Far away from you as I can git." He shot Waters a murderous look.

Water's face flushed beet red from his collar to his hairline. "You think yer fuckin' easy to live with? If you was my wife, I'd have shot ya dead by now."

"If I hadda marry you, I'd have blown my brains out before ya coulda shot me."

"At least I had a woman. You never could keep one fer long."

"I never beat the crap outta a woman to make her stay."

"A woman needs to know who's boss, just like a dog."

"Only cowards beat women and animals," Justin blurted hotly. It wasn't until every head in the cave snapped in his direction that he realized he'd expressed his anger out loud.

Porky looked amused. Poncho sat motionless. Taco's jaw clenched.

Waters pinned Justin with a look of Charles Manson intensity. "Who asked you, shithead?"

The old cowboy's hatred blossomed like a poisonous cloud, encompassing the entire cave, which had gone deadly quiet. Justin could almost smell his hostility.

"Enough. Everyone pack up tonight," Porky interceded, his raspy voice slicing through the tension. "Come morning, I ain't waiting fer nobody."

"What about him?" Waters sneered at Justin.

Porky concentrated for a moment on the blade of his knife, testing it on a deer bone. It cut clean through. He locked eyes with Waters. "He's coming."

"Hell he is!"

"The Mexicans can have 'im."

"If they don't want 'im, then we need to take care of 'im."

"Killing's yer game, Waters," he growled. "Not mine."

"You've always been yeller, Porky! Leaving me to clean up yer fuckin' messes."

Porky's hand moved so fast it was a blur, his knife a glint of silver slicing through the air. The blade thudded into Water's saddle between two of his fingers.

Waters whipped up his pistol but Porky already had his in hand, aimed and cocked.

"Put it down," Porky said.

Neck veins like wires, Waters didn't move.

"You kill me, no one gits paid." Porky's face was a mask of fierce control. "You too stupid to understand that?"

Waters neck muscles bulged with rage and a vein throbbed like a tiny stream in the center of his forehead. It took almost a full minute before he lowered his weapon.

"Taco, git his gun."

Taco obeyed.

"Take a walk," Porky hissed. "Don't come back 'til you cool off."

"Fuck you!"

"Git, before I change my mind and put two in yer head."

Leering, Waters lurched away from the fire. As he approached, Justin's heart pounded, and his breath caught in his chest.

The gnarly old cowboy strutted past him. Just as Justin lowered his defenses, Waters returned and kicked him in the side of the head. The ground came up and slammed into Justin's skull. He lay dazed. The firelight faded in and out. After a minute or an eternity, someone poured icy water over his head, startling him into consciousness. Nearly blinded by pain, he drew in a whistling breath and sat up slowly, head pounding, vision blurred, mouth filled with blood.

Crouched over him with a canteen in his hand, Taco murmured, "You okay?"

Justin shook his head and felt warm blood trickle from his mouth down his chin. He sat there for a moment, blinking himself back to reality, gritting his teeth, waiting for the red cloud to clear.

Casting him a sympathetic glance, Taco tucked the canteen into Justin's lap, backed away, and went about his business.

Justin rinsed his mouth with water, expelled more blood. His jaw ached, his right eye was swelling shut, and his fingers found a good-sized knot blooming under his hair. Chained like a dog, in a haze of pain and hunger, he was vaguely aware of the fire dying down and the others going to bed. Waters returned and disappeared behind his partition. Justin lay close to the pit trying to absorb the heat. Never in his entire life had he felt so capable of murder. He imagined strangling Waters, then shooting him full of holes, and finally, carving him into small pieces and feeding him to vultures. Tomorrow, he knew, it would be him, not Waters, who would be murdered. He saw no way out of his predicament. The *Matónes* would have no use for him, and Waters was itching to put a bullet in his head. If Justin could somehow find a way to take the sadistic cowboy down with him, he would do it. He knew God would forgive him. A man like Waters should not be running around loose, hurting people and animals.

Justin sank into a fitful sleep. He woke in the night, his body aching and drenched in sweat. He imagined a small stone fell from above and hit his blanket. Then a heavier stone hit his shoulder. He opened his eyes, expecting to see Waters toying with him. The glowing embers in the fire pit cast feeble light against the shadows. No dark figure loomed over him. Another stone hit his arm. He looked up and studied the crack in the ceiling. Some wild animal must be up there walking about. Through the opening he saw bright chips of stars piercing the black sky and he recognized part of the Big Dipper.

Something moved. The silhouette of an animal's head jutted over the edge. *Holy hell!* An arm appeared, waving. Shock jolted Justin's system. He waved back. He'd been found! He would be rescued!

The man tossed down something else, and it thudded on the blanket. A fist-sized chunk of bread!

Justin looked back up. The man was gone. Electrified, he trained his gaze on the crevice as he pulled the bread apart and ate it in small bites, savoring the flavor of nuts and fruit. If he was rescued and got out of this jamb, Justin swore he would never again take food and water for granted. He lay still, muscles taut, nerves exposed, listening for any small sound coming from above, or from the lava tubes. Any moment, someone would be coming to his aid, at least lowering a weapon on a rope. A gun! How long had the man been up there? Was he a cop with reinforcements?

Time passed. An eon. Justin waited, his eyes glued to the crevice. Stars moved slowly across the sky. The man did not return. Lying in the dark, listening to the snores and gurgles rumbling through the cavern, Justin's thoughts swirled in his mind like dust devils. Finally, it dawned on him that no weapon would be lowered. For good reason. In his current state, Justin might be tempted to use it. He'd only get off a couple rounds before getting himself shot full of holes. The smart thing for his rescuers to do was wait until morning. The gang would be out of the cave and mounted on horseback, away from shelter, and then they could easily be surrounded and captured.

CHAPTER FORTY-ONE

FEELING THE HUM of adrenaline in his veins, Sully descended the cliff to the riverbank below. The thin lip of beach was deserted except for a muscular bull elk dipping his head into the water, his head crowned by a five-point rack. The low, insistent hooting of an owl cut through the roar of water. Travis. Sully followed the sound into the cover of trees and found Travis waiting with the mule and horses. He looked relieved to see Sully in one piece.

"They in there?"

"Yeah," Sully said, breathing hard. "Heavily armed.

"How many?"

"Four. But one's just a kid."

"You were up there a good couple of hours. Hear anything?"

"You bet I did. We got here just in time. They're heading out at dawn to meet their buyers."

"Where?"

"Some fire road. An hour's ride from here."

"Did you see Justin?"

"Yeah, they've got him chained up. Some cowpoke named Waters is itching to kill him. He'd probably be dead if it wasn't for Porky, the ringleader."

"Waters and Porky. Sounds familiar." Travis mulled over the information. "I remember now. A couple years back they were wanted for murder in Beaverhead. They got off. Lack of evidence. Those two have been kicking around rodeos for years. Petty criminals."

"Not hard to see how they'd graduated to horse theft."

"Pays better. See any horses?"

"Yeah. There's a herd round the back."

"Gunner one of them?"

"Too dark to tell."

Travis pulled the satellite phone from his saddlebag and handed it to Sully. "Call the sheriff."

Sully dialed nine-one-one and got the emergency call center. They put him on hold while connecting him to Sheriff Turner's cell phone. Turner got on the line sounding sleepy. His voice sharpened as Sully filled him in. Turner shot him a few questions and asked for their GPS coordinates.

Sully said, "We'll be trailing them when they leave that cave at daybreak."

"I'll get a dozen men out there," Turner said. "Shouldn't be too hard to find you. Aren't many fire roads back in there. Update me when you get closer to their meeting place."

"Copy that."

"And Sully …."

"Yeah?"

"Don't act on your own."

"Copy."

***

The gang was up at first light, moving through the cavern with speed and purpose, rolling up bedrolls, carrying their tack outdoors. Justin felt no more shooting pains through his skull, just a dull headache and recurring dizziness, which he could control if he didn't move too suddenly.

When the cavern was empty, Taco unleashed him and ushered him out to the corral. The men were mounted and looked eager to set out, holsters strapped to belts, rifles in scabbards, hands gloved. Mounted on the high-strung stallion, Waters pinned Justin with his one good eye, lifted his hand, and fired an imaginary pistol.

Taco directed Justin to mount one of Hank's saddled quarter horses, a gray-dappled gelding named Bandit. Justin knew the gelding well. He was thankful he wouldn't be walking, but his gratitude was short lived. Taco tied his hands to the saddle horn and tied Bandit to his appaloosa on a lead rope. Christ. No way to escape if shooting breaks out.

Above the tree line, a band of gold was rinsing away the dark of night. The breath of men and horses mingled, steaming in the cold morning air. There was a creaking of saddles and clinking of bridles. Bodies pitched forward to head out of the fly-infested corral. With the stolen horses herded in the middle, the caravan followed a deer trail through a field of yellow grass, heading west.

A dozen miles disappeared beneath the hooves and the sky turned from pink to pale blue. Porky steered them onto a fire road, heading north. The road cut through stands of lodgepole pine and silver-trunked aspen. A cold wind blew out of the north and made the trees rustle like living things. Trees had been thinned back on each side of the road for fire control, and Justin peered a good hundred yards into the forest. No sign of a rescue operation. What's taking so long? A chilling realization hit him. His rescuers didn't know the buyers were *Los Matónes*. If the gang reached the cartel before the cops intervened, there would be hell to pay, and he'd be caught in the middle. His fingers gripped the saddle horn, white-knuckled. Despite the cold, sweat trickled down his spine.

The gang and horses entered a large clearing and Porky raised his arm, signaling the men to slow down. Just ahead under a canopy of giant ponderosa pines, three long horse trailers were parked with their back doors open, ramps down. Each was hitched to a white Ford-550. Six Mexican men, dressed like cowboys and bulked up with muscle, stood in a row in front of the trailers, pistols and rifles strapped to their bodies.

Porky halted his procession thirty feet short of the Mexicans. Fighting down a wave of nausea, Justin studied their hard-set expressions. Each looked like he could kill a man a dozen different ways with his bare hands.

"*Hola, Manuel,*" Porky called out.

Not a single *Matóne* cracked an expression. A stern-faced man with a compact build and trimmed gray beard stepped forward from the shadows. The grin on his face was fixed, joyless. "*Hola*, Porky. Right on time."

Porky dismounted and joined him. Manuel wore neatly creased jeans, a white chambray shirt, snakeskin boots, and an immaculate white Stetson.

Reed thin, hollow-cheeked, with scraggly beard and dirt-encrusted clothes, Porky faced him eye to eye. Justin had gotten used to the sour odor of unwashed bodies, but Porky must have smelled rank to the well-groomed Mexican. Equally foul-looking, the rest of Porky's gang sat taut in their saddles. Looking like they just crawled out of a cave, Justin thought without mirth.

They spoke in subdued tones. Manuel and three of his men examined the hooves and teeth of the stolen horses and ran their hands down their legs. Looking pleased as hell. Justin glanced up the cliff to the right, and then into the forest to the left. Nothing. The back of his shirt was damp with sweat.

CHAPTER FORTY-TWO

HIDDEN BEHIND a ridge of boulders midway up the cliff, Sully watched the proceedings below through binoculars. The Mexicans were examining the horses. A stab of unease worked its way between his ribs. Three other Mexicans stood watching from the shade of the trees. There was nothing amateurish in their appearance and posturing, or in the caliber of their weapons. They reminded him of the private security he'd seen in Afghanistan. Special Ops. Killing machines. He listened as Travis called in their coordinates to Sheriff Turner.

"We got the buyers in our sights. Six Mexicans armed to the teeth. Driving three white Ford 550s, each hauling a six-horse trailer. They look ex-military." Travis listened for a minute, making no comment. When he signed off, his expression was deeply troubled.

"Bad news?"

"We're fucked. The sheriff thinks these Mexican's are *Los Matónes*."

Frost crawled along Sully's spine. "The cartel that chops off people's heads?"

"Yeah. That one." Travis looked tense.

Sully had seen the cartel blasted all over the news for months. They were notorious for moving drugs through the U.S. by the tons, and for killing sprees in Mexican towns near the border. Their signature was a trail of mutilated corpses dumped along the border.

"Sheriff said they buy horses in the U.S. using drug money, then sell them south of the border to wealthy drug lords. Hundreds of cops down there are on their payroll."

Sully felt a keen sense of urgency. "How close is the sheriff?"

"The Mexicans knocked out a bridge. They're looking for another way to drive their trucks across the river."

"Shit." Three gristled horse thieves and a kid had turned into a heavily armed crime gang, and Sully's backup was running around stranded. He lifted his binoculars and scanned the unsaddled horses, hoping Gunner was one of them. He wasn't. Sully inched the binoculars over to the mounted rustlers and felt heat move up the back of his neck. His show-horse stallion was prancing nervously beneath the sadistic cowboy from the cave, Waters. Blood trickled from wounds made by the cowboy's spurs, and welts were visible on Gunner's hindquarters. Sully's trigger finger itched. "Gunner's down there."

Travis raised his own binoculars. "Christ almighty. Who's the bastard riding him?"

"Someone who's gonna get his ass kicked. Waters." Sully struggled to get his temper in check. Too soon to act. He needed back up. And lots of it. He scanned over to Justin, his hands tied to the saddle horn, face bruised and swollen. Sitting in the saddle like a man bracing for a deathblow. After witnessing Water's vicious assault on him last night, it had been all Sully could do to keep from firing down a shot. He could only imagine how Justin must feel; helpless to defend himself, or escape.

Sully surveyed the area under the trees. Behind one of the trailers stood two Caucasian men dressed like ranchers. One was unusually tall and muscular, his face hidden by his hat, yet there was no mistaking his identity. Sully's gut tightened. "Travis, you see what I'm seeing?"

"Hell, yeah. Hank's foreman. Sonuvabitch. Why am I not surprised?"

"You recognize the guy he's with?"

"Never seen him before." The other man, around Sully's age, had an athletic build and hefty arms. "We just found our middlemen."

Tumblers started turning in Sully's mind. "Makes sense. Bear does business all over Oregon."

"He knows all the ranchers, all the horses."

"Damn." Sully searched the distant terrain, but he didn't see any dust clouds rising from moving vehicles. "Where the hell is the sheriff? These *Matónes* aren't planning on peaceful negotiation."

"No reason to. There's enough muscle down there to take what they want. Unless he's dumber than hell, Porky knows he's facing an execution."

Sully lowered his binoculars. "We're gonna have to act."

"We'll try to save Justin and the Mexican boy. The rest of 'em can go to hell."

Feeling a cold watery feeling in his stomach, Sully looked his old friend in the eye and drew strength from his calm determination. Shit was about to fly. Travis wasn't fearless, but like Sully, he'd risk his life doing what was right.

"Let's roll," Sully said. Surefooted and quiet, he and Travis started down the steep terrain, needing to get within better shooting range while everyone was distracted.

CHAPTER FORTY-THREE

NO RESCUERS had materialized to save Justin, and now he wondered if his head injury induced hallucinations last night—the man appearing in the opening, the bread he ate ….

Justin watched two of the *Matónes* move over to the stallion Waters was riding.

"Fuck off." Waters spit dryly in their direction. "Ain't nobody taking this horse."

One of the Mexicans snickered. The other gave him the finger before they walked back to join their comrades under the trees.

"You got yer horses," Porky said to Manuel. "Where's our money?"

"Get the horses in the trailers," Manuel said.

"Not 'til you pay up." Porky had a dangerous note to his tone.

Something in Manuel's face stiffened.

Lined up like a squadron, the *Matónes* stood poised for trouble, fingers closing in on triggers.

Porky's raspy voice echoed through the meadow. "Bear, you gonna stand there and do nothing?"

After a long moment, Bear strutted out of the shadows into the bright sunlight. Kenny McKinley stepped out beside him.

Justin went rigid. *Jesus. I am so dead.*

"We did our part," Porky's voice called out. "There's about a million bucks worth of horseflesh here. We agreed on a quarter of that. We been waiting weeks to git our money. This how ya do business nowadays?"

Bear's voice rumbled into the quiet morning, straining with anger. "You screwed up, Porky. You killed a rancher two months back. Then you fucked up at Sterling O. Got only six horses. Shot at people. That put a spotlight on us, and a manhunt. Makes it difficult to get these animals out of the country."

"That killing warn't our fault," Waters yelled back. "The ol' man shot first. We gotta right to defend ourselves."

"What about the farrier? You saying he shot first? You ambushed Mateo!"

"He was gonna rat us out," Waters said.

"No killing! That was our agreement. Now the area's so hot, we can't do business here anymore. We got no use for partners like you. You're gonna pay for that mistake by giving us these horses free of charge. In exchange, Manuel's gonna let you live."

A hush fell over the men. Justin could see Porky's neck flush red.

Kenny broke the silence. "Leave the horses and get the hell outta here."

No one moved.

"Turn around," Bear echoed. "Ride the hell away!"

"So you can shoot us in the back?" Porky said.

"What? You don't trust us?" Graybeard laughed a mirthless laugh. He turned and spoke rapid Spanish to his men. Looking arrogant, his men laughed, too. They were cocksure of their superior position.

Acting so fast it was a blur, Porky whipped his Sig Sauer from its holster with one hand and pulled Graybeard back in a chokehold with the other, the barrel digging deep into his cheek. In an instantaneous clatter of metal, every Mexican and every rustler raised their rifles. The barrels of eight semi-automatics were leveled at each other. No one twitched.

Justin viewed the scene with an exquisite hyper focus of the details. Everything seemed to move in slow motion. Birds flitted in tree branches. A horse snorted. A fly landed on his chin and traveled up to his eye. He didn't blink.

As though in a photograph, Bear and Kenny stood frozen in the middle of the confrontation, unarmed, like him, their faces drained of color.

***

"Holy shit!" Sully whispered. Barricaded behind a row of corrugated boulders, he and Travis watched the tense scene below with their weapons raised and aimed. Sully felt the familiar heaviness in his chest, the pounding of blood in his temples. They were all in that quiet zone that anticipates an intense blast of danger.

Porky's voice sliced into the silence as he addressed the six Mexicans. "Put yer guns down, or your boss is dead."

Manuel's face flushed deep red. He struggled to breathe.

None of the Mexicans moved.

Porky lowered his Sig and fired a round into Graybeard's thigh. A sharp crack in the quiet morning. A red stain blossomed on Manuel's creased jeans and traveled rapidly down his leg.

"Guns down!" Graybeard gasped, his face screwed up with pain.

His men lowered their weapons.

"All of 'em!" Porky growled.

Pistols snapped out of holsters and were planted on the ground.

"Git me my money. Now!"

The Mexicans looked anxiously at each other, but no one budged.

Porky rammed his knee into Graybeard's thigh.

Manual shrieked and collapsed against Porky's chest, blood forming a widening pool around his boots. He gasped for air and trembled. "Get him the money!"

One of his men bolted into the cab of a truck, came back with a briefcase, snapped it open.

Already on the ground, Waters quickly leafed through the stacks of bills. "All here." He shut the briefcase, mounted his horse, and fired several rounds into the air. The explosions startled the unsaddled horses into a stampede. They headed straight for the trailers. The Mexicans dove for cover.

Porky pushed Graybeard away, shot him in the back, then slung himself into Juno's saddle. He took off at a gallop, followed by his gang. Leaning low over their saddles, the men wove in and out of the forest dodging trees at blinding speed. Taco's appaloosa raced at a dead heat, pulling Justin's horse behind.

A sudden continuous burst of automatic fire was unleashed at their backs. Even high on the ridge, Sully heard branches splintering and rounds thudding into tree trunks.

Sully and Travis fired their weapons. Their rounds exploded into fountains of dirt and ripped through the metal of trucks and trailers. Through the hazy dust, Sully made out three outlaws lying motionless on the ground. The others found cover, including Bear and the rancher.

Graybeard and two of his foot soldiers were dead. That left five men still alive and heavily armed.

A sudden hurricane of bullets blasted up the hill at their position. Chunks of steel-jacketed lead flattened against surrounding rocks with a deafening clamor. Crouching low, Sully and Travis were unable to get in a shot. Sully heard a grunt and saw Travis grip his left arm. Blood oozed between his fingers and streamed down his sleeve.

Sully had a sensation of being under water, life moving at quarter speed. He couldn't get to Travis fast enough. Then life resumed at hyper speed. Sully whipped off his neck scarf and wrapped it tightly over the wound.

"I'm okay," Travis gasped, his face stained with dust and sweat. With a determined expression, he pulled out his .357 Magnum, and cocked it with his right hand.

Chipped stone ricocheted in every direction. The air thickened with powdered stone and gun smoke. Then the fire from below lost its intensity. Sully shot a glance over the barricade. Two men were climbing up the hill, one from each direction. One was Bear. One was a Mexican. The other three shooters remained below, providing cover. Sully clipped a full magazine into his CX4 Storm and took aim at the advancing Mexican. Travis had one eye squinted, tracking Bear. They both fired.

CHAPTER FORTY-FOUR

AT BREAKNECK SPEED, Porky's gang backtracked down the fire road and veered onto a narrow deer trail. Porky signaled for the gang to slow down. They came to a stop in a small grassy meadow dissected by a shallow stream and encircled by conifer forest. Everyone but Justin and Porky dismounted at the water's edge. The panting, sweating horses stepped into the stream and lowered their heads to drink. Porky slid out of the saddle. Justin saw he'd caught a bullet in his left shoulder. The bumpy ride hadn't done the wound much good. Blood stained the front of his shirt and dripped over his jeans. Gripping his revolver, he lowered himself to the ground and leaned against the trunk of a fallen tree, his face pinched with pain. The two men and the boy stood anxiously watching him.

"I know first aid," Justin said to Porky. "I packed bandages in Juno's saddle bag."

"Untie 'im," Porky said, sucking air into his lungs.

Taco removed his bindings and Justin slid out of the saddle. Poncho handed him the first aid kit and Justin knelt in the grass next to Porky. "Give me your knife. I need to cut your shirt off."

"Keep an eye on 'im," Porky said to Waters, who had a tight hold on the briefcase.

Waters freed a hand and aimed his pistol at Justin's head. "Gimme one reason to blow your head off."

The Bowie knife swished out of its leather sheath. The long blade caught the sunlight as Porky handed it to Justin. Its razor-sharp edge sliced easily through the bloodied shirt. Justin examined the wound, which was as round as his thumb. He checked behind Porky's shoulder. No exit wound. The bullet was still in there. First order, stop the bleeding.

"This is gonna hurt."

"Do it."

Justin ripped open a packet of chemical hemostat, held the wound open, poured in the powder, and applied firm pressure.

Porky gasped, sucked in air, gripped the shaft of his pistol, white-knuckled.

Tough old bastard. After a gel seal formed over the wound, Justin taped a clean bandage over it. "I need something to make a sling."

"You boy, take off your shirt," Waters said to Poncho.

Poncho lifted his chin and his dark eyes blazed with defiance. "Theeze my only shirt."

Waters grabbed a handful of the boy's shaggy mane and yanked his head back. 'Take it off."

Taco stepped forward and hissed, "Let go my boy."

Waters shoved Poncho away.

Reluctantly, the boy removed his shirt. His thin body looked fragile, almost skeletal in the bright morning light.

Justin sliced into the fabric and fashioned a sling to support Porky's arm, tying it behind his grizzled neck. "The bullet's still in there," Justin said. "You need to get to an ER."

"Fuck that," Porky spat.

Frowning, Justin squatted at the stream and washed blood from his hands. Porky's knife was hidden up his left sleeve.

"Bring that money over here," Porky said weakly.

"Let's split it. I wanna head out of here." Waters sounded nervous, his walleye twitching wildly.

Porky raised his Sig. "Don't take a dollar more'n what's yours. Taco, watch 'im."

Waters knelt in the grass, unsnapped the brass latch, and lifted the lid. The two Mexicans leaned in closely, watching. Justin kept a respectable distance. The case contained multiple packets of hundred-dollar bills.

"Divide it in half," Porky said. "Then we each give the Mexican $10,000," Porky wheezed. "That seem fair?" he asked Taco. "Fer six weeks work?"

"*Si, si.*" Taco looked anxious, glancing around. "I keep two horses, yes?"

"Take the damn horses," Waters said. "Jes keep yer mouth shut. We don't ever wanna see you again. Comprende?"

"*Sí.*"

Waters divided the money, handed Taco his share, and the two men wasted no time stuffing their camp bags. Waters left Porky's share in the briefcase, snapped it shut, and placed it under Porky's arm.

Porky's revolver trembled in his hand and his face looked deathly pale as he pinned Waters with his steely gaze. "I cain't believe I'm lying here all shot up, and yer able-bodied. You kilt that rancher and his dogs. You killed Mateo, and you tried to kill Roth and Hank's girl. You're a murdering piece of shit, Waters. You should be lying here all shot up, not me."

Waters secured the straps on his saddlebag and smirked as he glanced over at Porky. "Life ain't fair."

Sickened by Waters callousness, Justin felt an irresistible urge, an itch, to wipe the smirk off his face. It was all he could do to restrain himself. He felt indebted to the crusty old cowboy who had kept him alive. If not for Porky's wily instincts back at the meadow, the whole gang would be dead.

Waters turned to Justin. "Mount up, asshole. You's coming with me."

Justin tasted copper on his tongue and felt a deep sinking sensation in the pit of his stomach. The time of his murder was approaching. Waters would no doubt shoot him as soon as he came upon a place to dump his body.

Justin looked to Porky for help but the wounded cowboy had slumped forward with his head on his chest. Unconscious, or dead. Justin bent over him and heard Porky's thin, raspy breathing. He laid his head back against the trunk so he could breathe more easily.

"How he is?" Poncho asked.

"Not good," Justin said.

The words were barely spoken before Waters grabbed Poncho by the arm and raised his gun to the boy's head. "Drop yer gun, Taco."

Poncho's eyes widened with fear.

Taco clenched his jaw tight. He carefully lowered his rifle to his feet.

"Gimme yer bag of money," Water's said. "And Porky's."

Taco hesitated, gazing at Porky.

"He don't need it," Waters said. "He ain't long fer this world. Hand it over, or I shoot yer boy."

Justin let the handle of Porky's knife drop from his sleeve to his hand, praying he could remain calm enough to accurately throw it.

Poncho's face had drained of color.

Taco placed the briefcase and his own bag of money at the cowboy's feet. Waters shoved the boy aside and bent over to grab the bags.

As Waters stood, Justin drew his arm back until his elbow was level with his head, then he snapped his arm forward in an even, smooth arc. The nine-inch blade struck Waters with force, buried in his gut up to the hilt.

The scrawny cowboy staggered backwards from the impact. He stared at the protruding handle, then peered at Justin, a comical expression on his face. Mouth gaped open. Eyes so wide the whites showed all around. With a shaky hand, he aimed his pistol at Justin.

A thunderous gunshot cracked the air.

Waters was thrown backwards into the tall yellow grass and a geyser of blood spurted from his chest. Startled birds flew from trees in a wild beating of wings. Waters lay spread-eagle, a gurgling sound coming from his throat, blood bubbling from his mouth.

Justin stood over him and waited until his legs stopped twitching before he pried the pistol from his fingers. He glanced at the edge of the forest and caught a puff of fading gun smoke.

Taco bent to pick up his rifle. Another shot rang out and a bullet thwacked into the log next to his feet. Taco and Poncho both raised their arms.

Leading their horses, two men came out of the trees with guns drawn, one limping. The other broke into a sprint. "Justin! Justin!"

Cody!

Cody flew into his arms, knocking off her hat. He held her so tight he felt her heart thumping against his chest. He pulled away and took her in. "Man, you look so fucking beautiful!"

Her face crumpled with emotion. Tears gave way and filled her eyes. "I was so worried."

"Hey, don't cry. I'm fine." He brushed her tears away with his dirty thumbs and left smudges across her cheeks.

"You look like hell. Who beat you?" she sniffed.

"The psycho lying there." Justin nodded at Water's body. "You saved my life. You're a hell of a shot."

"That wasn't me," Cody said. "That was Joe."

Her limping companion hobbled up and joined them, his handgun aimed at the two Mexicans. What the hell? Joe was an old man who appeared to have the use of only one arm. A small dog poked his head from a pouch hanging from his shoulders.

"Get their guns," the old man said sharply, nodding toward the Mexicans. Justin picked up the discarded firearms and packed them onto Juno. He tucked Porky's Sig into his waistband.

"Tie them up," the old man said.

"They didn't steal the horses," Justin said, wanting to let them go.

"I don't give a shit. Tie 'em, up."

Justin proceeded to tie up Poncho and Taco to a branch of the fallen tree. Without his shirt, Poncho looked as scrawny as a street orphan, his ribcage visible through his skin. He had shown bravery and loyalty to his father to the bitter end. "Sorry I have to do this, guys," he said, remembering their many kindnesses. Taco's expression remained stony. The boy's dark eyes welled with tears. Before he turned away, Justin winked at Taco. He had tied their knots loosely.

Justin pulled Cody into his arms again. After the foul company of the rustlers, she felt luscious, and smelled like a flower garden. "Jesus, you smell good. Sorry. I know I don't."

"I don't care. I just don't ever want you out of my sight again."

"Fine by me," he whispered. They stood with their foreheads touching. The world disappeared until the old man's urgent voice brought him back to earth.

"Where's Sully? Where's Travis?"

"I don't know who you're talking about."

"They came to rescue you and them horses."

Justin thought for a moment. "Were you on top of the cave last night?"

"No," Cody said. "We got to the cave this morning. You'd already cleared out."

"Must've been the guys you're talking about," Justin said. "Just now, there was a lot of shooting back where the Mexican's were."

"Take us there," the old man barked.

They mounted their horses and set off at a gallop. Within minutes Justin heard automatic fire and saw a haze of dust and smoke through the trees. Joe stopped at the edge of the clearing and assessed the situation. A shootout was going on at fever pitch. Shots were being fired up the hill from two points near the trailers, and two positions partway up the hill. Higher up, two men were shooting down the hill, returning fire with more precision and focus.

"The outlaws are down below," Justin said. "That must be Sully and Travis up there."

Joe said, "You keep the two guys by the trailer busy. I'll get the other two."

"Stay put," Justin said to Cody. Not waiting for a response, he followed the old man into the fray at a full gallop. He caught a Mexican outlaw by surprise. The man stepped out from behind a ponderosa pine and turned his assault rifle toward Justin.

Justin had the clear advantage as he squeezed the trigger of the Sig. It clicked several times on empty chambers. Shit. I'm dead.

The Mexican was propelled backwards against a trailer and blood spurted from his chest. He collapsed in a heap.

Justin saw Cody race past him in a blur, rifle raised. She directed her aim at the other man behind the trailer, pinning him down. Christ, she was a good shot.

Justin dismounted, grabbed the dead man's weapon and ducked behind the massive ponderosa. Before he could form another thought, a burst of automatic fire ripped into the trunk, one bullet coming so close Justin felt the movement of air against his cheek. The shooter behind the trailer! Justin's heart pounded as he returned fire, ripping up the dirt, pelting the side of the trailer. Holy shit! He'd never fired this kind of weapon before. Justin proceeded to swap rounds, keeping him too busy to shoot at Joe and Cody.

CHAPTER FORTY-FIVE

SULLY WATCHED two men on horseback appear in the clearing firing their weapons at the outlaws. Another rider had dismounted and was exchanging fire with the shooter behind the trailer. He and Travis were nearly out of ammo. He was down to half a magazine. Outmatched and outgunned, they wouldn't have lasted much longer.

"Help's here, Travis," Sully said. "We'll get you help soon."

"God willing." Slumped against a boulder, Travis's face looked clammy. His breathing was shallow and labored. He had only been firing off just a round or two before stopping to rest.

Positioned thirty feet down the hill, a Mexican outlaw continued firing at Sully while Bear turned his aim to the horsemen below. Sully had to act fast before one of the horsemen got hit. "Travis, I gotta get the Mexican to show himself."

The old Paiute nodded, a spark of fire in his eyes. He weakly fired off a few rounds as Sully darted from the protection of the boulders. The Mexican shooter raised his head a few inches above his barricade, took aim, and fired. Rounds exploded near Sully's feet and ricocheted off the rocks behind him. He felt something slam into his boot. His scalp suddenly burned as though sliced with a hot knife. As he flattened himself behind a low ridge, he heard a loud grunt and watched the top of the Mexican's head explode. The man fell over backwards and plummeted off the steep bank to the ground below. Only one cartridge could do that kind of damage. Sully peered at Travis, who was still poised with his .357 Magnum. Badass Travis!

The crime ring had been whittled down to two shooters. Sully heaved out a sigh, and felt blood running down his face. He removed his hat, stuck his finger through a bullet hole, and then touched the top of his scalp where a bullet grazed it. He whistled when he checked out his boot and saw a bullet lodged in the heel. Too close!

From his new position, Sully had a better view of the horsemen. He realized at once they weren't law enforcement. *Who the hell are they?* The palomino looked like Whistler. *Holy shit! It was Joe!* Sully's stomach twisted. *Thank God he hadn't been shot!*

Sully spotted dust clouds. A half dozen SUVs raced toward them from about a mile out. They couldn't get here soon enough. Anger at Bear coursed through him like venom as he turned back to the business at hand. With one eye pinned to the telescope of his weapon, he waited for the hulk to make a move.

***

Screeching to a halt, the Yukons formed a half circle around the trailers. Armed men poured from every door and took positions behind their vehicles. Through the layers of dust, Justin caught a glimpse of the sheriff crouching behind his open door.

The shooter Justin had been exchanging fire with suddenly darted from behind the trailer and made a run for the woods. *Kenny McKinley!* The ground ripped up behind him as Justin sprayed the area with bullets. Kenny clutched his butt cheek, stumbled, regained his balance, and disappeared in the brush. Justin sprinted after him.

As the lawmen positioned themselves behind their cars, Sully saw Joe and the other rider melt into the safety of the trees. He felt an immediate release of tension. *Dad was safe!* The firefight had come to an abrupt halt. The sudden silence was piercing. Gunshots still rang in his ears.

Sheriff Turner's voice cut through the quiet morning. "Sully, you okay?"

"I'm okay. Travis is hit," Sully hollered back. "One shooter's forty feet below me. Another is behind the first trailer."

"Put down your weapons," Turner commanded. "There's nowhere to run."

Silence.

"Show yourselves. Hands up."

No response.

Sully knew Bear and the other remaining outlaw had two options. Surrender, or die. How stupid were they going to be?

Turner signaled and a half dozen men blasted their firearms at the rocks below Sully. It sounded like Afghanistan. When the thunderous clamor ceased, ammo bursts echoed in his ears.

"Don't shoot! I'm hit." Bear's voice rumbled down the hill.

"Come out."

Bear rose unsteadily from behind his barricade, one massive arm raised, the other covered in blood, pressed to his gut.

A few deputies outfitted in SWAT gear rushed up to him, while others cautiously combed through the horse trailers and trucks. They brought out no captive. Must have been shot, Sully surmised.

Sully released the grip on his rifle, wiped his sweaty hands on his jeans, and took his first easy breath since the shooting started. He rushed over to Travis and found the old Paiute collapsed on his side, his breathing shallow. "We're getting you outta here."

EMTs worked quickly and methodically to stabilize Travis and Bear, administering IVs and oxygen masks. Sully stayed planted at the old Pauite's side, anxiously watching as two techs did their job.

Joe rode up on Whistler and slid out of the saddle with Butch hanging from his shoulders in a pouch. He looked sick with worry, ready to collapse. "How's he doing?" Joe asked one of the techs.

"Not good."

Joe squeezed the old Paiute's hand. "Hang tough, Travis. You can make it."

The distant sound of a rotor beat grew louder and a chopper swooped over the treetops. It hovered above the clearing, then descended to the middle of the field. The wind from the rotors flattened the tall grass and it rippled outward in waves. The EMTs loaded the two wounded men inside and climbed on board. Sully and Joe stood in the rotor current, shirts snapping back, holding onto their hats, watching the bird take off and disappear over the trees. Sully felt a quiet sense of desperation. *Please let him make it.*

"He squeezed my hand," Joe croaked.

Sully took in his father's wilted face and sagging posture. Joe made an exhaustive, rugged trip that even challenged Sully, and fearlessly rode into the middle of a battle. He saved the lives of Sully and Travis. Sully pulled his father into a bear hug and held him close, the only way he knew how to thank him and tell him how much he loved him. "You need to rest, Dad."

***

The light in the thickly timbered forest was dappled and muted. Justin's heart thumped in his chest as he moved cautiously from tree to tree, following the drops of blood scattered over the pine needles. Kenny was losing blood and had to be getting weaker. Justin came across his discarded rifle, out of ammo.

A movement in his peripheral vision warned him to bolt behind a tree. Rounds tore into the trunk and sprayed his face with sharp bits of bark. He felt warm blood running down his cheek. Sucking in a breath, he yelled, "Give it up, Kenny. You wanna die out here?"

Kenny fired off more rounds. Chips of bark exploded like wayward missiles from the trunks of surrounding trees. Justin's hands were shaking. Wind rattled the branches above him and he became aware of the sound of his own labored breathing. "There's nowhere to go, Kenny. Everyone knows you and Bear are involved."

Kenny unloaded his weapon, shooting wildly, rounds ripping up the forest floor.

When Justin heard the chambers of Kenny's gun click empty, he sprinted forward. He spotted the wounded man on his knees behind a downed fir, fumbling with his magazine, hands shaking worse than Justin's. Rounding the tangled arms of the root pan, Justin sent the weapon flying out of his hands with a swift kick, then he brought down the butt of his rifle squarely on Kenny's nose. Kenny fell backwards, moaning, his nose smashed to one side, gushing blood.

"That's for all the shit you've put me through," Justin hissed through clenched teeth. "Get the fuck up, before I spray you with more bullets."

CHAPTER FORTY-SIX

THE CLEARING was bathed in sharp light and it was hotter than hell. Bulked up with body armor, the sheriff's deputies fell into automatic protocol. Their shirts sprouted sweat stains as they swept over the crime scene, marking evidence and cordoning off areas with yellow tape. A couple of officers were snapping photos of the bodies from every angle. The stolen horses had wandered back into the grove and deputies were herding them into the trailers.

Pushing up the brim of his hat, Sully joined the sheriff, who had pulled his Yukon into the shade of the trees.

"We got a bunch of bodies out here," Turner barked into his radio transmitter. "I need a forensic team, the coroner, and body bags, pronto. In this heat, these bodies are gonna swell up faster than bologna on a skillet. Over." He looked up at Sully. "You Michael Sullivan?"

"Sully."

"Sorry as hell to take so long getting here. The *Matónes* took out a bridge. We had to go twenty miles out of our way to cross the river, twenty miles back." He shoved out his free hand and shook Sully's with a look of respect. "Looks like you did the job for us. No picnic out here. These guys look like seasoned killers. You military?"

"Marine. Travis, too."

"Helluva job." The radio crackled and the sheriff got back to work.

Sully saw Joe lying prone in the shaded grass, his hat covering his face, Butch cradled in his arm. He'd been through the grinder the last two days. Pride swelled Sully's chest. Hell, the old man still had it in him! He scanned the area looking for Justin and was surprised to see Cody Sterling. The other rider! Jesus! Annie Oakley!

Cody was looking from left to right with a panicked expression. She spotted Sully and the sheriff and rushed over to them. "Have you seen Justin?"

As though on cue, Bear's partner in crime limped into the clearing with blood oozing from his battered nose. He was panting through his mouth and he had a red sheen over his teeth. Justin prodded him forward with a rifle barrel to his back. "He's shot in the ass," Justin announced with great satisfaction.

Looking impressed, two deputies stepped forward and relieved him of his prisoner.

At the sight of McKinley, Sheriff Turner's lips tightened. His glasses caught the sunlight for a moment, and he barked into the radio. "Get another Medevac chopper out here. We got another gunshot victim." He said to Sully. "I'll be goddamned. Who would have thought? Kenny McKinley and Todd Behr. The two pricks behind all this mayhem. Both shot up pretty good. Serves 'em right."

Justin barely had time to lower his weapon before Cody rushed him like a defensive tackle and glued herself to his body. The two engaged in a long, steamy kiss.

Sully smiled, imagining the kiss he was going to give Maggie when he returned. When the two came up for air, the tenderness in their eyes as they looked at each other was almost painful to watch. Justin draped an arm around her shoulder, and they crossed the clearing to join Sully and the sheriff.

"Helluva job, bringing in McKinley. Helluva job." With a wide grin, the sheriff clapped Justin on the back.

Justin's face didn't relax under the praise. He said with a note of urgency, "There're more horse thieves down the road a few miles. One's dead. One's dying. There are stolen horses out there, too, and a big pile of money."

The sheriff's jaw dropped a little.

Justin hurriedly relayed how Cody and Joe showed up just in time to save his life. "Then all three of us rode back here."

Into a war zone, Sully thought, his throat tightening. Putting their lives at risk to save him and Travis.

"We need to get out there," Turner said. Static crackled from his radio and a voice came through, breaking up a little. Turner picked up the receiver. "We got another crime scene. I'm sending deputies over there right now."

"Thanks for your help," Sully turned to Justin and Cody. "Don't think I'd be standing here, if not for you."

A shy smile from her, a shrug from him. His face was bruised and bloody, and the area around his left eye was swollen, reminding Sully of Marines who'd been through fierce combat. Sully proudly shook his hand. "I'm Sully."

"I'm Justin. Was that you on the roof of the cave last night?"

"Yeah. Sorry I couldn't get to you sooner."

"No worries. It all worked out."

"Who's the old cowboy with the dog? I need to thank him."

"My dad," Sully said.

"I ain't so old," Joe said, limping over with Butch at his heels.

"I'm Justin. Can't believe you shot Waters from that distance. You saved my life." He thrust out his hand.

"I know who you are," Joe said.

Sully was struck by what happened next. Joe pulled the young man close to his chest and held him tight. After releasing him, he peered into the young man's eyes as though searching for recognition. "You got no clue who I am, do you?"

Justin looked bewildered. "No. Should I?"

Sully, too, was puzzled, and then it hit him with a burst of understanding. There was no mistaking Joe's genetic legacy. Justin's fierce blue eyes mirrored Joe's exactly. As he watched the tender look his father bestowed on his half-brother, Sully felt something prick at the back of his eyes.

Justin rubbed his chin, clueless.

Sheriff Turner interrupted their tender family moment. "Justin, can you take three of my deputies out to that crime scene? We're gonna get that chopper out there after it picks up Kenny."

"Sure, but vehicles can't get back in there. Only horses. A chopper can get down easily enough. It's a good-sized meadow."

"I'll ride over with you," Sully said. "My stallion's one of the stolen horses."

"Beautiful sorrel, white blaze and socks?" Justin asked.

"That's him."

"He's safely tethered."

Sully exhaled, relieved.

Turner turned to his deputy. "Ryan, mount up with Jesse and Phil. Follow these guys. When you get there, tape it off, take photos. Send coordinates for the chopper."

"Got it."

"I'm coming, too," Joe said doggedly.

Turner looked at Joe, his eyes flicking over the old man's haggard face and slouched shoulders. "I got something else for you to do. I need statements. I'll start with you and Cody."

Turner turned back to Sully and Justin. "Bring those horses back here. We'll trailer them, and give you all a lift to Sterling O."

"Sounds good," Sully said. They had all spent too much time in the saddle the last couple days, especially Joe.

The men started out on the trail. Riding side-by-side, Justin and Sully made light conversation. Sully observed his half-brother with open curiosity, picking up on familiar mannerisms and expressions that were obviously encoded in Sullivan DNA. He wasn't surprised to discover Justin was a pro bull rider and had ridden Hanks's champion bulls to eight seconds. Athletic ability ran in the Sullivan family. It still hadn't dawned on Justin that he'd come face to face with his own blood relatives. Sully wondered how long he should wait until he had "the conversation" with his half-brother, informing him that Joe was the father who abandoned him when he was three-years-old.

CHAPTER FORTY-SEVEN

THE COLD BEER tasted good. With food in his stomach, and his body scrubbed clean of grime, Justin felt half human again. He sat barefoot in the kitchen nook wearing baggy cotton pajamas while Maresol fussed over him like a hen with a chick.

"Eat, eat." She refilled his bowl with her hearty chicken soup and placed another cold Corona in front of him.

"Gracias, Maresol. I sure missed your cooking." His blistered feet were propped up on a chair, too swollen for shoes. His scabbed and swollen face was unrecognizable, and his lids felt lead-lined. He needed to pass out in his clean, comfortable bed and hibernate for about two weeks. His brain was numb and his whole body ached, but never in his life had he felt happier. He was alive. Bear was gone for good. Sterling O was now Justin's permanent home. Most miraculously of all, Cody loved him! Despite his weariness, little tremors of pleasure pulsed through him like the aftershocks of an earthquake.

His mind raced backwards over the events of the day. After the deputies hauled the horses and people back to Sterling O, there had been a happy reunion. Hot food, cold beer. Everyone grateful as hell the horses were returned. Sully, Joe, Cody, and Justin were hailed as heroes. It all seemed surreal to Justin, like he was living a mythical story out of a novel. Floating in a half-conscious state of exhaustion, he figured he'd wake up soon to find it all a dream. After one beer and some chow, clearly dead on their feet, Sully and Joe left for home. The celebration had been lost on them. Until Travis was out of the woods, they'd be weighed down with worry.

"A couple of decent, solid cowboys," Hank said with admiration as everyone watched them drive down the driveway. The affection they felt, and the debt they owed to Travis and the Sullivan men, could not be measured, or even framed with words.

The only one not celebrating was Sarah, who had placed herself in self-imposed exile, nursing her bruised ego and terrible judgment. It would take some time, Justin imagined, for her to get back on track, and hopefully find happiness without the necessity of a man. "She's got a lot to work out with her therapist," Hank confided.

Cody had vanished to her bedroom within minutes of coming home. Hank barred the hands from the kitchen so Justin could rest, then he plopped down next to him in the nook, and the two men had a candid conversation. Justin went into detail about his near-death experience at the hands of Waters, his rescue by Cody and Joe, and then his second near-death experience at the big shootout, rescued by Cody.

Hank listened with an alarmed expression. "You knifed a man? Cody killed someone?"

"I probably shouldn't have told you that part." Embarrassed, Justin stared down at his soup.

Hank heaved out a sigh, shook his head. "It's a lot to take in. Yeah, it scares the hell out of me to think what you kids went through. But I'm also proud of your quick thinking, and courage. You did what needed to be done. Kill, or be killed. You got rid of some real scum. Men who would have continued to hurt people. As far as Cody goes, it's clear she's not going to allow herself to be a victim again."

Reliving the whole chain of events, Justin felt numb. He wanted to block it out completely.

"Seems Cody is always saving your ass," Hank said with a touch of humor. "You better hang on to her, son."

"I intend to." The two men locked eyes and Justin knew Hank fully approved of their relationship.

"Finish your story," Hank said.

Justin went on to recap how he, Sully, and the deputies had ridden to the second crime scene only to discover the two Mexicans had escaped, taking their share of the money and two of Monty's horses. He did not disclose the part he played in their escape. That was a secret he would take to the grave. The father and son now had enough cash to give them a new start in life, far from the reach of *Los Matónes*. Porky was still alive, thanks to Justin's quick ER treatment, and he and Kenny were evacuated to a trauma center in Portland.

"Bear, Kenny, and Porky will be seeing the inside of a prison cell for a long time to come," Hank said.

"I plan to put in a good word for Porky at his trial," Justin said. "He's a thief, not a murderer."

"Follow your conscience, Justin."

As Justin worked his way through his second bowl of soup, Hank briefed him on the investigation of Jessica McKinley. "My P.I. cornered her while she was sitting outside a coffee shop downtown, accompanied by a baby boy in a stroller. My P.I. took a seat at her table and informed her she was facing arrest for sexually assaulting a minor, named Justin Powell, and she'd have to provide a sample of the baby's DNA. Jessica admitted nothing. In fact, she emphatically declared you're not the father, because she never had sex with you, and if charges were brought, it would be your word against hers. She left in a huff. My quick-thinking P.I. slipped the baby's pacifier into his pocket, and we had his DNA analyzed."

"Who's the father?" Justin asked with apprehension.

"Kenny."

"Kenny?" Justin shook his head. "Holy hell."

"That women's a piece of work."

"Yeah, she is. She was really making the rounds. What did Jabe have to say about it?"

"Doesn't know yet. We just got the results back. He still believes you're the father, and that you raped her. We'll report her to law enforcement this week." Hank paused a few beats before continuing. "Did you confide in anyone at the time that you were having sex with her? Any friends?"

"No. Never told anyone."

Hank rubbed the back of his neck. "There's not much we can do without evidence. The DA won't charge her if he can't win the case. You willing to file a complaint? At least it'll go down on record."

"Yeah," Justin said without hesitation. "It'll clear my name and let that psycho family know I'm not the father. When Jabe finds out Jessica was shagging Kenny under his roof, all hell will break loose."

"She'll pay for her sins one way or another."

"Amen." Relief washed through Justin in a warm rush. Two years of looking over his shoulder had come to an end. He could now go anywhere he wanted without worrying about being attacked. "I'd give my eyeteeth to witness Jabe's face when he finds out his son is also his grandson."

"Me, too. Hallmark moment."

"Thank you, Hank," Justin said with feeling. "For all your help."

"Get some rest." Hank squeezed his shoulder and left him alone to eat.

Justin finished his soup, shuffled to his room, and wasted no time getting horizontal between the sheets. The bed felt like a cloud; clean, soft, warm. Within minutes, he fell into a sucking quicksand of disturbing dreams. He tossed fitfully, and woke several times, thinking he was lying on the cold floor of the cave shackled like a dog, with Waters standing over him, the knife pulled out of his gut, ready to plunge into Justin.

Sometime in the black pitch of night, he felt the mattress compress beside him, and a warm body moved into his arms. He recognized Cody's shampoo. He held her close, dozing off now and then into short bursts of intense sleep; waking and touching her, being touched, listening to her murmurs of content. Everywhere her hands touched felt like it was being healed. He swept back her hair and brushed his lips across her ear. His hands moved softly over her breasts, tracing the seams of her scars, whispering she was beautiful. He drifted back to sleep until her voice ruffled the edges of his consciousness.

"I love you, Justin."

"I love you, Cody. With all my heart and soul."

CHAPTER FORTY-EIGHT

Four Months Later

GENTLY SWAYING in the saddle of a sweet old gelding named Sam, Maggie's gaze swept over the stunning landscape before returning to Sully, who rode Diego a horse length in front of her. They were crossing a flower-specked meadow on the lower flank of Blanca Peak. They had never ridden this far from the ranch, probably ten miles. After weeks of lessons in the arena and dozens of rides on easy trails, Maggie had demonstrated she could stay balanced on a horse. Today she had wanted to ride a horse with spirit, but Sully insisted she ride lumbering old Sam.

The trail widened and they rode two abreast to the sandy shore of Flathead Lake. Reflected on the surface were the autumn colors of the surrounding forest and the mountain's craggy snow-capped peaks. A startled throng of birds flew up from the grass and flitted out over the lake with a loud flapping of wings. The horses stepped into the water and lowered their heads to drink.

"God's country," Maggie said, soaking in the beauty.

Sully tipped his hat lower against the sun. "Travis and I used to camp up here when I was a kid. We used to fish all day, then Travis grilled our steelhead trout over the campfire with salt pork and potatoes. Some of the best meals I ever had."

"You're making me hungry."

He grinned. "Let's eat. We can spread the quilt over there in the shade."

They rode beneath the leafy canopy of a giant cottonwood.

"Hold on, let me help you down." Sully quickly dismounted and reached up for her.

"Sully, you have to stop worrying about every little thing. I'm pregnant, not helpless. Women have been having babies for thousands of years."

"Nothing wrong with being careful."

She knew he was right. At her age, being pregnant was a miracle. He caught her from behind as she slid down from the saddle, and pulled her against his chest, his hands roaming over her belly under her T-shirt. "I can't wait until you're as big as a watermelon, and I can feel our baby inside you."

"That's months away. Right now, our baby's the size of a pea pod." She leaned back against him, loving the feel of his rough hands on her skin. She turned to face him, and they kissed. Long, sweet, slow. His love poured in like sunshine, filling her entire being. "You're going to be a great dad." They kissed again.

"Let's have that picnic," he said softly. "Then I want to lie down and hold you in my arms under this beautiful sky. We'll head back soon. Mom needs help with dinner. Justin and Cody are coming at five."

She heard the slight edge to his voice. A lot was at stake. He wanted desperately to have his family reunited; his parents, and his half-brother. Tonight was an important first step, if everything went well. She and Sully had visited Justin at Sterling O numerous times. The half-brothers had quickly formed a deep bond. At the Sterling ranch, they had celebrated Justin's rodeo win that bumped him into tenth place in the world, and more importantly, his engagement to Cody, who was walking around with a sizable diamond on her finger.

The one sad note to these events was Justin's refusal to include Joe. Sully worked tirelessly on his father's behalf, gently shaping the idea that Justin should give Joe a chance. Maggie understood the young man's feelings. He had spent a lifetime scorning the man who abandoned him as a child. The fact that Joe saved his life as an adult, and now suddenly wanted to be accepted by him as his father, triggered a range of conflicting emotions. Justin's reluctant consent to bring Cody to dinner at Dancing Horse Ranch tonight showed he had a fundamental desire to forgive his father. The dinner would either be a love-fest, or an emotionally charged family confrontation.

Maggie helped Sully spread the quilt over the fragrant grass. They ate egg salad sandwiches, drank sweet tea in plastic cups, and spoke about their future plans. Her house was on the market. When it sold, the money would go toward the construction of their new home in the meadow at the ranch, as Sully had envisioned it, with a few modifications that suited Maggie.

After living alone for so long, becoming part of Sully's ready-made family was a blessing. Now fully recovered, Travis was teaching her how to make home remedies from medicinal plants. Maggie and Ronnie spent time gardening, cooking, and riding together. Though Ronnie was settled comfortably in the cottage on the creek, she was spending evenings in the big house with Joe, reestablishing old patterns. They were finding their way back to each other.

Wind rustled the branches above. The diamond ring on Maggie's hand sparkled in the dappled light. Six weeks ago, when she broke the news to Sully that she was pregnant, he was through-the-roof happy, and he suggested that they marry right away. Maggie said no to a quick ceremony at City Hall. Life slowed down in November at both ranches, and Justin would be taking a break after the PBR World Finals in Las Vegas. Perfect timing for a church wedding in the little white chapel in Wild Horse Creek, followed by a sit-down reception, with good food, music, dancing, and all their family in attendance.

Sully's voice drifted into her thoughts. "If our baby's a boy, let's name him Grant, after your granddad."

"If it's a girl?"

Lines of pleasure crinkled at the corners of his eyes. "Emily. After your grandma."

"I'll add those to our growing list." She smiled. Sully changed his mind about names every few days.

The long ride, the food, and the warmth of the sun made her drowsy. She lay with her head tucked into the curve of Sully's shoulder, his arms holding her close. They lay quietly. Soon she heard the familiar rumble of his soft snores and felt herself drifting into a peaceful sleep.

REVIEW *Hidden Part 2*

and

receive a FREE eBook by Linda Berry

Limited Supply

Contact Linda: lindaberrywriter@gmail.com

Also by Linda Berry:

THE KILLING WOODS

Book One of the Sidney Becker Mysteries

CHAPTER ONE

BAILEY'S LOW, INSISTENT growls woke Ann from a dreamless sleep. She found herself sprawled on the overstuffed easy chair in the living room, feet propped on the ottoman, drool trickling down her chin. Half opening one eye, she peered at the antique clock on the mantle: 11:00 p.m.

She heard Bailey sniffing at the front door, and then the clicks of his claws traveled to the open window in the living room. She opened her other eye. The sable hound stood sifting the breeze through his muzzle with a sense of urgency. Ann knew what was coming next. Sure enough, Bailey trotted back to the front door and whimpered, gazing expectantly over one shoulder. Damn those big brown eyes.

Normally Ann would be in bed by now, but she passed out after dinner, exhausted from carting her boxes of organic products to town at sunrise and standing for hours in her stall at the farmers market. By the time she loaded her truck and headed home, the pain in her calves had spread up her legs to her back and shoulders, and she felt every one of her forty-five years.

Bailey whined without let up. He knew how to play her. Ann looked longingly toward her bedroom before returning to the hound's pleading eyes. This was more urgent than a potty break.

No doubt, he had caught the scent of a deer or rabbit and wanted desperately to assail it with ferocious barking to assert his dominance over her small farm. Then he'd settle in for the night.

Since an unsolved murder rocked her town three years ago, Ann resisted going out after dark. Still, she felt a pang of guilt. She and Bailey had missed their usual after dinner walk. If the spirited hound didn't exhaust his combustible energy, he'd be circling her bed at dawn, demanding that she rise.

"Okay, Bailey, you win." Ann heard the weariness in her voice as she heaved herself from the chair. Fatigue had settled into every part of her body and her limbs felt as heavy as flour sacks. "Only a half-mile up the highway and back."

Bailey sat at attention, tail vigorously thumping the floor.

Still dressed in jeans, a turtleneck sweater, and sturdy hiking shoes, Ann grabbed her Gore-Tex jacket from the coat rack, wrestled her arms through the sleeves, pulled Bailey's leash from a pocket, and snapped it onto his collar. The boards creaked softly as they stepped onto the covered front porch into the damp autumn chill. The moist air held the promise of the season's first frost. Her flashlight beam found the stone walkway, then the gravel driveway leading to the highway. A good rain had barreled through while she slept, and a strong wind unleashed the pungent fragrance of lavender and rosemary from her garden. Silvered in the moonlight, furrowed fields of tomatoes, herbs, and flowers sloped down to the shoreline of Lake Kalapuya, where her Tri-hull motorboat dipped and bobbed by the dock. A half-mile across the lurching waves, the lights of Garnerville shimmered through a tattered mist on the opposite shore.

Following the hound's tug on the leash, Ann picked up her pace, breathing deeply, her mind sharpening, muscles loosening. Steam rose off the asphalt. Scattered puddles reflected moonlight like pieces of glass. The thick forest of Douglas fir, red cedar, and big leaf maple engulfed both sides of the highway, surrendering to the occasional farm or ranch. Treetops swayed, branches dipped and waved, whispered and creaked. The night was alive with the sounds of frogs croaking and water dripping. The smell of apples perfumed the air as she trekked past her nearest neighbor's orchards. Miko's two-story clapboard farmhouse floated on a shallow sea of mist, windows black, yellow porch light fingering the darkness.

Ann didn't mingle with her neighbors, few as they were, and she took special pains to avoid Miko, whose wife had been the victim of the brutal murder in the woods adjacent to his property. The killer was never found, but an air of suspicion hovered over Miko ever since. Ann detested gossip and ignored it. She had her own reasons for avoiding Miko—and all other men, for that matter.

When they reached the narrow dirt road where they habitually turned to hike into the woods, Bailey froze, nose twitching, locked on a scent. He tugged hard at the leash, wanting her to follow.

"No," she said firmly, peering into the black mouth of the forest—a light-spangled paradise by day—black, damp, and ominous by night. "Let's go home."

Bailey trembled in his stance, growled with unusual intensity, and tugged harder. The hound had latched onto a rivulet of odor he wanted desperately to explore.

Ann jerked the leash. "Bailey, home!"

Normally obedient, Bailey ignored her. Using his seventy pounds of muscle as leverage, he yanked two, three times until the leash ripped from her fingers. Off he bounded, swallowed instantly by the darkness crouching beyond her feeble cone of light.

"Bailey! Come!"

No sound, just the incessant drip of water. Ann's beam probed the woods, jerking to the left, then the right. "Bailey!" She heard a steady, muffled, distant bark.

He's found what he's looking for. Bailey's barking abruptly ceased. Good. He's on his way back. She waited. No movement. No appearance of Bailey's big sable head emerging through the pitch.

Ann trembled as fear took possession of her senses. She bolted recklessly into the woods, her light beam bouncing along a trail that looked utterly foreign in the dark. Her feet crushed wet leaves and sloshed through puddles. Her left arm protected her face from the errant branch crossing her path. A second too late she saw the gnarled tree-root which seemed to jump out and snag her foot. She fell headlong, left hand breaking the fall, flashlight skidding beneath a carpet of leaves and pine needles. Blackness enveloped her. Shakily, she pulled herself to her feet, left wrist throbbing, trying to delineate shapes in the darkness, the moist scent of decay suffocating.

The forest was deathly still, seeming to hold its breath.

Soft rustling.

Silence.

Rustling again.

Something moved quietly and steadily through the underbrush. Adrenaline shot up her arms like electric shocks. Ann swept her hands beneath mounds of wet leaves, grasping roots and cones until her fingers closed around the shaft of her flashlight. She thumbed the switch and cut a slow swath from left to right, her light splintering between trees. Her beam froze on a hooded figure moving backward through the brush dragging a woman, her bare feet bumping through the tangled debris.

The man kept his face completely motionless, eyes fixed on hers in a chilling stare. The world became soaked in a hideous and wondrous slowness. He lowered the woman to the ground and hung his long arms at his side. He was quiet; so was Ann. He radiated stillness. The stillness of a tree. It was hypnotic.

Ann felt paralyzed. Tongue dry. Thoughts sluggish. Then threads of white-hot terror ripped through her chest and propelled her like a fired missile into motion. Switching off the beam, she turned and sprinted like a frightened doe back along the trail.

His footfalls crushed the earth behind her, breaking through brush, snapping branches, his breathing thunderous. Any moment, he would yank her by the hair and pull her down.

Ann's world narrowed to a pinpoint. Everything except survival ceased to exist. She darted off the trail, skidded down a steep ravine, hobbled and splashed across Deer Creek, heard the man bulldoze through thickets, plummet down the slope, stumble, fall, curse, regain his balance, resume crashing after her like a bear through a woodpile, heaving, staggering, steps slowing down as he splashed through the creek.

Ann ran light-footed and sure, shoes springing off the deep mulch of the forest floor. She understood the features of the marsh that lay ahead. The smell of peat moss and a current of frigid air guided her steps. Her footsteps sank deeper into wet earth and soon she was wading into the black shallows through dense clumps of reeds. When she reached a monstrous fir that lay like a great beast across the wetland, Ann crawled beneath the carcass of rotting wood. She backed into the hollow where Bailey once hid and refused to come out. Jagged wood scratched her skin and cold water swelled through her clothes and hair, shocking her flesh. Imprisoned, she listened, trembling. No sound. Then the heavy weight of a man splashed into the marsh and sloshed along the full length of the fallen tree, circled back, and stopped.

Ann's body went rigid. Threads of nausea reached up around her throat and she tasted bile on her tongue.

With a short guttural sound, the man hoisted himself onto the trunk of the tree and it compressed a few inches into the bog. The ceiling of Ann's hiding place pressed down upon her. Water crept higher, and with effort she kept her nose in the desperately thin space above the water line. The weight of her prison shifted as the man marched up and down the length of the tree. Agitated. Did he know she lay within? Was he taunting her? Or was he using the tree as a lookout to scan the surrounding wetland and woods?

A ghastly creeping terror rose from a place beyond thought. Her heart knocked so furiously against the cage of her chest she felt certain the man would hear. She heard him jump off into the shallows with a big splashy crescendo and the tree bounced up higher above the water line. For a breathtaking moment she didn't hear him move, and then he waded away and the tree settled firmly into the oozing earth. Silence sealed itself back over the forest.

Buy THE KILLING WOODS

Book One of the Sidney Becker Mysteries

https://amzn.to/32px75b

ABOUT THE AUTHOR

Linda's love of literature and the visual arts led her to a twenty-five-year career as an award-winning copywriter and art director. Now retired, Linda writes fast-paced mysteries and thrillers. She currently lives in Oregon with her husband and toy poodle.

To learn of new releases and discounts,
add your name to Linda's mailing list:

www.lindaberry.net

Follow Linda on Twitter:
https://twitter.com/LindaBerry7272

www.ingramcontent.com/pod-product-compliance
Lightning Source LLC
Chambersburg PA
CBHW021224250626
47155CB00008B/2935